WEDDING ROULETTE
Leandra Logan

D0210192

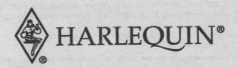

HARLEQUIN®

TORONTO • NEW YORK • LONDON
AMSTERDAM • PARIS • SYDNEY • HAMBURG
STOCKHOLM • ATHENS • TOKYO • MILAN • MADRID
PRAGUE • WARSAW • BUDAPEST • AUCKLAND

For my friend Karin Cierzan
Founder of the delightful
Early Morning Breakfast Club

ISBN 0-373-16960-4

WEDDING ROULETTE

Copyright © 2003 by Mary Schultz.

This edition published by arrangement with Harlequin Books S.A.

® and TM are trademarks of the publisher. Trademarks indicated with ® are registered in the United States Patent and Trademark Office, the Canadian Trade Marks Office and in other countries.

Visit us at www.eHarlequin.com

Printed in U.S.A.

"I need a fiancée-of-convenience for this convention in Las Vegas, and you're the perfect choice."

Krista was at a loss for words. Was this man seriously asking her to play the role of his wife-to-be?

"I realize there's little in this…arrangement for you. There will be a level of intimacy involved. You and I, virtual strangers, sharing a room."

"We'll be sharing a room?" she gasped. "Maybe this isn't such a good idea."

Now would have been the perfect time to tell him she wasn't the force behind sultry seductress Simona Says, but something inside Krista didn't want to disappoint him.

"So, Krista, do you agree to be my wife for the duration of the convention?"

His face was inches from hers now. He was so strong, so masculine, so determined. Pure, ambitious hunger set Michael Collins apart from other men.

It was time to take a chance. After all, this could be the adventure of her life, her biggest gamble yet.

Dear Reader,

It's that time of the year again. Pink candy hearts and red roses abound as we celebrate that most amorous of holidays, St. Valentine's Day. Revel in this month's offerings as we continue to celebrate Harlequin American Romance's yearlong 20th Anniversary.

Last month we launched our six-book MILLIONAIRE, MONTANA continuity series with the first delightful story about a small Montana town whose residents win a forty-million-dollar lottery jackpot. Now we bring you the second title in the series, *Big-Bucks Bachelor*, by Leah Vale, in which a handsome veterinarian gets more than he bargained for when he asks his plain-Jane partner to become his fake fiancée.

Also in February, Bonnie Gardner brings you *The Sergeant's Secret Son*. In this emotional story, passions flare all over again between former lovers as they work to rebuild their tornado-ravaged hometown, but the heroine is hiding a small secret—their child! Next, Victoria Chancellor delivers a great read with *The Prince's Texas Bride*, the second book in her duo A ROYAL TWIST, where a bachelor prince's night of passion with a beautiful waitress results in a royal heir on the way and a marriage proposal. And a trip to Las Vegas leads to a pretend engagement in Leandra Logan's *Wedding Roulette*.

Enjoy this month's offerings, and be sure to return each and every month to Harlequin American Romance!

Melissa Jeglinski
Associate Senior Editor
Harlequin American Romance

ABOUT THE AUTHOR

Leandra Logan is an award-winning author of over thirty novels. A native of Minnesota, she enjoys writing stories with a midwestern flavor, full of realistic characters of all ages. She presently lives in the historic town of Stillwater with her husband and two children.

Books by Leandra Logan

HARLEQUIN AMERICAN ROMANCE
599—SECRET AGENT DAD
601—THE LAST BRIDESMAID
732—FATHER FIGURE
880—FAMILY: THE SECRET INGREDIENT
960—WEDDING ROULETTE

Don't miss any of our special offers. Write to us at the following address for information on our newest releases.

Harlequin Reader Service
U.S.: 3010 Walden Ave., P.O. Box 1325, Buffalo, NY 14269
Canadian: P.O. Box 609, Fort Erie, Ont. L2A 5X3

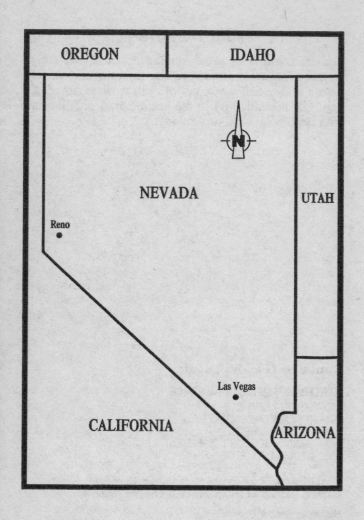

Chapter One

"I am so glad you're back!"

Krista Mattson had breezed into her inner office without realizing Bigtime Promotions' receptionist, a flighty nineteen-year-old girl named Courtney, was on her heels.

"Is there a problem?" Krista whirled round to ask.

Courtney stopped short of the boss woman smartly dressed in a navy-skirted suit, her long black hair woven into a braid. Because of Krista's imposing stature, her serious slant on life, employees of the small company tended to call her Ms. Big—behind her back, of course. Krista knew all about it, however, as she was so remarkably thorough. But even Krista at her most formal could only cut Courtney's general enthusiasm by half.

"There's no problem," the girl assured. "I have the best kind of news. In the name of efficiency, I've created a new message system for our company."

"You always leave the pink slips on my desk. I have no complaints."

"But I have streamlined the process down to a more exact science."

Krista's raven brows arched as she surveyed the girl, bouncing from one platform sandal to another. Courtney's outfit was especially striking today, a canary-yellow dress with black bolero jacket. It was quite a carnival of color with her red curls.

Practical Krista probably wouldn't have awarded the exuberant Courtney her job if she'd been conducting the interviews. But her partner Judy Phillips had chosen their current receptionist *because* the girl had energy and vitality, in her estimation what a promotions firm should reflect. All in all, it was tough to argue the choice. Clients seemed delighted with her. She never missed work, was never late. Krista had grown to highly approve of Courtney. So at times like this, when her patience was strained, Krista tried to be understanding.

Perhaps this particular modification was Krista's own fault. She'd made the mild suggestion that Courtney put more effort into the pink notes, polish her language skills and penmanship. Courtney, always overeager to please, apparently had gone the extra mile. "So tell me about this system."

"It's my idea to recite messages to you," Courtney said excitedly.

"That hardly seems necessary."

"Let's try it, please. I can read my own writing better than anyone. And I may be able to add a certain tone, give you an idea of the caller's aura."

Krista smiled faintly as she set her briefcase on her desk. "Very well."

"We'll start with business...." Courtney shuffled through the pink slips, snapping her chewing gum. "It would be easier if we had different pastel-colored pads for different kinds of messages. You know, blue for business, green for personal and pink for passion. Don't you think that the color pink should always be reserved for romance? I wore a pink dress to prom and my mom grows pink roses, a whole garden full of them."

Krista regarded her with mild exasperation. "Courtney, everyone uses the pink notepads, it's just the way it is."

"I put colored stars on the top right corner of each note, for our own use, of course. Ten blues, eight greens—" She drew a breath. "And I'm afraid no pinks again today."

Krista bristled slightly under Courtney's pitying look. The girl had been working for Bigtime Promotions for three months and never in that time had Krista received what could be construed as a passionate message from anyone.

Under the circumstances, they couldn't afford to use all the pink paper in stock exclusively for mash notes.

Krista sank into her chair and rummaged round the cluttered glass desktop for her glasses. She'd had a rough morning, which included losing her left contact lens at a downtown St. Paul bookstore where she was arranging a huge signing for a celebrity science-fiction author. Acting as go-between for author and store manager, she'd negotiated M&M's and some obscure bottled water for the author and a round-table discussion with die-hard fans for the manager. Then it was back across the river to a Minneapolis charity, a block down from their Nicollet Avenue office, to draft some press releases for a homeless shelter charity drive.

Along the way she'd apparently brushed up against some damp paint. She suddenly noted a white stain on the sleeve of her navy suit jacket, wondered if the laundry service could remove it.

"The first message is from Ms. Phillips," Courtney announced, surreptitiously removing the gum from her mouth. "She jotted it down on her way out the door."

Krista grew alert at the mention of her partner.

"The clown got sick, went to take his place at Hawkson Motors."

"Judy is pinch-hitting for a clown?" Krista's dark-blue eyes twinkled.

"That's right. For a live TV remote advertising the Boom-Bang-Best-Car-Deal-of-the-Century. She's hoping you can drop by the Bloomington dealership sometime this afternoon."

"Wouldn't miss it," Krista murmured.

Courtney plowed through the first string of messages

tagged with blue stars, reciting them with importance. "Now for the personal messages."

"I'll take those—"

"All eight are from your aunties. Rachel and Beverly Mattson. I only call them the 'aunties' because that's what they called themselves. I don't mean any disrespect."

Krista exhaled impatiently. "Courtney, what did they want?"

"I'm not sure. They took turns calling, just kept saying, 'Code Red.'"

Krista sat back in her chair, appearing rather deflated. "Oh, I see."

"I asked them if they needed the police or anything. But they said it wasn't that kind of emergency."

"I'm sure they're perfectly fine."

Courtney turned a rather smug smile. "I can't help but notice I'm not the only one who uses colors in her message system."

"Well, they are limited to the color red." And one color for the rambunctious pair was quite enough.

"You going out again?" Courtney asked as Krista rose from her chair.

"Yes, to see the aunts." Sensing curiosity in Courtney's huge brown eyes she added, "It's nearly twelve-thirty. I can use a free lunch."

It was a short drive to the Mattson sisters' Lake Calhoun neighborhood. Their grand old Victorian home was two blocks away from the lake on a very desirable street of turn-of-the-century homes. Their dwelling was painted a stately gray with maroon trim, set on a nicely sized lot shaded by two large oaks and some smaller maples. It was nearing the end of September, and the leaves were ablaze in reds and golds.

Krista usually parked in the back alley, in the shallow driveway fronting their small garage. But today she saved time by pulling up at the front curb under a large elm. Dashing through fallen leaves she scrambled up the wooden porch steps as fast as her high heels could carry her. Having spent many a childhood summer and winter vacation under this roof, eventually relocating to the Twin Cities for college, she wasn't compelled to ring the bell. She burst through the front door into the hushed mahogany entryway.

"Bev? Rach?" She clattered across the tiles, peering into the library on the left, the living room on the right. There she found the television alive with Rachel's favorite soap opera, Beverly's half-finished crossword and bifocals on an end table. Only their cat, Mr. Bellows, was on hand, curled up in a corner.

She dashed down the hall to the back of the house, to find the sisters in the kitchen preparing lunch. Krista paused in the doorway, gaping like a small girl. "Hey, why didn't you answer me?"

"Took you long enough to answer us," Beverly retorted, setting a blue ceramic plate holding a hot beef sandwich and potato chips on the round kitchen table with a *thump*.

"We didn't know what to think," Rachel chirped in agreement, setting a matching plate beside it with a small tossed salad and some wheat crackers. "Especially when you wouldn't even answer your cell phone."

Their respective lunches reflected their distinct personalities. Beverly was plump, hearty and brusque. Her gray curls were kept rolled tight against her head and her clothing always baggy on her full figure, like today's outfit of dark gabardine pants and floral rayon shirt. Rachel was only two years younger than Beverly but behaved decades off, keeping her birdlike figure with diet and exercise, her loose ringlets tinted golden, and her clothes up to date with clingy knit outfits like today's zebra-print pants and purple T-shirt.

But the sixty-something sisters were definitely of the same family tree as they did their henlike fuss-and-hustle routine about the kitchen.

"My phone ran out of power and I lost my contact lens," Krista offered in excuse, smiled wanly, girlishly, as she always did under their tutelage. "It's been a rough morning."

"Got stuck going round and round with your silly receptionist," Beverly complained. "When she sensed I was upset, she blamed it on my astrological sign."

"We've waited lunch hoping you'd come," Rachel said with a sniff. "We could've eaten on TV trays in the living room during *All My Children.* But now it's too late."

Krista bobbed and weaved around them to reach the cupboard holding glassware. She reached for three tall frosted glasses from the second shelf and filled them with lemonade from the full pitcher on the counter. "So, do I still rate a lunch? Or shall I just go stand in the corner?"

The aunts paused, staring at her as she leaned against the counter, innocently sipping her lemonade.

"Of course you have to eat," Beverly chortled. "You're a stick."

"She is not too thin," Rachel objected, "but surely hungry by this hour."

Exchanging a competitive look, they wondered exactly what she wanted for lunch.

Krista hesitated. "How about a salad...and a half sandwich," she said diplomatically. The aunts set to work to fill the order. Krista transferred the glasses and some condiments to the table. As she went on to apologize profusely for the delay in communication, her lunch got larger and larger. "That's plenty of food," she finally said, beckoning them to chairs.

Properly placated, the pair warmed up considerably. Rachel noted the stain on Krista's jacket sleeve and Beverly vowed to remove it after lunch.

Krista poured some French dressing on her bed of lettuce. "So, what is the Code Red about?"

Beverly hopped up to bring a quartered section of newspaper and the pitcher of lemonade to the table. She set the paper, folded to highlight the "Simona Says" column, at her niece's elbow. "Read this."

Krista did so, aloud.

"Dear Simona:

Help! My boyfriend, Doughman, has asked me to marry him. I impulsively said yes. Since then I have begun to doubt that he is my Mr. Right. He is strong and handsome and personable, the owner of a popular bakery franchise. I have come to realize, however, that he is a loner under his charming facade, a workaholic who spends endless hours at his shop. A lifelong dieter who enjoys the club scene, I'm afraid I am doomed to a future of lonely one-sided conversations over my frozen dinners. Even worse, our passion has always been on a weak sizzle. He says fireworks take time, that I must be more patient in lighting our fuse. What say you, Simona?

Irritated In Illinois

Simona Says:

Mr. Right, you say? Wrong! You're trying to light the fuse of a dud. Ditch your sweet-tooth loner Dough-man and redirect that fire to a real stick of TNT."

Krista finished on a sigh. Her eyes lifted from the paper to land on the duo who were, in fact, the flamboyant sex advisor Simona Says. "This ran a couple of weeks ago, didn't it?"

Beverly humphed in confirmation. "So, what's your impression?"

Krista paused for a diplomatic reply. "It's certainly... flippant."

"Simona's trademark, naturally. But I assure you, we gave the dilemma much consideration before ministering advice."

Rachel's golden head bobbed. "We're so different ourselves, that every query is about turned inside out."

Beverly laid a plump hand on her full chest. "As much as I would die for a beau who ran a pastry shop, plainly, as Rachel pointed out, this young woman isn't taken with the business."

"And Doughman hasn't any time for a nightlife," Rachel inserted, "one of Irritated's main interests."

"Surely once people marry," Krista objected, "they pull back on the club scene to nest. Together."

"But Doughman is never at his nest with his business a top priority," Beverly said.

"I am surprised you swung so hard in the female's favor. Generally you leave room for interpretation, for compromise!"

Rachel's eyes grew. "How could we in all conscience advise one of our own species to settle for a slow-burning fuse? We girls all deserve some real sizzle, wouldn't you agree?"

Krista took a swig of lemonade. "Gee, I don't know." She was uncomfortable talking about sex with the aunts, mainly because she had very little to go on about. And in this case, her sympathies automatically swung to Doughman as he sounded a lot like her, a workaholic cautious of romantic entanglements. And it was wise for entrepreneurs to be cautious with amour. Krista had learned the hard way that most of her partners proved threatened by her job, determined to compete with it, or, in the worst cases, eager to mooch off her success. If there was a stable, confident hardworking partner out there for her, Krista had yet to meet him.

To Krista, Irritated sounded like a typical whiner who would spend her entire life self-absorbed and dissatisfied. But it would be a foolish exercise to start up a defense of cautious workaholics. The aunts didn't understand the breed.

"Doughman is to blame for his own trouble," Beverly blustered on. "A man must tend to the fire under his own roof before anything else."

Weary of the runaround, Krista pushed harder. "How has this particular column led to a Code Red?"

The aunts exchanged a sheepish look. When they weren't at one another's throats, they were conspiring.

"There has been a complaint," Rachel admitted.

"Who complained?" Krista demanded. "Someone at the newspaper? Some of your more opinionated readers?"

Beverly spilled the beans. "Doughman himself. He wrote us a very mean letter."

"A registered letter," Rachel added. "He called our advice to his fiancée careless and damaging. Irritated has broken off their engagement and he blames us."

"He's threatened to sue," Beverly admitted bluntly.

Krista was aghast. This was the first time in the aunts' seven-year run as Simona Says that there'd been any real threat of a lawsuit. There were minor complaints, of course, but avid readers across the nation seemed to realize that Simona was a free-spirited character who tried to entertain and perhaps comfort, rather than stand up as a serious psychology guru.

To the best of her knowledge, the aunts were the only ones who took their own advice even remotely seriously. Until now.

"I would declare Doughman a dud even under oath," Beverly declared heartily, her double chins trembling. "We cannot be held liable for his inadequacies."

"What exactly does he hope to base his lawsuit on?"

"Alienation of affection," Rachel replied, looking truly afraid. "He claims we put crazy ideas into Irritated's head. That she was fine until she read our column."

"But her plea for help certainly suggests otherwise," Beverly bellowed.

"What, exactly, does this have to do with me?" Krista dared ask.

Two fingernails, one pointy, red and artificial, the other flat and plain as nature intended, stabbed Simona's photo on the column's masthead.

The photo was of Krista. A vamp glamour shot of wild black hair, flashing eyes and sly gypsylike smile; an image so unlike Krista that no one outside a small circle of confidants had ever connected her to the photo.

The arrangement was simple: the aunts doled out advice with Krista as their sexy front woman.

It had all started out as a lark, really. Aunt Rachel's longtime beau, Bob Freeman, was the managing editor of the *Minneapolis Monitor*'s Variety department. Seven years ago the seasoned newspaperman had an opening for a columnist. Sister Seamstress was retiring, and he needed someone to fill the space. The daily sewing column had grown mundane; he wanted something with a bit more zip to attract a younger audience. They already had one syndicated advice guru who prided herself on the practical, who tackled serious issues. What Bob wanted was a second advisor, with an exotic, more tantalizing attitude.

So it was in Rachel's four-poster bed, over two bottles of champagne, that Rachel and Bob created "Simona Says." She would be a sexy fantasy figure who catered to the lovelorn with glib entertaining advice. Rachel originally intended to run solo on the project, craft the daily column herself, reveal her true identity to the public. As much as Bob adored his spunky retired-waitress lady friend, he doubted Rachel had the skills to put her good ideas to paper with the necessary clarity. So it was his idea to include former schoolteacher Beverly in the scheme. Together they could provide a good balance of talent and temperament to round off Simona. It was also Bob's idea to keep Rachel— as well as Beverly—in the background, their identities secret. No offense, but hip young readers would relate better to a contemporary. Recalling a photograph of a nineteen-year-old Krista dressed up for a Halloween party, he suggested she pose as Simona Says.

Krista had been a little hesitant at first. She was, after all, a serious student at St. Paul's prestigious Hamline University, majoring in business administration. But even she had to admit that after submitting to a full makeover, she didn't look like herself at all. To her own nervous delight, she even appeared a bit dangerous.... So she agreed to all of their terms. She would pose for the column's photo, make the occasional fleeting guest appearance, do the odd radio interview. And their secret would be shared only by the Mattson women, Bob and a few of his closest associates at the newspaper.

For Krista's trouble she was to be paid nineteen thousand dollars the first year, with a thousand-dollar raise each subsequent year. It had been a godsend as she finished college and started up her business with Judy Phillips.

At age twenty-six she was up to twenty-six thousand dollars now. So, she supposed, it was no mystery as to why they felt justified in involving her in this crisis.

Bravely, she raised a hand in surrender. "Tell you what, I'll call this guy if you like. One of you would pose a better defense, but I do have a youthful voice."

Beverly's full bosom rose and fell. "That would've been our choice of amends, as well. Unfortunately, the situation has escalated beyond that option. Instead of allowing us to handle the call, Bob Freeman did so with a man-to-man approach."

"Bob was only trying to help," Rachel said hotly.

"But your boyfriend blew it! Doughman was insulted that Simona didn't make the courtesy call herself." Beverly's puffy face pinched in anger. "Bottom line, Krista, Doughman's due here for a face-to-face meeting with Simona."

"He'll be at the *Minneapolis Monitor* building around eleven a.m. tomorrow," Beverly verified. "So you can see why this is a full-blown Code Red. We need you, Krista 'Simona' Mattson, in place, at a *Monitor* desk, acting like a columnist."

"Acting like our image of Simona," Rachel added. "Sexy, sassy, jiggly."

Jiggly? Krista glanced down at her modest-size breasts.

She could push them up, but they weren't going to put on a show even if she jumped up and down on a trampoline. All in all, she was as modest as her breasts. Her pulse jumped wildly at the idea of confronting a furious jilted lover. "I'm not sure I can pull it off."

Beverly was taken aback. "Uncertainty is never once mentioned in the Mattson family credo. We go the extra mile to get results. In this case, we need Simona to make a personal appearance. If we cannot nip this man's temper in the bud, we might very well lose our jobs. Any inkling of a scandal and someone is going to dig a bit deeper into Simona's identity. Bust open our game!"

"If this man decides to go on full attack in court, you're liable to lose your nest eggs, as well," Krista pointed out. Noting they were perplexed, she explained. "He can sue for a lot of money, any amount he chooses. If he can convince a judge that you've destroyed his life, who knows…"

The sisters paled.

"You'll just have to save us," Beverly declared.

They bolstered her with proud and dewy eyes, as they had so often over the years. Krista was their brother Joshua's only child, the only child of her generation to carry on the Mattson name. When Krista's mother died in childbirth, the aunts offered their maternal influence without hesitation. Joshua started early in delivering Krista cross-country from California to Minnesota a few times each year to give the females of the family time to bond.

The pair had always been in Krista's corner, albeit in their grating, know-it-all, bossy fashion. She adored them, always wanted to please. But the timing of this crisis was terribly ironic. She'd grown tired of the charade and wanted out. She'd been working up the courage to tell them. The personal appearances were especially a load of nonsense, shimmying around, dodging questions with glib one-liners and a throaty laugh. They had promised at the onset that her participation was only temporary. And she was so busy now, with a promotions business to run. A business, she was proud to say, that was doing extremely well.

But this was no time to broach the subject of a dissolution. They were far too distressed to endure another upset. "I'll do my best by you," she promised, to their open relief. "So, have you considered our strategy?"

They blinked in confusion.

"You know," she clarified, "concessions you are willing to make to encourage him to go away."

"We are right. He is wrong. Simple as that."

"This jilted lover is taking time out of his schedule to descend upon us and you want me to simply tell him he's wrong?"

Rachel puckered her lips. "There are ways of seducing a person into submission."

"It'll take a little more than a fake jiggle to put this forceful man off."

"You have my good looks and Beverly's brains, yet you refuse to use this powerful combination with the opposite sex. It's nothing short of tragic."

Beverly agreed wholeheartedly with her sister. "We'd each kill for your combo. If we could merge into one woman we could topple an empire."

Krista resisted pointing out that together they couldn't even efficiently run an advice column. "I'll do what I can for you. But don't expect a miracle."

Chapter Two

Hours later Krista found the time to seek out her business partner and friend Judy Phillips. Night was closing in as she drove down the freeway in her silver Saturn, exiting at a Bloomington exit near the Mall of America, following the searchlights to Hawkson Motors.

Three salesmen jogged in her direction as she came to a stop in the large lot crammed with automobiles. With elbows up and feet flying she managed to dodge them for a dash to the brightly lit showroom.

Krista smiled her first big smile of the day. There among a circle of children stood Judy. The fragile fair-haired, fair-skinned woman was barely recognizable in a bright-purple wig, full face makeup, billowy dotted pantsuit and huge floppy black shoes.

She and Judy had been sorority sisters at Hamline University. They'd clicked their freshman year, discovering they shared many of the same interests. Both were ambitious and determined to earn a business degree. Working on campus on various volunteer committees they discovered they had a knack for promotion. With the aid of Krista's Simona Says salary, they were able to start a business of their own right out of college.

Krista stood by patiently, while Judy shook hands with the last of the adults and gave hugs to the children with zeal, directing them over to a senior citizen named Mr.

Duff, whom they'd hired from a temp agency to distribute helium balloons.

"It's seven already? I need a cup of coffee!" Judy led Krista through the showroom to a private lounge in back, next to the parts department.

The room was stark and smelled faintly of motor oil. They sat on molded plastic chairs, balancing paper cups full of bitter coffee from a huge urn. Judy placed a small paper napkin on Krista's blue skirt, then passed a clear plastic platter of small hard cookies with the aplomb of a duchess. "A sweeting, milady?" she said primly.

Krista laughed, taking a ginger cookie. "This reminds me of the sorority teas we gave to loosen up stodgy professors."

"Remember the time the house mother asked you to make some Russian tea cakes?" Judy said, setting the platter back on the wooden table beside the urn. "They were worse than these little bombs."

"They weren't!"

Judy's huge painted green eyebrows jumped on her creamed white face. "They were."

Krista winced. "Maybe they were a little hard."

"You just hate ever being less than perfect, ever losing control of a situation."

"Speaking of losing control..." Krista pushed her glasses up her nose and glanced round the break room to make sure they were still alone. Satisfied, she went on to relate the aunts' dilemma. Judy had been in on the charade from the start, encouraging Krista to be daring enough to take the role. She'd offered steady encouragement at every rough spot over the years.

"Surely you've got this Simona gig perfected by now," Judy said, bending forward to pat the cold hands in Krista's lap. "You'll be fine."

She smiled faintly. "I hope. The aunts have decided they don't trust me an inch. I just got a fax at the office outlining any number of scenarios I may encounter with Doughman, and how I am to respond."

"How is that?"

"It all boils down to outwitting him and appeasing him without admitting any wrongdoing or compromising Simona's principles. They feel the man is a dud and expect me to fight their position to the death."

"With what weapon?"

She blushed. "My sex appeal."

Judy laughed. "Well, you are a knockout as Simona."

Krista waved fingers in a fluster. "Thanks, but I intend to lead with brain power. On that I know I can rely."

"At least be prepared for erotic combat. Have Romano himself do your hair and makeup."

"Already set up a morning appointment. He's charging me double, but he's the soul of discretion and willing to make a house call."

"Which Simona ensemble have you decided on?"

"I have only four. The black lace evening gown with slit up the thigh. The white satin blouse with long flowing skirt. The royal-blue sequined mini tunic. And the red knit shift with the metallic threads running through it. Plus the silver shawl that coordinates with everything."

Judy gave the matter sixty seconds of consideration. "I suggest you wear the red shift. The color is so striking with your hair and the cap sleeves on the shoulder can be pulled down, in case of emergency."

"I suppose I could. But I will be bringing along the shawl."

"Chicken!"

"It's the best I can do, feeling so out of place in that sort of slinky clothing."

Judy stood up and put a reassuring hand on Krista's head. "C'mon, it can't get stranger than spending the day in a clown suit."

Krista shifted in her chair to stare up at her partner.

"Wish we could've traded places. I'd gladly have taken the clown role."

"I love you, Kris, but you just don't have the jolly carefree spirit for it."

Krista grinned, but the observation hurt her, just a little bit. Did no one on earth appreciate her fun streak?

IT WAS DRIZZLING LIGHTLY the following morning as Krista, a.k.a. Simona, alighted from a cab along Marquette Avenue at the entrance of the *Minneapolis Monitor* Building. Under an awning stood her anxious aunts Beverly and Rachel, dressed in raincoats and plastic hats to protect their stiff sprayed hairdos, as well as Rachel's managing editor boyfriend, Bob Freeman, in sports jacket and slacks.

Bob didn't look like a ladies' man with his balding head, thick waistline and ill-fitting clothing. But he had a remarkable personality and gentlemanly manner. He wasted no time moving across the sidewalk to pay the driver.

He guided Krista to the aunts as if she were some kind of precious commodity. "Here she is, safe and sound. Looking adorable."

Adorably trapped perhaps, one white-knuckled hand gripping a tote bag, the other at the collar of her buttoned-up raincoat. A part of Krista still could not believe she'd agreed to this.

"There's little time to lose," Bob said brusquely, handing the ladies their visitor ID badges. "Rach, get our captivating Simona up to room 1411. I've made arrangements to meet Michael Collins in the lobby."

"That is Doughman's name," Rachel explained to Krista as they whirled through the revolving doors on a human wave.

Krista thought she saw a couple of women with *Minneapolis Monitor* ID badges in hand come to attention at Bob's mention of Simona, but she couldn't be sure. She understood that Bob was nervous about the whole affair, but he shouldn't have made the slip. Krista was an enigma at the newspaper. No employees had ever seen her up close.

The three Mattson women crowded into an elevator car, which emptied by the time it reached the exclusive executive floor. Rachel knew exactly where they were going and steered them down a maze of corridors.

Room 1411 was upscale with decorated leathers, polished oak and rich blue carpeting. Both aunts gratefully tore off their damp rain gear, but Krista resisted. Her small outfit was…chilly.

"This space belongs to a vice-president on vacation," Rachel explained with a tinge of self-importance. Then she scampered over to the desk on her high heels. "Quick, Krista, let me show you how the phone system works."

Krista glared at the console full of buttons. "Does it matter?"

"Yes, oh, yes." Rachel used a long red nail to depress a large button at the top of the console. "This is the intercom. You want to keep it on."

"Why?"

Rachel was exasperated. "So we can listen in the room next door."

Beverly, standing by with a hand on her ample hip, agreed. "And give you a jingle if you get off track."

Krista balked. That wasn't part of the deal!

Before she could protest, the phone gave a single sharp ring. "That's Bob's signal," Rachel trilled, pushing her sister toward a connecting door on the opposite wall. Together they called out parting instructions.

"Ooze with charm, dear."

"Try and be sexy. Best you can, anyway."

MEANWHILE, IRRITATED CHICAGOAN Michael Collins was getting the VIP treatment from Bob Freeman, who was escorting him through the lobby to a private elevator. As they whizzed smoothly upward in the paneled car he felt a little sorry for the Variety department managing editor he'd tussled with by telephone. Freeman was being so gracious, just as he'd been on the wire when Michael had been spouting off at the top of his lungs. But it had rankled Michael that Simona hadn't called him personally. For the second time, Freeman was apologizing for that, taking the entire blame, claiming Simona gladly would have contacted Mr. Collins if asked to. But Freeman was in the habit of protecting Simona from the public. Most cranks—er, ah, complaints—held not a fraction of significance.

Michael once again assured him that his complaint was serious, indeed. As was his threat to sue anyone in sight. His future was in the balance.

The car stopped on floor fourteen, with Bob leading the way. Offices located in the core of the building had long windows on the corridor walls to give them a less claustrophobic feel. Room 1411 was one of these rooms.

As the men glanced through a pane with mini-blinds at half-mast, Krista was facing the opposite way, slipping a damp black raincoat off her shoulders to reveal a svelte figure in a little red dress. The dress hemline rode high to reveal long legs sheathed in dark hose, the backline plunged low to reveal a length of ivory spine.

Completely unaware of her audience, she flung her coat on a nearby chair and shook the raindrops from her loose black hair. Then she sauntered over to the desk holding her tote bag and did a supple deep bend, pulling out a long silver shawl, which she draped ever so gently over her shoulders.

The males, suddenly bonded in male appreciation, didn't spare a breath between them.

Bob Freeman snapped back to reality first, clearing his throat, touching the rim of hair above his ear.

Michael wasn't so quick on the rebound. He swallowed hard, hoping to clear his ringing ears. Simona was exquisite! Her grainy photo in the newspaper didn't begin to do her justice.

His body's instant response to her charms was frustrating. But it was a natural reaction. Simona was most desirable, at least behind the safe wall of glass.

With effort he stiffened his back. He would do well to remember his anger, his outrage. Beautiful women like Simona used men as chew toys, then tossed them away! Even men she didn't know got the treatment—through that wretched column of hers.

Oddly, Bob Freeman also seemed affected by their unintentional window peeping. He had to be accustomed to Simona's moves and he was her boss. But there was no mistaking Bob's slow recovery as he grasped the doorknob, swung in the heavy paneled door and plunged inside with the finesse of a chubby schoolboy.

"My favorite columnist," Bob said a bit too jovially.

She spun round then, regarding them with surprise, instinctively tightening the shawl on her shoulders.

Michael was dumbfounded. Caught in an unguarded moment, she emitted a dizzying swirl of vibes: vulnerability, modesty and, remarkably, a twinkle of intelligence. Qualities in direct conflict with the sloppy gooey advice she doled out each and every day in her column.

As if recovering, a protective mask fell into place over her face, concealing anything of value. "Thanks, Bob." It was a throaty dismissal, which Bob obeyed with a hasty exit.

Suddenly the couple was alone, in a room alive with electricity.

Michael took a good hard look at his nemesis. Her dark eyes were a rather unusual shade of midnight blue. Her mouth was a pleasing size, with just a flash of white teeth. Her complexion was bronzed to an exotic hue, expertly blended with a number of earth tones.

This was going to be a battle of the sexes. A heated, intense battle.

To his credit, Michael had never suffered from any complaints about his own looks, with a towering build, thick blond hair and dark-gray eyes. He was representing himself well today, in a new gray suit, hair clipped short and neat. He sensed a note of approval in Simona's gaze. No matter how unconscious her gesture, it felt good, considering the stinging slap his ex-fiancée's letter and Simona's reply had caused him.

"I'm Michael Collins," he said formally, extending a hand.

Krista slid her hand into his larger one, offering him a grip firm enough to make his brows jump. "I am Krista Mattson."

"So you don't care to be addressed as Simona?"

She shook her head, causing her loose mane to sway. He couldn't help noting the henna highlights in her hair were similar to the metallic threads in her dress.

"I'm guessing you don't care to be called Doughman, either."

"No, I don't. In fact, I prefer to keep that particularly humiliating tag between you, me and Irritating In Illinois."

"You mean, Irritated In Illinois."

"Depends upon your perspective," he grumbled.

"Well, if you insist on a lawsuit, all will come out." She flashed him an infuriating smile.

"Maybe we can avoid opening the floodgates on our personal business," Michael acquiesced.

"Have a seat, Mr. Collins." She gestured to one of the huge leather chairs fronting the desk. "Let's see what we can do."

Michael bristled. Was the directive to sit the kind of deliberate ploy often used in business to gain the upper hand? How would an airhead like Simona know of such things? Out of pride and curiosity he sat down in the chair adjacent to the one she'd selected for him. And she noticed. A frown marred her lovely features as she took her place behind the desk.

Krista settled back in the leather desk chair, which seemed too large and low for her. "Please, carry on."

"Believe me, I wouldn't be here at all if your stupid

advice to my fiancée hadn't completely wrecked my life, put a strain on my future success!''

Her artfully shaped brows arched. ''Exactly how did I accomplish all this?''

He shifted in his own chair, which seemed too small for his towering posture. ''Well, I own a Decadent Delights franchise in Chicago, am set to attend their upcoming convention.''

''Ah, the doughnut company.'' Krista's tone held appreciation. ''Though the chain hasn't reached the Twin Cities, I've tasted them several times on trips to Manhattan. The shops are bright and inviting, done in pristine green and white tile. The air is warm and sweet, a virtual sugar dough heaven.''

''Sounds like you can appreciate a good doughnut and a well-run place.''

Her smile suggested as much.

Michael started as he caught a flash of movement out of the corner of his eye. His head snapped sideways to find a group of spectators at the double windows along the corridor. ''You sell tickets to our show?''

Krista followed his gaze with open dismay as at least twelve people, an equal balance of male and female, peered inside the room without a qualm. So, the women in the lobby had overheard Bob Freeman. Bracing herself, she gripped her shawl closed and rose fluidly. Navigating her sinfully high heels as best she could, Krista sauntered to the windows and snapped down the mini-blinds on the dozen agog faces. Taking a steadying breath she returned to her chair.

''Do you ever sacrifice a chance at the limelight?''

She hesitated, then smiled slyly. ''Can I help it if the public is interested in me?''

''I would have thought that a matter this serious would warrant your complete attention.''

''It does!'' She resumed her place at the desk, wearing

an expression of polite concern. ''Now, please, tell me about your situation.''

Appearing rather disconcerted, he continued. ''It's difficult to explain the importance of these conventions to an outsider. But to franchise owners like me, it is the rare chance to shine for company founder Gerald Stewart. He hosts a lavish convention for his employees every few years in his hometown of Las Vegas. I've been attending regularly since I started working part-time for shop owners Norah and Allen Larkin, then on through my culinary school years, ultimately to the opening of my own franchise. With every convention, I made it my business to interact with Mr. Stewart. Year after year, I've played the DD game by routinely sending in a personal anecdote for his monthly newsletter.''

''Is the newsletter a big deal?'' she asked.

''It's the electrical current running through the company. Gerald Stewart is big on family values and the newsletter is his way of humanizing his huge corporation. Unable to have children, he chose to adopt his employees nationwide to make up his extended family. The unfortunate death of his wife several years back has made him all the more sentimental about his people. It isn't easy for a private man like me to reach out with folksy anecdotes. But it's a system that works, that I can respect.''

Krista found herself following his logic, approving of his business tactics with nods of understanding. When she realized she was slipping out of character, she tossed her head back and fluffed her hair.

He leaned over the desk in urgency. ''In short, I've tried to make mine the best Decadent Delights franchise possible. I love my job. I'm proud of my success.''

''As you should be, Mr. Collins,'' she managed to say.

He appeared buoyed by her support.

She leaned back in her chair, heady with seeing her earlier suspicions confirmed. This masculine hunk was born in her own image—a male version of her!

It was all too tempting to imagine what it would be like to be in Irritated's place, dating such a dynamic go-getter. The idea of discussing one's dreams and the challenges of the day over a variety of Decadent Delights doughnuts was so very appealing.

Michael Collins was very appealing, indeed.

A sharp peal brought her back to reality. She glanced at the telephone console. Button three was lit up. It had to be the aunts, primed with complaints.

"Aren't you going to answer that?" he asked.

"I don't think so." It rang five more times, though. She finally picked up the receiver. Unfortunately, that didn't stop the ringing. Krista pushed some buttons at random but couldn't figure out what was wrong. In her defense, the system didn't resemble her own at Bigtime Promotions.

"This system appears similar to mine." He stood up and examined the console. "Oh, you seem to have the intercom on. That's the problem."

"I didn't even notice," she rallied. "Must have been the cleaning staff's mistake."

He jabbed the black button, then the glowing white one. The ringing stopped and he sat down again.

Beverly's voice boomed in her ear. "This isn't an *A & E Biography* special. Listening to this dud's résumé is a precious waste of our time."

"This particular recipe is more complicated than you know, Aunt Beverly," she improvised cheerily. "You have to start with a dollop of honey. Now I know you aren't especially fond of anything sweet, but—"

"I'm a regular sweetie pie when I need to be. Got all my lessons from an expert tart named Rachel a long time ago. We both want you back on track, bringing this man to his knees, begging your forgiveness! Now cut short the businessman's special and do it the old-fashioned way. Drop that shawl, give those cap sleeves a tug south!"

"Maybe I already have."

"Don't kid a kidder. Now get to it—and push the intercom back on!'' *Click* and *buzz*. It took Krista a moment to recover from the scolding and surreptitiously nick the intercom button with her knuckle. Michael Collins really couldn't see the phone console clearly unless he stood up. ''Aunt Beverly's making a new bread recipe,'' she offered lamely.

Michael expressed interest. ''You from a family of cooks, then?''

''We dabble,'' she laughed. They enjoyed a comfortable moment. She felt secure enough to let the shawl slide to her elbows. Michael appeared frozen in appreciation. ''As you were saying?''

He cleared his throat to recover. ''Anyway, this year's convention starts next week. It's the most important convention yet, the stakes are unusually high.'' Closing a hand he gave his chest three self-righteous beats. ''I had my plans set, was geared up for the challenges. Everything was perfect—'' he took an incensed breath ''—until you butted in!''

''Exactly how is this convention so different from previous ones?''

''There's a big contest among about fifty franchise owners to make the next DD doughnut flavor to be distributed nationwide. The winner gets a hundred thousand dollars and a fair amount of fame, with his photo displayed in every store. Without question, this is the highest honor ever offered by Gerald Stewart.'' His expression could only be described as reverent. ''We contestants are to gather in a kitchen at the convention site to prepare our recipes. A small elite panel of chefs will judge the entries, with Gerald Stewart himself having the final say.''

Behind her lashes she could envision a kitchen full of sweet smells and the sharp scent of keen competition. She couldn't bake her way out of a nursery school with an Easy-Bake Oven, but she still understood the spirit of it all. What she didn't understand was how his jilted fiancée affected the convention.

"Are you trying to tell me you can't cook without this woman at your side? Is she your inspiration or what?"

"I've explained!"

"Not about her you haven't."

"Oh? Guess it's really simple. With Gerald Stewart's family values policy, no unattached bachelor has a chance of winning that contest."

The business angle again. Not what Krista expected to hear from a crushed Romeo. "Rather than condemning Simona Says, maybe you should be threatening to sue Gerald Stewart for rigging a contest for discrimination," she suggested helpfully.

He waved off the idea. "It isn't blatant discrimination that I can prove. And Gerald Stewart doesn't mean any harm. He just has a soft spot for family. Let's just say the odds are against a bachelor winning."

"I've read about Gerald Stewart," she admitted. She knew Simona probably wouldn't have, but it seemed a necessary admission to back up her point. "He sounds like a shrewd straight-shooter. If your doughnut recipe is good enough, you will win on your own merit, despite your single status. Plainly, you've managed quite nicely within the system so far as a bachelor."

"Being a bachelor has been fine. I guess. But things have changed. To Mr. Stewart, to the whole corporation, I am as good as married."

"Why?"

He hesitated briefly. "I impulsively sent in a brief teaser to last month's company newsletter, announcing my upcoming nuptials."

"You're a fast worker, calling attention to your rushed engagement to a calorie-conscious whiner." Krista's midnight-blue eyes rolled.

He made a defensive squawk. "At the time it seemed wise. I wanted Gerald Stewart to acknowledge my engagement come convention time. And it worked beyond my wildest expectations. He's honoring Irritated and me, among others, at the convention's kickoff cocktail party. Who knows how much trouble he's gone to. Plainly, he'll be annoyed to learn his efforts were for nothing, that I couldn't hang on to my woman. I'll be much worse off than the average bachelor contestant, let me tell you.''

''You will appear the bungler,'' she said, half under her breath.

''Thanks a lot.'' Then he gave a wave. ''Oh, what's one more insult? You've already called me a dud in your syndicated column.''

Krista was especially sorry that the aunts had resorted to such name-calling. Michael, or any man for that matter, deserved a chance to prove himself more than a dud. As it was, his intense silver gaze searing clear through her scanty costume and minuscule lingerie made the man and the moment far from dull.

Despite family loyalties, salaries and skating lessons, she felt a magnetic pull over to his side. It took effort to keep in mind her aunts' position. ''As much as I might appreciate your dilemma, I must say your fiancée had no business taking the column so literally. It is an entertainment piece. Showbiz. Simona's remarks are meant to stimulate and titillate rather than educate or inform. There are other columns more grounded in reality—''

''But my girl chose yours! Like hundreds of other Americans must do every day. Though I can't think why. I went to the library to examine some of your previous columns and was appalled by the glib, romantic gibberish you dole out time after time.''

''It's all done in the spirit of fun. Maybe that's what is lacking in your life. A spirit of fun.''

''I can be. Fun.'' Despite his claim, he erupted in a very ill-humored growl. ''I've worked so hard to build a solid life plan here. Then to have a ditz like you come along and pull out a linchpin. Have you no conscience about that?''

Chapter Three

Krista nervously began to drum her red manicured finger-nails on the desktop. She for one had a conscience and was ultimately in charge of this meeting.

What next? Plainly, she wasn't going to be able to fix this mess as neatly as the aunts hoped. He certainly wasn't going to be leaving on the tail of an apology. And she didn't think he should.

"Have you any concrete ideas about what I can do for you?" she dared to ask.

He pivoted on his heel, pinning her with a look of amaze-ment. "Finally! I wondered if and when you'd find the guts to ask. Once I got a good look at you, I must confess I suspected you might hope to make me surrender on bended knee."

"No woman in her right mind would expect such a thing," she scoffed, studying the desk's ink blotter.

He leaned closer. "Not even a sex kitten like you could have made me do it."

She'd never been called a sex kitten before. It made the blood sing through her veins. Made her panty hose feel tight.

"As it is, I do have some ideas," he went on curtly. "To start with, you can call Irritated personally. Report to her our meeting and grovel out a suitable act of contrition highly favorable to me, including an assurance that I am, in fact, quite interested in her. Then I want you to draft an open letter to your readers, saying, in effect, that you sometimes jump to conclusions, get a little too cute with your advice. Admit that this behavior has gotten you into trouble with a reader, and you sincerely wish for any other injured parties to accept your blanket apology.''

"Wow." Krista sat back and waited for the unavoidable sound of the bell. When it did ring, Michael jumped up in frustration. Steadying herself, she pushed the intercom and snagged the receiver. "Yes. Oh, hello. I'm afraid I'm very busy right now."

"His demands are as far from crawling as you can get," Beverly complained.

"You set your hopes way too high in the first place, Mr. Bellows," she added, using the name of the aunts' cat.

"Or maybe we sent in a girl to do a woman's job."

"Don't push it."

"Hang on a minute while we decide what you should do," Beverly said in an aggrieved tone.

Krista could hear her aunts murmuring in the background. Then Beverly returned to the wire. "Go ahead and make the phone call for him."

"I refuse to flirt with disaster." She was watching Michael pace and couldn't miss his glare of disbelief. "It's my stockbroker," she hastened to tell him. "Always wants me to take wild risks."

"Look, Krista, it's a compromise we don't like, either. But we see no other way out. He is over twenty-one. If he wants to play footsie with Irritated, who are we to stand in the way? In fact, he's so determined to wreck his life, he intends to sue us for the right."

"I only wish we could find another *stock* option."

"Don't cry to me. You're the one who's failed to manipulate him. Now we have no choice but to play his game. Call the ex right now. See if perhaps you can do a better job sweet-talking her."

"Still, in my opinion—"

"Your opinion doesn't mean diddly here. You are not really Simona."

"What about the other directive?"

"The printed retraction? In his dreams. Simona's never copped a public *mea culpa* in all her born days. Serve him up our compromise and be done with it."

"But—"

"Make the call," Beverly ordered. "Ditch the dud."

Krista stared up at Michael, a lone sentry in a sober gray suit, raking his clipped blond hair with a huge powerful hand. Her heart squeezed and her pulse jumped.

Dud, indeed. The man was a genuine hottie. She'd forgotten what instant combustion felt like, the instant rush of desire. Her aunts and Irritated were fools not to appreciate his potent animal magnetism.

Krista was struggling hard in her role now, caring more than ever to do the right thing. Her most important consideration was that, despite his jilted lover pitch, he was not in the throes of sincere romantic anguish. His was a bottom-line business dilemma. He hated losing, he hated rejection, he hated having his business affairs upset.

There was no fooling Ms. Big of Bigtime Promotions. It took one workaholic to know another.

Under the circumstances, Krista could not bring herself to cooperate. The aunts might view her as a puppet to their whims, but she had her limits. There was no way she was going to phone up Irritated in order to help Michael Collins ruin his own life.

She was suddenly surging with power and confidence. Only she would and could save him from himself. And that meant standing firm against his self-destructive demands.

She rose from her chair on a wave of euphoria, allowing her protective shawl to slide to the floor. She rounded the desk, ever so subtly giving her cap sleeves a bit of a tug off the shoulder.

In all her life, she had never felt sexier.

He had been roaming all over the room, but at the sight

of her lazy feline approach, found himself rooted to a spot near some file cabinets. Touching his lapel, she spoke in a husky firm voice.

"Michael," she began in a hush, "I'm afraid it is against my policy to ever print a retraction."

He inhaled laboriously, touching the bloodred nails climbing his jacket. "Fine, forget it. The retraction was strictly for my ego. The phone call, however, is a necessity."

She felt him give her hand a gentle squeeze. Shimmering with sensuality and bravado all at once was no easy feat, especially when delivering bad news. "I'm afraid I must refuse to make the call, as well."

He was flabbergasted. "But a word from you would mean so much."

She stole her hand back. "That's the problem. Your former fiancée might actually respect Simona enough to give you another chance. Not a responsibility I want."

"Why do you insist upon taking her side?"

"I don't mean to—"

Realization suddenly flooded his face. "So it is the sex."

"The sex?"

"You bought all that baloney about my not lighting her fuse fast enough."

Oops. Krista had forgotten all about that crack. The aunts took way too much pleasure in doling out that sort of earthy double entendre.

He crowded her against the file cabinets, dipping his face close to hers. "Maybe Irritated was a little too anxious about our progress in that department. And maybe I was a bit too distracted this close to my convention. But let me assure you, when I do have the time and inclination to light a fuse, it burns fast and it burns hot."

Krista didn't doubt it. Her own legs were weak. She had to press her thighs together to keep from melting to the floor.

He continued in a tight, confident voice. "You're a meddling egotist to hold your ground, to refuse to mend my fences. There was nothing wrong with Irritated that some square meals and a few dazzling nights in Vegas wouldn't have cured. Why, given the chance I would have..."

She gulped in his minty breath and spicy aftershave as he hovered close and laid into her about his courtship plans in the nation's most pulsating city.

He curled his mouth in self-deprecation. "What a waste this trip has been. I thought if I came here in person to plead my case, I could get my point across."

"You have made a point, though not the one you intended. Your every move today has convinced me all the more that you and Irritated are a mismatch. If a forceful man like you truly loved a woman, she would know it without a doubt. The very idea that she would be insecure enough to write to an advice columnist just doesn't fit."

He reared in offense. "I proposed to her with sincere intentions."

"You were staging an engagement of convenience!"

"Hey, I truly care for Irritated."

"You're far more excited about impressing the boss."

"You make me sound ruthless."

Her voice softened. "Not if you fooled yourself, too, Michael. You probably got caught up in the excitement of it all without realizing. Doesn't it strike you as the least bit strange that you fell in love at a time when you needed a wife most?"

"The fact that our relationship blossomed as opportunity knocked was a lucky stroke of fate."

She was clearly skeptical. "How long were you fateful lovers dating?"

"Three whole months."

"Hah! I don't trust a dry cleaner or a manicurist for the first six months."

"Maybe that's because you're a crummy con," he sputtered, "on the lookout for your own kind."

"Am not!"

"Are too!"

"Not!"

He glared at her incredulously, his face flushed with fury. "You have reduced this argument to an embarrassing level of childishness. I better get out of here before I give you cause for a countersuit," he fumed. "But you'll be hearing from me again, I promise."

Krista stared at him in dismay. "What are you going to do?"

"Something," he vowed, charging for the door with fists squeezed to his sides. "Something to make you squirm."

When the outer door slammed shut, the aunts came rushing through the inner office door.

Krista crumpled. "Guess that didn't go too well."

"Where did we go wrong with her, Beverly!" Rachel lamented. "The girl knows so little about manipulating men."

"Never trust youth and inexperience." Beverly sighed hard at Krista. "All you had to do was follow our instructions. We breathe life into Simona and therefore know exactly how she should behave."

The aunts stood together like a couple of uneven bookends, sizing up their niece in disappointment.

Krista was too wound up in her own emotions to immediately tune in to their wavelength. "Did you hear the way he talked to me? To *me*? I'm not some dummy to be squashed!"

Rachel shook her finger with a quick reminder. "This isn't all about you, dear! It's about us! Our column!"

Krista conceded that it was about all of them. The aunts and their column. Krista and her obligation to the aunts. But it was her diagnosis of Michael Collins, a man so wound up in his career that he couldn't discern his business moves from his personal ones, that really made her simmer. Even though she herself was a fanatic about putting business affairs first, she was outraged that her charms hadn't taken him in. The very idea that the seduction challenge had come to mean so much once she got revved up was surprising and disturbing. She never allowed men to shake her up to this point. It made her feel too vulnerable, distracted her from her work.

"It's a shame he and I couldn't reach some understanding," she said in fumbled apology. "I tried. I really tried."

"But you failed," Beverly chided.

"Just as you failed with your advice to his fiancée," Krista fired back. "Don't overlook the fact that he's only mad at me because he doesn't know about you."

"Apparently a more seasoned temptress was needed." Rachel tilted her blond head from side to side. "Perhaps with a little theatrical makeup and a dark wig, I could have—"

"You play the young nymph, Simona?" Beverly clapped her ample bosom. "Dear lord give me strength."

Rachel glowed. "In her place I would have put him on the scamper."

"He'd have scampered for cover! You're old enough to be his mother."

"Big sister, maybe."

"He is thirty, you are sixty. Do the math."

"Still, I would have been better than Krista."

The idea that they didn't appreciate her sex appeal one bit hit a strong nerve in Krista. She stuttered angrily above their bickering. "I was to, sexy. You just don't understand the executive mind. He was way too smart to fall for a surface dazzle like this one. Face it, he was too smart for me—for you! But I did it up sweet, fantastic. Just look at these shoulders," she said with a snap of one stretchy sleeve. "I am a turn-on and tuned in."

The aunts regarded her with skepticism, and worse, unmistakable pity.

Krista stomped a heel. "C'mon, you couldn't even see me in action!"

"But, dear," Beverly said, "we heard everything."

"Everything but the necessary male panting of desire," Rachel added.

"I'm telling you, no woman could've gotten through to him!"

Rachel held her determined, if not dewy, gaze. "The bottom line is indisputable. You didn't pull our butts out of this sling. When you realized you couldn't handle him, you should've made the phone call."

But Krista didn't feel compelled to make the call. In her customary role as boss she'd made her own gut decision. The very idea that they were blaming her youth and level of experience in the matter was silly. But it was predictable because to them, she'd always be that made-up girl in the photograph. This seemed the perfect time to reveal that other gut decision she'd been repressing for too long.

"I'm sorry this didn't work out." Krista marched over to the desk to gather her things. "But it's left me with the feeling that I've stretched the role as far as I should. I'm not good at faking things the way you two are. It's high time I retire my shawl and my voodoo hairdo. Use my picture if you like, but I am finished with the Simona schmooze, no more personal appearances like today's fiasco."

"But Doughman isn't finished with you yet," Beverly protested. "He said so."

The very idea of unfinished business with Michael Collins sent a tingle down her spine. She eased on her raincoat, fighting the sensation. "He doesn't have my number, and I prefer to keep it that way."

"He'll probably be determined to sue us now."

"Don't be so dramatic. He'll probably come to see the obvious, that the wrong wife at an important convention would do him more harm than good."

"The wrong wife…"

"Versus the right wife…"

Krista looked up in time to see the yin and yang sisters exchanging their trademark look of inspiration. She never ceased to be amazed at the way these two completely different women could merge into one dangerous entity.

"That's right," Krista went on. "A dynamic man like Michael Collins shouldn't be in any hurry in choosing a mate. He needs a sensible wife who understands the complexities of running a business. Someone who confronts him on issues. Who likes doughnuts, for Pete's sake!"

"You do know your doughnuts," Rachel said sweetly.

"I daresay that he does need a wife like me. But he'll no doubt grow old chasing wishy-washy waiflike party girls full of self-doubt who feel the need to consult a columnist for redirection!"

"Perhaps we've been a bit too hard on you, dear," Beverly clucked maternally. "You were only trying to support our original stand, which made the most sense."

Rachel stroked her niece's hair. "And we're very sorry if we offended you with our remarks about your sexuality."

"O-kay…" Krista eyed them warily.

"You do have the Mattson charm and good looks." Beverly preened.

Rachel sighed consolingly. "Trouble is, you've been riding a bicycle with training wheels all these years and we were wrong to yank off those training wheels so abruptly. Seducing a workaholic like Doughman would be no easy feat, even for an experienced diva. It was wrong to expect a rookie like you to let it all hang out on such short notice—with no practice."

"Hang on there!" Krista took a deep breath and counted to ten. They were trying so hard to make amends that it was getting downright insulting. "Look, I need to go home now, see if it's possible to transform myself into a professional for a one o'clock appointment."

The aunts beamed, at a good five hundred watts.

"You go along, dear."

"Yes, you have a life, too."

Once in the elevator car Krista realized she'd misbuttoned her coat. A mistake that proved her distraction.

What a morning. Even now, with the dust clearing, she was sure she had done the right thing with Michael. Her only regret was that he wasn't content with her judgment call. He had found her sexy, of that she was certain. But how much more firepower would it have taken to make him take his medicine and like it?

She moved through the lobby and out into the lingering drizzle. Oh, damn, he probably didn't find her sexy at all.

KRISTA A.K.A. SIMONA was a lethal weapon. A heat-seeking missile on a search-and-destroy mission.

These were Michael Collins thoughts over a lonely room-service dinner that evening at the downtown Holiday Inn.

He jabbed a forkful of green beans from his plate and chomped them down. It was all so very puzzling. In some respects Krista Mattson was the quintessential Simona Says—sassy, brassy and smug. But at times her mind operated like a steel trap, full of sound deductive reasoning that belied her frothy advice column. A frothy column that would be better served by her more practical side. But as she admitted herself, her column was showbiz. Perhaps a more serious column wouldn't have been such a hit in syndication. Her schtick was catchy, he imagined, for the average American reader over morning coffee.

He took a gulp of his mineral water and set the bottle back on the hotel desk with a slam. Here he was, actually finding points in her favor! Certainly an unconscious move. And intolerable.

Never had he been mesmerized and scandalized by a single woman.

He was a chump who no longer knew his own mind. To think how crystal clear he'd been on everything before marching into Simona's office. She'd wriggled under his skin with that dazzling sensuality, then thumped him over the head with ruthless logic.

She'd actually had the nerve to suggest that she was saving him from himself. From a doomed marriage…

Dammit, he'd come to realize she made a valuable case.

How could he ever have considered marrying a girl who carried a calorie counter in every purse? Who slogged through the day at a menial job just to change dress and burst onto the club scene? Who at her worst refused to take a single bite of a Delectable Delights doughnut, his crowning glory? His reason for living?

So blinded by the idea of finally settling down, having a wife to come home to, and more immediately, a dazzler on his arm for the convention, he'd overlooked the obvious differences in their personalities.

Part of him wanted to sue the panties off Krista Mattson for waking him up. Another part of him wondered exactly what kind of panties she'd worn under that tight knit dress today.

He was contemplating the matter when there was a knock on his hotel room door. Krista? Bob Freeman?

He opened the door wide to find the bellman carrying a giant goodie basket. Digging into his pants pocket he extracted a couple of loose bills and accepted his delivery.

The contents were far more to his liking than the bland roast beef platter he'd been munching on. It was brimming with fresh fruit, assorted cheeses and crackers, even a bottle of wine.

He used two long fingers to scissor the large note card buried between two bright-red apples. Tearing open the envelope he found a stiff white notecard embossed with *Simona Says* in silver.

His hand shook slightly as he read the card over and over again. Bless this wild woman's heart! She'd had the nerve to shoot down his whole game, but ultimately had the sensitivity to come up with a reasonable solution. Considering his rudeness, this was quite a gesture. Of course, his threat of a lawsuit was bound to have had some bearing on her generosity. But not a lot, as a quick call to Irritated In Illinois would've gotten her off the hook. The possibilities jacked him up, sent him into a near tailspin. He couldn't wait to speak with her. There was no phone number on the card, but the envelope bore her address.

Plainly, she wanted to discuss this in person rather than over the phone.

Basket in hand, he dashed out the door.

Chapter Four

It was a routine brainstorming session for Bigtime Promotions. Krista and Judy Phillips were at Krista's Minneapolis town house, huddled together at her dining room table over a huge sheet of paper loaded with scribbles. It was the favored creative exercise for the pair. They began with a nugget of an idea, a core phrase written in the center of the paper, then formed a cluster of related buzzwords around it until they had a substantial concept to present their latest client. In this case the client was a local chain of electronics stores.

It always was a casual session when held after hours, away from office formality. Judy was dressed in red capris and white knit shirt, quite practical for her dash over from her own town house, three blocks over in the same development. Krista was wearing some threadbare jeans and a gray Hamline U T-shirt. Both had their hair gathered in high bouncy ponytails.

They worked contentedly to the soft backdrop of jazz. Each sipped a diet cola, anticipating dinner as the appetizing scent of supermarket lasagna and garlic bread heating emanated from the oven.

Presently their cluster was leaning toward a sci-fi theme, with the main focus on a robotic character who could conceivably hand out a giveaway sack, including perhaps a store coupon, a cheapo calculator, and maybe a CD featuring the afternoon drive show of a local radio team.

They were discussing who could possibly play the role of the robot on the cheap, namely Judy herself, when the doorbell rang.

"Saved by the bell!" Judy said sweetly.

"A temporary fix," Krista vowed. "You've given yourself away as a natural greeter with that clown appearance at Hawkson Motors." Tossing her pencil onto the table with a clatter, she moved through the small living room to the door. A glance through the peephole and she was scurrying back to Judy.

"Ah, ah…" Her mouth hung open. Wide.

"What's the matter?"

"It's him. Doughman!"

"No kidding." Judy's laughter rang out, as she'd been treated to a vivid description of the morning's events at the newspaper.

"What could he possibly want?"

"How did he even find you? You aren't listed in the phone book."

Krista was thoughtful. "The aunts must have done something, Jude."

"Would they dare take it to the next level after today's fiasco?"

Krista gasped. "Certainly! They're bigger promoters than we are. Remember the time they signed us up for voice lessons so they could get a free blender?"

"The teacher was so mean, and it only had three speeds."

"Remember the time their handsome neighbor needed dates for his homely twin sons and they lured us to that dance?"

"Those hideous gardenia corsages they pinned on us at the house should've been a bellwether."

"Remember the time I had engine trouble at the State Fair and called them to find me a professional mechanic?

Instead they summoned Rick into action, that old boyfriend of mine they liked so much just because his mother once shook hands with Susan Lucci?"

"That must have been an awkward tune-up, as you had another date at the time."

"I ended up with no dates for weeks!"

"Okay." Judy relented. "The aunties are poor operators at times."

"All the time! Which is why it's high time I slip out of their clutches."

Judy halfheartedly tried to conceal her amusement. "Well, they've gotcha at least one last time."

"Really?" Krista folded her arms and jutted her chin stubbornly. "I believe I'll simply pretend I'm not here."

"He's seen the lights. Probably heard the jazz."

She knew to the depths of her sensible soul that she had to respond, but couldn't help fretting. "After the way he stormed off on a threat this morning, who knows what he wants now!"

"So slip into Simona and find out!" Judy enthused. "Sounds more exciting than our work."

Perhaps it did. A little bit...

Suddenly Krista clapped her hands to her bare cheeks. "But I can't in this condition. Simona wouldn't dress this grubby if she were the last woman on earth, or wear her hair like Little Bo-Peep, or be caught dead without makeup."

"She would if she was just out of the shower—no, make that a scented bubble bath," Judy amended, on a roll. "I will answer the door, while you hide in the bathroom. Count to fifty, then come out in a robe, your hair concealed in a towel. That way, he won't expect the full hairdo and face makeup." Noting that her friend seemed paralyzed, Judy gave her a push toward the hallway. "Scoot!"

Michael was startled when the door finally popped open and rather than the tall, willowy, dark-featured Krista, there stood a petite blonde. Judging by her cute appearance, he first thought she might be a teenager. But as she moved under the entry light he realized it was her size and hairdo that had thrown him off. Like Krista, she was well into her twenties.

"Hello," he began slowly. "I'm not sure I have the right town house. Does Krista Mattson live here?"

"Why, yes."

"I'm Michael Collins. An acquaintance," he added awkwardly.

Judy expressed delighted surprise. "The man from the newspaper. Well, come right in." She stepped out of the way as he crossed the threshold into the tiny entryway. "I'm Judy Phillips, Krista's best friend."

"Nice to meet you." He followed Judy into the living room, toting the goodie basket.

Krista's guest, a levelheaded friend no less, proved to be only his first surprise.

There was the home's stark decor to appraise, white walls bearing some abstract prints, champagne shaded carpeting, tan leather furniture and some low, practical end tables.

Hardly the sultan's harem he'd envisioned, with Krista awaiting him on a purple satin sofa, dressed in something suitably flimsy to help cajole him into submission.

A secret part of him had been looking forward to that.

"Krista's bathing at the moment," Judy explained.

The announcement snapped him from his reverie. He could hear the annoyance in his own voice. "Is she planning to go out this evening?"

Judy considered this and winked slyly. "Perhaps later. She's hard to pin down after dark."

The notion of pinning down the sexy Simona after dark sent an unwelcome tremor of desire through him. It wasn't fair that he found Krista so attractive when she was in the process of wrecking his life.

In her favor, though, she'd made a valiant attempt at amends.

Still, all things considered, wasn't it the very least she could do?

His feelings for her rose and fell like a wild roller coaster. She was bad, she was good. Back and forth. He was feeling as anxious as a schoolboy picking up his first date.

What fun she could have with his attraction to her, considering that it backed her theory that his fiancée wasn't right for him.

Krista's apparent insight into his psyche was a number one frustration.

Her sexuality was a close second, however. But surely his feelings were physical, whimsical. They had no footing in reality. The woman flounced around in costume, doled out daring irresponsible advice to strangers. She was too much like a carnival gypsy for his comfort.

Judy was watching him curiously. "Maybe I'll go tell Krista you're here."

"She's expecting me, of course."

Judy's eyes widened a fraction. "Is she?"

He beamed. "A man doesn't receive a basket like this one, a message like hers, every day."

"Please, take a seat."

Krista jumped as Judy eased through the bathroom door. She had shucked down to her white cotton bra and panties and was wrapping a towel round her head turban-style.

"You were only supposed to count to fifty."

"I'm too nervous to count. Have any clue what he wants?"

Judy leaned against the vanity. "He says he got a message."

"From whom?"

"From you."

Krista stared at her stricken reflection in the huge wall mirror over the vanity. "Wonder how hard the aunts have pushed it?"

"Fairly hard, I imagine, to get this man off his high horse

and over here. Good lord, he's humming with assurance. And what a hottie. Easy to see why you're shaken up.''

''How angry is he?''

''Angry? Who said anything about angry?''

''He isn't mad?''

''Nope. He's…excited.''

Krista stared at her own blank-faced reflection. ''I can't think why.'' But the very idea sent her pulse racing. She took a fortifying breath. ''May as well get this over with. Quick, hand me my robe.''

Judy touched the white velour wrap on the door peg. ''Is this the only robe you have?''

''It is a bathrobe. I am supposed to be bathing.''

''Simona's only use for velour would be to give her shoes a quick polish.''

Krista moaned. ''You are so right.''

''C'mon, you've got to get into the spirit of things.'' Judy looked around the bathroom suite, opened the linen closet. ''Have you anything else?''

''I have the scarlet kimono we both bought on our trip to Hawaii last year.''

''Where is it?''

''On the shelf of my bedroom closet, near the back.''

''Hope it's not in its original packaging.''

Krista scoffed defensively. ''Oh, just fluff it up a little bit!''

Judy gave her head a rueful shake. ''Mine has wine stains and a rip in the sleeve from a private dance session with that assistant director from Uptown.''

''You played around in a two hundred dollar robe?''

''Yes. It was worth every penny.'' Judy turned to grip the doorknob. ''I'll be back in a flash with the goods. In the meantime, run an inch of water in the tub and sprinkle in some oil for effect.''

Krista raised a dubious brow. ''Surely that won't be necessary. He won't be coming in here.''

Judy spoke in a light singsong. ''I don't know. He seems

set on a real visit. Brought along refreshments, a goodie basket, complete with a bottle of merlot. Oh, and by the way, the basket is from you.''

Krista's heart skipped a beat. ''Hmm…better bring the matching scarlet slippers, as well.''

''I'll bet those are in their original box, too.'' With that shot, Judy left, returning a few minutes later with the packages.

Krista eventually mustered the nerve to make her appearance in scarlet. She entered the living area to see Judy and Michael in the dining alcove, poring over their cluster still spread out on the table. Had he discovered her true vocation? Surely Judy wouldn't let that happen. Not on purpose. But Michael was sharp.

''Krista!'' Judy spotted her first. ''Michael noticed the Visons Electronics campaign. I was just telling him all about *my* company. He thinks it's awfully nice of you to help me brainstorm whenever I need an extra muse.''

Not a bad story, Krista decided. Michael appeared to be buying it, quite engrossed in the cluster they'd created.

As for her physical appearance, she hoped she'd found a balance between Simona and herself, dressed in this exotic ensemble, with the amount of face color she generally wore to work. Nervously she concentrated on readjusting the sash cinching her waist.

''So…Krista.''

Her gaze jumped up at his croon. His eyes held the same lusty weight, as he wasted no time giving her a full body search.

He had a lot of nerve treating her this way! Then she reminded herself that he was treating Simona this way, that Simona invited just this sort of male attention. He would assume she liked it.

It was possible that she might come to like it.

''Hope I haven't come at an inconvenient time.'' He gestured to the cluster drawing. ''You're a lot busier than I had expected.''

"Nothing pressing."

His eyebrows lowered. "Judy already explained that you go out most nights."

Krista was startled by the unexpected curve. "I don't go out all that—"

"Early," Judy inserted smoothly. "I tried to make that clear to him," she told Krista.

He openly struggled to suppress his annoyance. "I assumed the goodie basket made for two was for the two of us."

Krista glanced at the basket sitting on a dining room chair. That certainly had been the Simona team's intention. The aunts frequently hand-packed goodie baskets for peace offerings and romantic encounters. Beverly supplied comfort food; Rachel, alcohol and greenery.

He gestured to the bottle of wine. "This merlot is particularly nice."

Rachel's favorite, Krista noted wryly. The trap was a good one, and no graceful escape that she could see. "You are right about my intentions, of course," she felt compelled to say. "Care to sit in the living room for a chat?"

"I believe I'll just go check on dinner," Judy said. "Of course you'll stay, Michael."

"Something smells great," he called after Judy. "I understand Krista is a great cook."

Judy gaped, but recovered enough to make a smooth exit.

Krista led him into the living room, aware of the sensual caress of the satin fabric against her skin. It made her feel like someone else, the sort of woman he believed her to be.

Michael watched her perch on the arm of a chair, then sat down on the nearest end of the sofa, setting the basket on the end table between them. "I also feel I must apologize for my criticism of your writing talents."

She stared at him blankly. "Why?"

"Because of the lovely note you sent me, of course."

Sure enough, wedged between the block of cheddar and

box of chocolates sat a white square envelope. A message. A trap. "I believe I'd like that glass of wine now," she said in a bright rush.

Michael handled the uncorking expertly, filling the pair of wineglasses she picked out of the basket. He lifted high a glass of the rich red liquid. "To your thoughtful and generous offer."

Her mind screamed in panic behind her frozen smile. Simona had made him an offer?

Somehow, she had to find out what sort of offer. Fortunately, she hit upon a way as he began to tilt his glass into hers for a clink. With the flick of a wrist she tipped her glass, managing to splash some merlot onto his beige knit pullover. She felt awful about it, and grateful as he jumped off the sofa before it could splash onto her cushions.

She was so very sorry. But desperate measures called for desperate action. "Oh dear, oh no." She made all the right sounds, pushing him in the direction of the kitchen, calling out to Judy to ready a damp towel. As Judy appeared in the doorway to assess the damages, Krista plucked the envelope from the basket and waved it in the air so Judy would get the picture and stall him. Then she tore free the crisp white card inside.

Ah, the official Simona stationery.

My dear Mr. Collins:

I honestly tried to do a good deed today. Perhaps I didn't deliver my message properly. I was too sexy. Hope you won't sue. No matter what you decide, I am finished with the Simona schmooze, no more personal appearances like today's fiasco. Believe me, I am tuned in and turned on to your dilemma. You are a dynamic man, too smart for me in some ways. Still, I maintain that I have some insight. The wrong wife could do you more harm than good at a high-pressure convention. I daresay, you need a wife like me at your side. I'd show you.

Yours,
Simona

She sat dumbfounded, holding the card in a loose grasp. The aunts were diabolical. They'd managed to cleverly lift a series of her remarks out of context to form this—this pandering piece of junk mail!

No wonder Michael had come zipping over. His ego had to be the size of a blimp right now.

As for the offer, was he seriously considering allowing her to play the role of his wife for the Decadent Delights crowd? With shaky fingers she returned the card to its envelope and jammed it down near the cheese.

"Taking back some of your favors?" a baritone voice asked.

Caught with her hand in the basket. "You can't trust me," she lilted.

He sat down on the sofa again and eyed the upturned envelope with suspicion. "You were handling your own note?"

"No. Yes. I—"

"Okay, what's the game now? May as well tell me where we stand. My toast took all the color from your face. Not to mention its effect on your dexterity," he added, touching the damp spot on his shirt. Judy had done a fairly good job removing the stain.

Before she could respond there was some clattering from the kitchen and Judy appeared in the adjoining dining room to gather up some belongings. "I believe I'll skip our dinner," she said, breezing in on them with the cluster sheet rolled in a tube. She patted Michael's arm as she passed by him. "Good to meet you."

"Yes. Thanks for the rescue."

"Just get that shirt top cleaned properly."

"Don't forget your tote bag, Jude." Krista walked her to the foyer.

"Ooh, Kris," Judy enthused in a whisper, "he is delicious. Not at all the dud the aunts believe."

"I know it."

"Seems unusually bright, too, aside from his faith that you can cook. What a harebrained idea!"

"That isn't the only harebrained idea he has."

"Oh?"

"He believes I've volunteered to play his wife!"

"Gee, for real?"

She squinted at her pal. "I imagine for the duration of the convention."

"Still, gee."

"What should I do? Say?"

Judy bit her lip. "This is a crossroads. You either have to bust the aunts' game wide open or stand by their generous offer."

Krista looked at her helplessly. "I am simply too stunned to think."

She gave Krista a quick squeeze. "Talk it over with him at dinner. Just so you know, your kitchen is now a gourmet haven. I transferred your store lasagna from its aluminum pan to your glass cake pan, the bread from its sack to some foil I found folded in a drawer. Oh, I also prepared that premixed salad in a bag you had—put it in your popcorn bowl."

"That salad was our lunch for tomorrow."

"So bring one of those expired soup mixes from the back of your cupboard."

Krista blew out a nervous breath. "Okay. Thanks. I'll call when he leaves."

"You bet you will. No matter how late."

Krista found Michael had wandered into the kitchen and was peeking in the oven. "Looks just about ready," she said over his stooped shoulder.

He closed the oven and straightened to full height, about six inches above her five-foot-six stature. Krista noted that he was beginning to show signs of wear, traces of vulnerability underneath his confident show of strength.

He'd brought wine along and now handed her a freshly filled glass. "You girls seemed to be having fun. Get a good laugh out of the lonely pastry mogul's love life?"

"Certainly not. Judy and I aren't in the habit of tramping all over men."

"I agree, she doesn't seem the man-killer type."

The inference was that Krista *was* the type, but she had no defense. She was playing the role of a vamp. A part of her was repelled by the idea, but another part was intrigued by her ability to pull it off even this far.

Imagine, a male actually thought her a threat to mankind!

Suddenly, the room was hot. Whether it was the force of the oven, the potency of the wine or a blend of their own desperation was uncertain.

"I believe we were discussing your proposition," he declared coolly.

Krista sensed there would never be a better time to set him straight about the force behind Simona, while she was pumped up with self-righteousness. Beverly and Rachel had no right to send him that note without her permission. Theirs had always been a collaboration. This was coercion. This was out and out coercion! What was the wisest course of action?

She felt a frown of indecision settle upon her face. Michael's voice grew slightly anxious. "I understood the note correctly, didn't I? The offer of a wife to replace my fiancée at the convention?"

"That's how it reads," she hedged.

There was no mistaking the joy in his expression. Grateful words spilled from his mouth. "Let me say up front that it was extraordinarily kind of you to even consider playing the role. Also, I'd like to apologize for my behavior this morning. Maybe if I hadn't been so hot-tempered, you would've been comfortable making this suggestion right off the bat. But on the other hand," he relented rather sourly,

"I didn't immediately see you as any sort of solution maker, probably wouldn't have given your offer the chance it deserved."

"You are on the way to wrecking this all over again," she warned.

"I don't mean to insult you. All I mean to say is that once I calmed down, I realized this is mighty decent of you. When you didn't care for my solution you went to work and came up with one of your own. Even if it is under the threat of a lawsuit and it is only a temporary fix to my relationship loss, it's a nice and thoughtful idea."

Yes, those busy-bee aunts of hers had been quite busy.

He went on with gusto. "I realize there's little in it for you. There is the free trip to Vegas. And I will be off your back—and the newspaper's—permanently. Still, it has to be an inconvenience, taking vacation unexpectedly. All things considered, I'll make things as easy as possible."

A whole week away from her career. Krista hadn't considered how that would affect her. She didn't take time off as a rule. At least, never more than a day or two in a row. Why, her job was the centerpiece of her whole life. Her days revolved around any number of projects.

"There will be a level of intimacy involved," he continued. "You and I, virtual strangers, sharing a suite of rooms at the Imperial Majestic."

"We will be sharing a suite?" she gasped. "Maybe this isn't such a good idea, after all," she said slowly. "Simona—I can be too darn impulsive for my own good sometimes."

He merely smiled, unfazed. "Even for a live wire like you, I imagine this is a stretch. But believe me, I'll make every effort to give you space and privacy when we're not on display at convention functions. All the convention suites are large. With two separate bedrooms spaced far apart," he assured, spreading his arms wide.

Krista doubted the bedrooms were that far apart, but she got the message, he wouldn't be hitting on her. With professional acumen he was off on a fresh campaign to persuade, shame and, lastly, commend the engagement-wrecking Simona. "To be perfectly honest," he finally admitted, "I can't imagine going along if our roles were reversed."

"I would feel better if I knew really you," she admitted.

"Though I am not the dud you first pegged me to be," he assured, "neither am I a wolf. I run my affairs with smarts and confidence. I set a goal and get it done. With efficiency. Our arrangement will be handled the same way."

She believed him. And again marveled at how similar they were. "How crazy this scheme must seem to a man like you," she said.

"It's best described as a crazy business necessity; a phrase that's never applied to me before. But life is full of surprises." He gave her a loopy grin. "So, Krista, do you agree to be my wife for the duration of the convention?"

His face was inches over hers now. It was a handsome face, with just a trace of bristle roughing up the jaw. Again she inhaled the rich spice scent of his skin. He was so strong, so masculine, so determined. So unlike the sort of semi-ambitious men she'd attracted since her hungry college days. Yes, pure, delicious hunger set Michael Collins apart from his thirtyish peers. He hadn't lost that energy source so common in men ten years his junior. He was eager, intense, devoted. A potent blend when aged to perfection.

This could be the adventure of her life. If she had the guts for it.

"Well?" Grasping her arms, he gave her a gentle shake.

"I do," she murmured dreamily. "I mean, yes!"

He gave her the businessman's handshake, firm and sure. "Good deal. Let's eat. I'm starved."

Michael didn't seem to notice that Krista was all thumbs in even the meal's most basic preparation. Accustomed to handling food, he darted round the kitchen, removing the lasagna from the oven along with the bread, tossing the salad. Krista filled water glasses, amazed at Judy's inventiveness to make the meal look home cooked. The strip of foil on the bread was a wrapper from some take-out place. And the glass pan, a gift from a client, was generally used to store stray pencils and rubber bands.

As they settled into chairs at opposite ends of the table, Krista demurely expressed doubt that she could represent herself as the sort of wife expected at his convention.

"Not as you are, of course!"

Certainly not the polite retort she had expected. Her fork clattered to her plate. "Excuse me?"

"After running wild your whole life, you're hardly prepared to hold a candle to the ideal executive wife. But I will coach you personally. In no time you will be the image of perfection, everything Gerald Stewart or I could ever expect."

Krista couldn't help comparing his image of Mrs. Right with the robot she and Judy were concocting in their latest promo campaign. "This model wife image you have, is it just for Gerald Stewart's sake or are you serious about it yourself?"

He hesitated, a forkful of salad greens poised in the air. "What do you mean?"

"It seems to me you are looking for an unusually co-operative mate."

"All men prefer cooperative women."

"Yes, but eventually they wake up in the morning and accept it was only a dream."

He laughed. "Marriage is all about cooperation, of course."

"Give and take on both sides, though."

"True. But I have every right to put a personal spin on my own expectations. My dream mate is someone willing to support my business."

"But what if your wife has a solid career of her own?"

He was dubious. "All the serious career women I've

dated have proven way too busy to even consider my feelings, much less marriage.''

"There are a few out there who aren't complete monsters.''

"Sure, but what are the odds of a busy man like me meeting one? No, after several years at the hunt, I have my sights set exclusively on a woman looking to share *my* dream.''

"Happily ever after as Mrs. Decadent Delights?''

"Exactly! I know you're being sarcastic, but such arrangements can be very happy. Take for instance my friends the Larkins, Allan and Norah.''

"The mentors from Chicago.''

"Right. Allan had a dream and Norah respected that dream, made it her dream, too. Allan's a lucky man, let me tell ya.''

"Is Norah satisfied?''

"Definitely. She loves her role as much as Allan loves her.''

"So tell me the truth, did you ever consider Irritated In Illinois this sort of dream material underneath her party girl exterior, or were you just that desperate to show up at that convention with somebody?''

"I originally had high hopes. She disliked her clerical job, seemed open to a new venture. And she had the social skills to handle all the public contact. With customers to wait on, events, charity functions and employee programs to organize, her fear of loneliness was ridiculous. And if ever she wanted to hold my hand, I'd have been right there waiting across a doughnut display case.'' His features narrowed as he eyed Krista across the table. "But rather than give me a chance to sell myself, she cried to you. And chop! Off came my head. In print. For the amusement of millions.''

She flinched as his hand chopped the table. "For your own sake, don't you think you should forget about Irritated In Illinois? Move on?''

"You've left me no choice, have you."

Properly shut down, Krista leaned back in her seat and busied herself with her pasta.

The silence wore on. Finally he sighed deeply, staring across the table. "Truth is, I do want to move on. I probably shouldn't be telling you this, as it might weaken my case for a lawsuit, but I'm relieved you didn't call my fiancée today. I cooled down after our talk and realized any woman who couldn't confide her troubles to me isn't bound to make a good match. No matter how sincere I might have been, no matter how hard I might have tried to build a fulfilling marriage, it amounts to nothing without communication."

"You can trust me on this, Michael," she said warmly, "your mate will come along one of these days, by surprise, with an explosion of chemistry."

"I doubt it. My recent mistake was made just that way. I fell into trouble because I was desperate. All that's about to change, though. No more nightclubs or blind dates for me." He stared off into space. "I see my girl, walking through the door of my shop one day, looking around and spotting me. Our eyes will lock, we will talk. She will show an immediate and avid interest in the shop. She will be glad to join my team."

She tipped her water glass at him. "Happy hunting," she said drolly.

"I happen to think a lot of women might very well find my master plan quite appealing."

"So they might," she relented, though she herself gave it a cool zero on the marriage meter. She was so accustomed to leading the charge as he did, to calling the shots, pouring all her energies into her business, that she viewed his dream as one of antiquated autocracy.

Krista also couldn't help noting that the issue of love had never come up, not at the newspaper, not even now as he realigned his goals. How sad, as *love* was the four-letter word that made the world go round. Granted, she wasn't setting the singles world on fire herself. She rarely took a date seriously these days, her biggest agony of late being whether to replace Bigtime Promotion's photocopier. But she was wise enough to know love was a necessity for the long haul.

She couldn't help wondering what it would be like to ultimately sweep Michael off his feet. To be the one who opened his eyes to the joys of love. She could only imagine how he would react to such a discovery, imagine sharing his joy, amazement and abandonment.

But it was only self-torture to consider Michael a possibility. His Antiquated Autocracy Plan assured he would marry blindly and stupidly.

Even Ms. Big didn't expect her big romance to fall that neatly into line.

Chapter Five

Michael returned to his hotel room to find the red button on his phone flashing a message. The voice mail proved to be from Allan Larkin, his friend and mentor, presently stationed in Las Vegas—Gerald Stewart territory.

"Hello there, Mikey. Just got home from the shop. Norah tells me you called from Minnesota this afternoon with some nonsense about maybe skipping the convention. What's that all about? And what are you doing in Minneapolis? Call, no matter how late."

Michael sat on the edge of the bed and dialed the Larkins' familiar number.

"Hey, Allan! Yeah, it's me. I'm fine, really. No, I'll be coming, after all. Just had a touch of the flu or something. But I'm feeling better already. Can't you guess why I'm in the Twin Cities? It's where my fiancée lives! No, her name's not Colleen. You're confusing my girlfriends. Her name is Krista Mattson. Can't wait for you and Norah to meet her. No, haven't known her long. Of course she's interested in the business. A lot like Norah." Feeling guilty over the first lies he'd ever told Allan, he winced. "Of course, we know there is only one Norah. Yes, I'll see you in a few days. Kiss her for me. Bye now."

With a shaky breath, he replaced the receiver on its cradle. Hopefully he hadn't overplayed his hand. But Allan would expect his fiancée to be the supportive kind. Michael had never kept secret his admiration for the way Norah supported Allan's career, putting herself wholeheartedly into first his Chicago shop, and then his Vegas branch. He'd been barely sixteen when he was hired on by Allan as an apprentice baker. Allan and Norah had changed his life with their support and approval. For the first time in his life he'd felt wanted, needed, important.

Now, on top of the stress of the contest, he desperately wanted the Larkins to like Krista. Even if it were only for a matter of days. Certainly they'd eventually hear of their breakup, but he wanted his mentors to admire his choice in a wife just the same.

No, the larger-than-life Simona was nothing like the simple soul Norah, as he'd claimed. But she could pass inspection with a little direction. Dropping the *Says* from her title was his first order of business. If she cut back on the chatter, it would go a long way toward clinching the charade. There was a lot to be said for keeping quiet; it left people open to assume the best in you.

But how could he possibly hope to shush a woman who actually offered up opinions for a living? Inflammatory opinions. Impulsive opinions. Downright rotten opinions! The sort of opinions that had started his troubles in the first place.

Indulging in this sort of panic attack wasn't going to help, he realized. He needed to approach the task—transforming Simona into a subdued lady worthy of the Decadent Delights family—as a business venture. In her favor, she hadn't seemed quite as overbearing at home tonight, probably because she was tired. She'd be back in form for the convention, no doubt. He was set to return to Chicago tomorrow to get ready for the trip, and then it was back here to Minneapolis on Friday to spend a single day preparing her for her role. The next week was bound to be the craziest of his life.

Later, as he drifted off to sleep, Michael tried to imagine Krista the proper lady, subdued and polite, dressed in a two-piece suit. But no matter how hard he tried, his mind held fast to the image of her in that little red robe and slippers, shimmering with sheer indolence.

The image was a guilty pleasure, without a doubt—one he could not afford right now. He was busy. Upwardly mobile. There was no place in his life for a reckless nymph. How ironic that just such a woman was to be his savior. She was wrong for him in every conceivable way. Still, there was an intriguing buzz between them that he'd never experienced before.

KRISTA GAVE HER BOTTOM DESK DRAWER a thump closed as her aunts entered her inner office at Bigtime Promotions the following morning. "I am not speaking to you."

"That's silly.

"Especially at a time like this."

Krista straightened in her chair and surveyed the pair: Beverly, her plump face alive with anticipation; Rachel, her mascara-coated eyes dewy behind a lacy kerchief.

"We just got the wonderful news from Bob," Rachel gushed. "Michael Collins called him first thing this morning all cheery and nice. Mapped out your plans, first-class all the way, it seems. Imagine, our little girl, on the way to Las Vegas. It's a dream, a lifelong dream."

Beverly inhaled tolerantly. "Not the way we would have preferred the good news, of course. Perhaps you meant to call us yourself but sprained your dialing finger."

Krista balked. "You two are the ones who sprained something—between the ears! How could you move forward without my permission? I was floored when Michael showed up at my door last night with one of your custom baskets, that teasing mash note!"

"The basket was an innocent peace offering. As for the note, it was in your own words, dear," Beverly claimed self-righteously. "If you meant for your sentiments to be confidential, you should have said so."

"The words may have been my own—"

"Oh, they were," Rachel assured. "Beverly's razor-sharp memory is quite a phenomenon. It was simply amazing the way she started spouting off all your remarks. I had to use my old waitress shorthand to get it down."

"But you took my remarks out of context, completely changed my meaning!"

A tense silence fell over the room. The aunts had the grace to avert her gazes.

"All right," Rachel whined in confession, "we pulled a fast one. But you would've said no to the whole neato deal."

"Naturally! Michael and I are complete strangers who have no business playing house!" Indeed, this had been her first thought of the morning as she sat up in bed. How had she allowed herself to catch a satin slipper in such an intimate trap! But wearing a satin slipper in the first place had much to do with it, along with the satin robe, the wine consumption and the late hour. Things had gotten a little too cozy for clear thinking.

Here and now, in the light of day, her own duplicity in the masquerade stunned and terrified her.

"He's safe enough," Beverly stated urbanely. "Bob did a check on him. He's every bit the straight shooter he seems, a hardworking man who'd much rather nibble on a doughnut than a dish like you. Even if he finds you attractive, he'd never jeopardize offending you during the charade with a come-on, risk losing your cooperation. As long as his business is on the front burner, you're bound to be nothing more than a cute accessory on his arm."

"Playing pretend can be such fun if you let go," Rachel cooed. "Bob and I do it all time. Sometimes he's the sheriff and I'm the dance hall girl. Or he's the train robber and I'm the dance hall girl. Or he's the drifter and I'm—"

Beverly cut in sharply. "That is more than we want to know, Miss Kitty. Though," she added with a stroke to her fleshy chins, "it does explain some rather strange snippets of talk I overheard one night last week."

"And of course it is strictly business in your mind, as well, is it not?" Rachel challenged Krista while ignoring her sister's comments. "You'll feel no real emotion in the playacting, will you?"

"Certainly not," Krista said slowly, unable to shake off the sparks she felt reliving their talk in her kitchen, the way he filled up the space and her senses. Michael had such authority about him, such strength, such sex appeal. With difficulty, she found her voice. "Even so, if I were to go through with this trip, I'd lose precious time at work." She gestured nervously to her littered desk. "I would be letting so many people down were I to leave. It's easier to never take a vacation. To keep hard at it. I have my plans, my schedules, my comfortable framework."

Rachel waved a jeweled hand. "You are exaggerating your importance around here, surely."

"Always were too intense," Beverly concurred. "You think you have to oversee every little detail of every little job."

"Hello, ladies." Judy eased through the door with an armload of files and a good-humored smile. "Is this some sort of holiday? Like 'gang up on the nearest niece' day?"

Rachel smiled at Judy. "We're only trying to convince Krista to keep her word."

"You have a nerve demanding it, after the way you twisted my words. I was to, sexy," Krista mimicked.

Beverly took rather impressed. "We threw everything in that we could think of," she admitted. "Though we sure didn't expect that particular line to have an effect on Mr. Snooze."

Judy shot Krista a shocked look. "It's true. They don't think Michael's sexy."

"But we do think Krista would have fun," Rachel said. "A getaway to a flashy town would be a lark for her."

"On that much we agree," Judy said to Krista's surprise. Easing a hip over the edge of Krista's desk she added, "As usual, you're thinking too much. Plainly, you've let your doubts overpower you. Last night, when I spoke to you on the phone, you were absolutely pumped about it.''

''So Judy, she called you instead of us,'' a wounded Beverly fumed.

''I am her friend—''

''Hey!'' Krista cried. ''This conversation is supposed to be about me, my situation.'' Satisfied they were contrite, she continued. ''You haven't even given me the chance to tell you the worst part. Before we ever set foot in Nevada, Michael intends to mold me into the wife of his dreams. It's the condition that holds me back most. I can't even imagine allowing a man to call the shots that way, while I demurely cooperate!''

The aunts exchanged an amazed look.

''She still doesn't get it.''

''Too many years with her nose to the grindstone while her peers played the field.''

Krista pounded her desktop. ''What are you two rambling on about!''

Rachel deferred to Beverly. ''You explain it. You're better with her.''

''Make no mistake about it, Krista. Allowing Michael, or any man for that matter, to believe he's in the driver's seat, is the surest way to control *him*.'' Satisfied with this nugget of brilliance, Beverly buffed her colorless fingernails on her coat lapel.

Krista glanced at Judy for her reaction.

''Bev does have a point,'' Judy confirmed. ''The idea will be to allow Michael Collins to believe he's manipulating you, when, in fact, he's totally relying on you. At this late date, you alone make his scheme possible. And unbeknownst to him, you already know exactly how to present yourself in an intelligent way to impress his peers.''

Krista was uncertain. ''I wish I could just tell him who I really am, who you really are. I would still go along,'' she said above the aunts' howls, ''but at least I would get the respect I deserve as a fellow professional.''

"Such a confession could blow the whole deal!" Beverly bellowed. "Don't you know anything about a successful man's fragile ego? After some kicking and screaming, Michael Collins has finally adjusted to the story we've carefully fed him, is by now most likely neck-deep in the fantasy of molding you into a proper lady. We can't rob him of the chance to play Svengali."

Even Judy agreed. "It is a little late to backtrack. He's under a lot of pressure and has this scheme set in his mind. He might just crack if he were to discover that Simona is just a couple of broken-down old women. Uh, sorry, ladies," she finished awkwardly.

Rachel tossed her golden head. "I take offense to that."

"Oh, sister, get real," Beverly advised. "We're in our sixties, on the autumn side of life. This young man would in fact be mortified to learn we're the steam behind the Simona engine."

Krista fell silent. This was her own fault, really. She had had the chance to straighten him out last night, before things got out of hand. But she'd been too flattered by his interest to think straight.

"Krista," Beverly went on evenly, "if you are going to play at all, you must play it as it lays. You are Simona, flashy siren in need of a total redo."

"But exactly how to play it…" Krista looked uncharacteristically lost.

"You must pretend to be impossible," Rachel advised.

"But not too impossible," Beverly countered.

"Flashy."

"But not trashy."

"Available."

"But not desperate."

"Flighty."

"But not stupid."

Krista still stared at them blankly.

Judy snapped her fingers. "Hang on. I think I can help." Pressing a button on Krista's intercom, she summoned their receptionist. Moments later, Courtney appeared. Today's outfit was orange leggings and a sheer jacket. The red hair was piled high on her head in a floppy knot.

"What's up?"

"Please take Ms. Mattson's water pitcher and refill it," Judy requested. "Her aunts are thirsty."

"Oh, so you are the Code Red ladies." Chewing hard on her gum, Courtney took a closer look at the pair. "Thought you might be. Don't look much alike for sisters, though. Most of my aunts look like sisters, even the cousins. Though some look like their brothers who are my uncles. Except we don't include Uncle Arthur because he did a little time in the workhouse for stealing a car. He still claims it was a misunderstanding, and I tend to believe him. It is harder for me, as his favorite, to pretend he's not my uncle even though my grandparents cut him out of the will. I mean, you girls know how it is."

"The water, Courtney," Judy urged.

"Oh, yeah."

"And ditch the gum."

She took it out of her mouth, pinched it between two fingers and marched over to get the water pitcher. "Be back in a flash."

"What did you notice about Courtney?" Judy asked after the girl left.

Krista shrugged. "Nothing unusual."

Judy grew impatient. "Snapping gum. Hip-jerk walk. Inappropriate observations. Mouth runoff."

"All the things we try to tolerate because she is bright and devoted?"

"Exactly. And isn't it possible that she needs a little tune-up, as Simona might need one?"

"Ah, I see," Krista said with new understanding. "I will be on safe ground with Michael's makeover campaign if I act like Courtney, then allow him to reshape me into the real me."

"Right. Just be careful not to overdo the real you."

Krista glared at her friend. "What do you mean?"

"You will be tempted to tamper with his image of the perfect mate."

"That image is total bull."

"But it is his show. You are playing a role."

"Okay, okay."

Satisfied, Judy dusted her hands together. "Follow these basic instructions and before you know it, you will be taming our Mr. Collins."

KRISTA WAS BREATHLESS when she answered her front door at ten o'clock on Friday morning. "Hello, Michael. Come on in."

He moved past her into the foyer with a boxy briefcase. "Did I awaken you?"

The query was sincere but incredibly naive. She'd risen at five, suited up, met Judy at the office forty-five minutes later, and worked three hours clearing her desk. Then it was on to Romano's for some basic hair and makeup tips, then back home to slip into short white shorts and a small pink T-shirt worthy of Simona at leisure. As the doorbell rang she was popping some chewing gum, borrowed from Courtney's desk, into her mouth.

"Don't worry about it," she said chewing hard. "I'm wide awake."

He smiled approvingly. "Great. Let's have some of that coffee I smell."

Despite her lack of culinary skills, Krista did make a darn good cup of coffee. She filled two mugs and called out, "Cream? Sugar?"

"No. Just hope it's hot and strong."

"That's exactly how it is." Another trait they shared.

He'd set up shop in the living room, sitting on the sofa, placing his briefcase on her coffee table. She dropped a coaster onto the table and put his mug on top.

He sipped his coffee appreciatively. "Hmm, perfect. The brew on the plane was warm and bitter."

She stood over him with hands on hips. "You come straight from the airport, then?"

"Yes. Won't be needing a hotel room this leg. Bob Freeman is picking me up here later for my flight to Vegas." He noticed that she was slightly taken aback by the news. "Anything the matter?"

"No," she lied. Poor Bob. She hated to see him anxious with his high blood pressure. But she understood. Until Michael was safely back in Chicago, post convention, there was the chance that he could blow the whistle on them, topple the column, the aunts and Bob himself.

These consequences swam round Krista's mind as she plunged deeper into her role with a snap of gum. It was bound to be a complete bust if she didn't manage to relax a little.

"So what's in the case?" she asked. "Is it sort of a Pandora's box?"

"No." With some amusement he unlatched the case's brass locks and lifted the lid. Visible were some magazines and a yellow legal pad bearing some kind of list. He patted the sofa. "Come, sit beside me."

She obliged, deliberately giving the cushions a little extra bounce.

He began by handing over her airline ticket. "I already brought Bob up to speed. Your flight is late Sunday morning. The convention officially starts that night, though, like me, a lot of owners are gathering early to spend the weekend together."

"Don't you go find a replacement for me over the weekend," she joked.

"Not likely. You are one of a kind." He reached for his legal pad and began to study his notes.

She glanced over to find it was a checklist concerning her. The crazy control freak.

"I don't recall you chewing gum at the newspaper," he remarked with a frown.

She gaped at him. "Oh? Guess I was fresh out that day."

"You may want to leave it home altogether. None of the wives will be chewing."

She sighed laboriously. "All right."

He gestured to the magazines, *Fashion Review* and *Businesswoman's Monthly,* lying in the briefcase. "I picked those up for you at an airport kiosk. They are chock-full of suitable clothing."

She set an issue on her lap and began to leaf through it. He leaned closer, looking particularly smug. "I circled some of the better bets."

"So you have."

"Darker shades are always nice, don't you think? Take this green suit with the narrow skirt, for instance. It needs more than a scarf under the jacket, of course. Imagine, if you can, matching it with an off-white blouse. My accountant for the shop has something similar."

Truth be told, she liked the look. And with her long body she could carry it off—did so in similar suits all week long. The trouble was, she was being told she *should* like the outfit. As she figured, taking direction was proving to be irritating.

He extracted a pen from his shirt pocket. "Can I put you down for a dark suit? Can I count on the green?"

"I won't agree to it in writing, if that's what you mean." She paged through the fashion magazine. "I suppose I'll need some formal wear, some nicer dresses, some sportswear."

He tapped the fat fashion periodical. "Just follow the circles." When she remarked on possible matches to her own clothes, he put pen to paper.

"You don't need to write all that down, Michael."

"Oh. Well, I'm accustomed to writing everything down."

All too frequently she was accused of doing the same thing, but that was beside the point. "You're overdoing it. You've even noted, *Check luggage.*"

"Thought I'd have a look at your suitcases."

"They are not polka dot or anything, if that's what worries you."

His expression suggested as much. He quickly drew her attention back to the magazine. "So, what do you think of this dress?"

"Green again?" She eyed it with Simona's critical eye. "I'd say that if you stood me in the hotel lobby I might be mistaken for a potted plant."

He made an exasperated sound. "Are you going to challenge me on every point?"

"I didn't say I wouldn't wear such an outfit," she said with a gum snap.

He growled. "I can't think with that noise. Please, give me the gum."

Intent upon looking particularly pained, she removed the gum from her mouth. Most likely the palm he held out was an unconscious gesture, but she couldn't resist dropping the sticky wad right in the center of his hand.

He stared at it. "Why, thank you."

She stifled a smile as he looked around waving his hand, not sure what to do with the gum. In a fumble he sent it to the carpet between his loafers. "Oops. Sorry." He leaned over to retrieve it, ever so reluctantly pinching it between two fingers.

"So we're clear on the clothes?" she asked sweetly.

"I had planned... Thought I could take a look at your closet, if you don't mind."

"No way!"

"I don't mean to pry. I just thought we could piece together...pieces. Together." He faltered under her furious gaze.

"Forget about it."

"Why?"

Because he'd find about fifty suitable pieces to mix and match to perfection. "Well..." she hedged, lifting her chin high. "I simply don't allow men in my closet."

"That's silly."

It would seem an odd quirk for a temptress. She paused thoughtfully, drawing on something Courtney had once said about claustrophobia. "A fortune-teller once told me that because I'm a Taurus, I must never get into tight spaces with men. Tight dark spaces, in particular." She fluttered her fingers and tried to look blank and helpless. "Something about the atmospheric condition..."

Suddenly he threw his head back, roaring in laughter. "You really believe that?"

"Of course. And I don't care to be made fun of."

"I'm just fascinated."

Perhaps she could keep her sense of humor, after all. It was most flattering, the way he was watching her without another thought to the chewing gum he was unconsciously kneading to a mushy goo between his thumb and forefinger.

"Will you feel better if I leave the clothing to you?" he asked kindly.

Funny what a little seduction could do. The tables were turning in her direction, ever so slowly. "There's no need to worry." She patted the magazine on her lap. "I know what you want." Fueled with her new sense of power she asked sweetly, "Is it all right if I bring the underwear of choice?"

"If your fortune-teller doesn't mind."

She smiled, he kneaded. Their eyes locked in a warm cozy place.

"Moving on. Damn!" He stopped short, finally noticing the gum. He began to pick at it, only succeeding in drawing it into a web between several more fingers.

"Let me get you a tissue—"

"Some gum chewer you are. That would only make it worse. I need some ice." He popped up. "I'll get it myself."

When he returned some minutes later, he was still a bit rueful. "Didn't you notice the gum?"

"Maybe I'm just a little fascinated with you, too."

He smiled faintly as he glanced at his list again. "Now, about your makeup."

"Too heavy?"

"Seems so. I'm no expert, but I can imagine you with just a dash of blush and lipstick, in a lighter shade of rose than you are accustomed to." He dug deeper into his briefcase and produced a cosmetic kit of subtle pinks. "I dropped by Marshall Fields on the way and picked this up."

Free makeup? The kit was nice, the kind she didn't feel she could indulge in. "I'll make good use of this, I promise."

"Great. Now, about your walk."

She reared in affront. "I've been walking for years."

"Yes. It's just that your style is…mixed. I've seen you walk different ways."

She could offer no rebuttal. With all her different moods of the past few days, she'd most likely been all over the map.

"If you don't mind, I'd like you to demonstrate your most comfortable walk."

She stood up, tugged at her short shorts and gave him a socket-popping shimmy across the room.

As he watched her long bare legs scissor atop high cork-heeled sandals, a funny sound gurgled up his throat. "Okay. Now, that's a whole lot of what we can't use."

She whirled round, scurrying back to him in distress. "Oh. I thought that was good."

"It…is," he admitted, tugging at his polo shirt collar as though he were choking. "But not appropriate for an executive wife-to-be. Would you mind trying again, easing up on speed and swing this time?" She turned and walked again, grinning as he added, "Think of your hips as frozen solid, so they can't move at all. No, I still see movement."

She pivoted again to face him. "Then, maybe you are watching me too closely," she taunted in a purr.

He stood up. "Watch me." He proceeded to glide across

the room like a corporate giant in slow motion, on his way to bankruptcy court.

She fell in behind him to do a fair imitation of his stiff, swinging arm gait. He turned short and she barreled right into him, crashing her nose against his chest. She spoke directly into his shirt pocket. "We're perfect, if our last name is Frankenstein."

"That's absurd."

She stepped back with twinkling eyes. "Hey, I'm sorry, but you don't walk like any girl I've ever seen."

"I was only trying to prove a point—that any human being can move along without shaking a hip out of joint."

"All right. I'll work on the mummy march on my own time."

"It's just so necessary that you don't stand out, cause the wrong kind of talk. My recipe, my store record, is where I hope to shine."

"I'm prepared to help you pull off this madness. But someday, some hour when you least expect it, some girl is going to shake you out of joint but good."

He grasped the fist she was shaking, and a trace of yearning, perhaps even fear, crossed his eyes. She sensed that just maybe, he hoped that girl might be her.

"What now, Svengali?"

"May I have this dance?"

She smiled shyly. "I'm not sure I have the right music."

"No problem. I've got Frank Sinatra—"

"In the briefcase," she finished with a laugh.

They spent a long while in each other's arms. Both were decent dancers but had to learn to mold in all the right places, discover a mutual rhythm as they moved round the floor.

A very intimate exercise, dance, Krista decided. Even as they stumbled through faster numbers like the fox-trot and rumba to find their best bets, she felt closer to Michael than she'd felt to a man in years. Even during sex.

As they rounded off their second hour with some slow,

meaningless meandering, Krista couldn't help feeling they were retracing unnecessary steps. But she wasn't about to complain. No way...

When he was preparing to leave her town house around three o'clock, she gave Bob Freeman a call at the newspaper and offered to drive Michael to the airport herself. Bob declined, insisting upon picking him up.

Thirty minutes later, she spotted Bob's Town Car at the curb out front, his short boxy figure moving up her sidewalk. The man had a wide variety of tweed jackets, but somehow they all looked the same.

She led Michael into the foyer. "Guess this is it."

He gazed down upon her affectionately. "Not a bad day's effort."

"Not bad at all." Suddenly she sensed he might want to kiss her.

The moment was fleeting, lost as Bob rapped once and walked in.

"Hello, you two," he said, pressing the joviality. "Michael, would you mind waiting for me at the car? I'd like a word with Krista about a business matter at the paper."

An unsuspecting Michael strolled down the walkway.

Bob stepped through the entryway. "Everything okay, Krista?"

"Yes, Bob. Though I wish you had just let me take him to the airport."

"No, you are put out enough. Besides, I wanted to see you in person, make sure you're okay with saving my hind end and all."

She folded her arms over her chest with a sigh. "I am perfectly fine with saving your anatomy. Please don't worry so much."

"I won't, now that I see how well you're handling things." He moved back to the stoop. "I could come back here on Sunday, if you like, take you to the airport?"

"Judy's bringing me so we can discuss some last-minute business."

"Okay." He squeezed her hand. "Thanks."

"Just wish me luck."

"The way this Collins fella is eyeing you, he'll need the luck."

Chapter Six

Las Vegas was indeed the land of Lady Luck.

Or so Michael Collins decided as he spotted Krista crossing the entrance of the Imperial Majestic on Sunday afternoon in a smart travel ensemble of blue gabardine, her raven hair pulled away from her features with a silver headband. If he didn't know better he'd guess her pantsuit was tailored for her, the matching black leather luggage in the hands of a bellman, custom-made.

She'd transformed herself not only into a proper lady, but into one of elegance and refinement. She didn't walk, she glided. She didn't gawk, she perused.

By the quirk of her mouth and the gleam in her eye, however, he suspected that she was holding dear to her truer sassy Simona nature deep inside. The dynamite combo of lady and temptress made his pulse quicken.

He moved across the busy lobby with genuine delight, calling her name when she was in earshot.

Krista gave a little cry of surprise as he swept her into his arms. Another when he planted a kiss upon her open mouth.

Holding her close, he murmured in her ear. "Guess we never did get to practice that part."

Her voice was as soft as his. "I don't think you need any practice. But some warning would've been nice."

He touched some small stray hairs at her forehead. "No

time to prepare, with half a dozen nosy conventioneers mingling in the lobby.''

The lobby was grand in size and splendor, decorated in a sultan's palace theme. The floor was sunken marble with a circle of small staircases flanked by golden railings. There were twin spurting fountains in the center court, as well as some bronzed statues scattered about.

Several other men were wearing polo shirts like Michael's, red in color, embroidered with DD for Decadent Delights. Even now, one of them, in the company of a woman, was closing in. He was about thirty, with a husky build and brown hair; she was near the same age, slender, with a shock of burnt-orange hair.

The bellman was standing by patiently with the luggage. Admiring Krista a little too much, Michael decided. He sent the young man along to their suite with his key. "Here come Randy and Beth Norquist," he reported quickly. "They're out of Chicago like I am. Good friends, in fact. And he'll expect you to have heard his name. So wing it as best you can."

"No problem."

Introductions were enthused, suggesting the Norquists were genuinely thrilled to meet Michael's fiancée. Jokes were made about Michael's long bachelorhood, the number of times the Norquists had tried to set him up, to no avail. The usual gibes expected from good friends.

Randy seemed a bit hesitant, half convinced Michael had mentioned a name other than Krista in connection with his fiancée.

"Must have been a pet name," Krista improvised.

"Yes," Michael chimed in.

"Started with a *C*, I think. Colleen?"

"Oh, Randy," Beth huffed. "You always get names wrong. A bad habit, being in the service business."

Randy laughed. "Sorry. Maybe it was one of Michael's old girlfriends I'm thinking of."

Beth swatted his arm. "Randy!"

"What now?" he squawked.

Beth smiled apologetically at Krista. "He's such an oaf."

"Don't worry about it," Krista murmured, slipping an arm through Michael's. "I am totally secure in our relationship. Michael absolutely adores me. Don't you, sweetie?"

"I sure do," he murmured.

AS THEIR EYES LOCKED, Michael allowed himself to pretend it was real. For the good of the charade, of course. There was no way he could ever hope to end up on the same page with her, but pretending she belonged to him felt strangely thrilling.

The couples exchanged parting words, agreeing to meet up at the convention's kickoff cocktail party that night. Michael took Krista's hand. "C'mon, I'll show you our suite."

"Ooo, tiger," Krista purred, to the Norquists' pleasure.

Michael was still holding her hand as they rode up in the crowded car, liking the way it fit snugly in his, impressed with her firm grip. Perhaps tapping a keyboard all day was good exercise for the fingers, even if the messages she was releasing to the public were dangerous tripe.

"So did you like that touch?" she asked, once they were alone in the tenth-floor corridor.

He deliberately gave her a blank look.

"The tiger thing."

"It was fine. Fine." What Simona would expect of a real tiger was anyone's guess. Michael was so frazzled that he nearly went beyond suite 1078. The door stood ajar and the bellman was inside, taking his sweet time unloading the luggage from the cart. Again, Michael sensed another male's appreciation of Krista. Feeling rankled, he peeled off some bills and got rid of the young male employee posthaste.

Krista, who had wandered around for a closer look, returned just in time to see the brusque dismissal. "Something wrong?"

"I didn't want him hanging around. Not the way he was inspecting you."

"Me?" She pressed a hand to her heart in surprise.

"Maybe your real boyfriends like that kind of thing, but I don't. For the next few days, you are my woman. I intend to draw a very protective circle around us." He was immediately embarrassed by his outburst. The sentiments and passion behind his words were completely foreign to him. On top of it all, she laughed.

"Oh, Michael, we are in a city full of showgirls who strut around in tassels and garters." She gestured to her conservative pantsuit. "I doubt I had any affect on that twenty-year-old kid."

"Maybe in one of your obvious Simona getups, he would've passed you by. But there is a lot to be said for subtlety, for keeping feminine assets covered. It stimulates the imagination. C'mon, you know you're beautiful."

Absolutely radiant now, she linked her arm through his. "You have nothing to fear. I promise not to do any tricky hip rolls or tease my hair or plaster on the makeup—"

"But can you possibly keep such promises?"

"On Girl Scouts honor."

"You were a Scout?"

She lifted her chin proudly. "Sure. It was a very memorable time in my life."

"I'll bet the Scout leaders remember it, too."

"Probably do, as I won more merit badges than anyone else in my troop."

He shook his head. "One minute I think I understand you, the next I don't have a clue."

"Mysteries can be fun."

Too true. Heaven help him, he was already way too curious about all her secrets.

"In any case, we are off to a decent start," she said. "The Norquists seem very nice."

"Oh, they are," he said absently. "But did you see the way some of those other DD owners were looking you over with raw envy?" He rubbed his hands together with glee. "This whole thing is going to be so great!"

She lifted a dubious brow. "What happened to the circle of protection?"

"You're in it, of course. But you can't blame me for showing off for the guys I know."

She rolled her eyes. "Boys will be boys."

"C'mon, I'll show you your bedroom." He picked up her suitcase and garment bag. She followed with her tote and purse.

The room was garish, done in silver and royal blue with traces of purple.

"It certainly is bright."

Michael shrugged, setting down the cases. "I suppose they don't expect people to do much sleeping in here."

Her eyes immediately fell to the round king-size bed that resembled an adults-only trampoline with its chrome coverlet and velvet accent pillows.

"Because of the games," he clarified.

"Games?"

"In the casinos."

"Yes. Those games. I imagine this color scheme would go far to drive people downstairs."

It didn't seem the right time to admit that he had expected her apartment to be decorated along these very lines.

Krista sighed. "I suppose once I close my eyes, I can pretend the room is a relaxing white."

Michael left her to the chore of unpacking. He'd just spread the contents of his briefcase on the living area's desk when he heard a cry of dismay. He raced back to the bedroom to find Krista on her knees in the center of the huge bed, desperately pawing through an open suitcase.

"What's the matter?"

"I've forgotten some shoes."

"That's all?"

"The shoes for tonight's big cocktail party."

He growled in dismay. "The event is so important. Gerald Stewart intends to honor us in a toast."

"I remember, I remember." She inched off the bed and gestured to the closet door. "I was just setting my dress out and didn't recall packing the shoes. Now I'm sure they aren't here."

His annoyance faded slightly as he scanned the dress hanging on a hook attached to the door. It was an off-white gown with simple lines. Not too flashy, not too inconspicuous. "This is perfect. Just perfect."

"You don't have to look so surprised!"

"Sorry, this is no time to bicker, anyway. Let's go down to the main level and find you a pair of shoes. There are several shops to choose from. In fact, it'll be my contribution to your wardrobe."

"I can buy my own shoes," she said, brushing past him through the door.

"If you'd packed well, no one would be buying them. I never forget anything. Make a checklist. Then check off each item as I stow it away."

"Gee, let's stop off and cable Irritated In Illinois, let her know of the fun she's missing."

He couldn't help chuckling. "We're sounding more like a real couple every minute."

Shopping was a strength that Krista knew she could carry off well under any persona. A little later, as she and Michael stepped off the elevators to join the bustle of people on the main level, she went straight to the reservations desk to pick up a hotel directory. All but casting aside her anxious escort, she studied the shops listed, their locations in the complex, and set out to buy some shoes.

By shop number five, Michael had had his fill. "Please. Krista. Choose some shoes here."

She couldn't help thinking how cute he looked, full of weary yearning. "You could go up to the suite and wait."

"And trust you? No, I think I'll hang on awhile longer."

She was reminded that he'd expect her to make an unusual choice. Lost in her mission, she'd forgotten that. "Why don't we split up?" she suggested. "You try the displays on the left while I try the right side." Once out of his reach, she punched in her work number. Judy answered. "Jude, it's me."

"I knew you'd be calling to check on us. You were supposed to leave our business in my capable hands!"

"I can't bear to be totally cut off. Quick, tell me if you heard from Baxter Interiors about my sky writing idea for their grand opening."

"No word yet."

"Has my T-shirt order for Life Form Fitness Center arrived?"

"Yes. I plan to deliver them to the center myself. So, how are things going with the scam?"

"Okay. We're shopping for shoes to go with my cream cocktail dress and Michael doesn't trust me to choose them without his help." She glanced nervously at Michael, just out of earshot by a clog display. "That's another reason I called. I need Courtney to recommend some shoes, something inappropriate, something Michael can inflate his ego by correcting."

"Hang on. Our resident bohemian is doing some filing."

Courtney was soon on the line. "Hello, Ms. Mattson. Still can't believe you just took off on a holiday. Especially to Vegas. Neither can my mom or my boyfriend—"

"Courtney, I brought along my cream dress, the one I wore to the Christmas party. If I want to add some pizzazz to my look, what sort of shoes would you suggest?"

"A Taurus like you doesn't take risks. You are deliberate, methodical."

"What would *you* do about the shoes?"

"If I were a Taurus, you mean?"

"Yes!"

"Your colors are pale blue, green and pink. Any of those would work."

"Okay."

"I can't be sure without my charts, but I think according to your sign, Venus is in Cancer."

"Does that have a bearing on my shoes?"

"No. Just thought I'd throw it in. You being on vacation and all. Be aware that you're bound to be full of sensual passion. Possessiveness can be a problem. It is also a time for Taurus to apply business sense to the business of relationships."

The hints of possible sense in that jumble of nonsense gave her a little shiver. Which she promptly shook off. "Thank you, Courtney." She disconnected as Michael approached.

"Who were you talking to?"

She hesitated. "Judy."

"I like that girl's savvy. Could be a stable influence, if a person let her."

"Don't gush too much. She'd think twice before jumping into a deal like this."

"Ah, but she'd never get me in a jam in the first place. Now don't blow a fuse," he begged as she geared up. "I think I found something." He held up a stunning suede pump with a medium heel and smooth line.

They looked perfect, the sort of thing Krista bought frequently. Not about to give in easily, however, she continued to roam the shop. "Hang on to those while I take one last loop around."

He was anxiously at her side as she picked up one glittery shoe after another. It was a bit of fun, watching the confident executive gape and blanch over the most inappropriate possibilities. Ultimately, she chose some dainty slippers with high heels. They were light green in color with a crystallized texture. "You're sure to like these, in your favorite color."

"Green isn't my favorite color. I just read someplace that it makes a good impression on people."

"But I should be taking a fashion risk here, being a Taurus full of passion."

A hint of fire lit his face at the mention of passion. "They are dazzling." Just the same, he planted the suede shoe in her hand. "We're taking enough risks as it is. Let's try these on."

The moment the salesman slipped the shoes on her feet, she was aware of a snugness in the toe. Then she stood up and walked back and forth to verify a very pronounced pinch.

"They aren't the best fit," she told a very disappointed Michael. The salesman had to be commissioned, for he too looked disappointed. "Have you a half size larger?"

"They run only in whole sizes. The next size up would be too large."

"Are they terribly tight?" Michael dropped to his knee at her chair and held her foot in his hand.

Krista felt a spark run up her leg as he absently caressed her calf. "Not terribly tight, I guess."

"They look so wonderful. You will look so wonderful...." He gazed almost reverently upon her slender feet.

"I can take a pinch for one evening," she relented. "Let's take them."

KRISTA OPENED THE DOOR of her bedroom at 6:45 to find Michael waiting for her dressed in a very expensive blue suit.

"A woman who is on time," he marveled.

She did a pirouette. "You like?"

As during their crash course, Michael was not shy about offering his open appraisal. And once again Krista felt the same old tingle, as if he were physically touching her with his penetrating eyes.

She'd dressed carefully, making sure the cream sheath dress fell smoothly over the curves of her body. Jet hair was piled high on her head to expose her slender neck.

Gold earrings adorned her lobes and a simple gold chain hung at her throat.

"I like." Not a hair was out of place, but he couldn't resist touching one of the tendrils that teased her temples.

She drew a sharp breath as his fingertips lingered on her face, didn't realize she was holding her breath until she tried to speak. As it was, her words spilled out in a rush for air. "Exactly how are we going to play it tonight?"

His fingers still warmed her cheek. "I am going to be crazy for you and you will stand by in quiet beauty."

She smiled. "Afraid of my irrepressible wit?"

"I call it the Simona sass. I see it bubbling up right now. The least bit of stress and anything is liable to pop out of that lovely mouth of yours."

"My feet are the only thing about to pop." She shifted uneasily in the pumps.

"Are they that tight?"

"Maybe they'll stretch with time."

"You aren't going to frown in pain all night, are you?"

"Only if all the jokes are bad."

"Laugh, no matter how bad."

"Don't worry, I'll be nice to your little doughnut club." She reached up to straighten his tie.

"Be especially careful if conversation turns to the contest. Don't reveal a thing about my entry to anyone."

She lifted her shoulders. "I don't know anything about your entry."

"Guess that's right. Well, we won't worry about that now. Just do me the favor of talking about things like the weather, the hotel, gambling."

"All right." When he extended his hand to shake on it, she leaned into him, instead. "By the way, my original question on how to 'play it' was directed at our level of intimacy for the evening."

"Oh. That." He beamed.

"You plan to kiss me again in public?"

"I don't know. I've been more concerned about our mental strategy."

"If you decide to do so, I'd like some warning."

"Yeah. You did look a bit like a doe in the headlights the last time."

"And you looked like a buck showing off for the boys," she shot back, embarrassed that he so readily nailed down her reaction. "In any case, I fumbled because I was caught off guard."

"Guess it is my fault we didn't practice those kinds of moves in advance."

She fluttered her lashes. "You were too busy with my appearance."

"You can't argue that I did a good job at it. You look like a dream. Still, you have a point. We better give the kiss action a quick run-through." He placed one hand on her waist and another at the back of her bare neck.

"Ah! Careful not to muss the merchandise."

With a small grunt he pulled her close. "Now, the next time I kiss you, I'll be holding you just like this. I'll slide my hand round your throat like this, take hold of your chin like this..." He put his mouth down on hers with warm pressure.

Krista hadn't meant to encourage the real thing. She had only been speaking in general about kisses. And it was no small frustration that like the last time, her knees were once again growing uncontrollably weak.

He was faking it all, and had the power to make her weak! Feeling threatened, she pushed him off with an unfair critique. "You might want to raise one hand up my back a little next time, for better leverage. And a little less force on the back of the neck. Oh, and as we will be in public, don't move your lips around too much. It'll muss my lipstick."

"It was only one little kiss."

She forced a lilt into her tone. "I suppose you don't even want to discuss where *my* hands should be."

"You know," he said succinctly, "I may avoid kissing you ever again."

Her murmur was light and amused. "I highly doubt it."

The reception was in a ballroom on the hotel's fifth floor. Its decor continued the sultan theme with its white and gold. Chandeliers were huge and plentiful, offering an abundance of glitter and light. There was a stage at the front of the room where a small orchestra played. Well-dressed people numbering close to five hundred mingled and nibbled on champagne and appetizers.

Michael scooped her into his arms. "Let's show off a little."

For several blissful numbers, they moved around the dance floor in fairly good harmony. Finally, to save her feet, Krista insisted on a break. It was only a short while later, when she was taking a bite from a cheese puff, that a man moved center stage to the microphone. He was wearing a pale-blue tuxedo, a white ruffled shirt, black shoes and a thick brown toupee combed in a high unnatural wave.

"Gerald Stewart?" Krista whispered in Michael's ear.

"In person," he confirmed.

She laughed softly. "I am astonished by his gaudy outfit."

"When you're that rich, you *set* the fashion."

"But the hair, Michael. It's probably more than he had at eighteen!"

"Probably," he whispered back. "It has doubled in size since his wife died a few years back. I suppose no one has the courage to set him straight."

The music stopped, the lights dimmed a notch and the microphone made a crackling sound. Then they heard Gerald Stewart's voice: "Welcome to my…" His message was quickly drowned out by thunderous applause. He raised his hands over his loyal flock to still the enthusiasm. "Welcome, everyone, to my hometown and to the tenth Decadent Delights convention. This is sure to be the most rip-roarin' get-together yet. As you all know, I've raised the stakes of excitement with my little doughnut makin' contest. It's my understanding that fifty-two DD owners have tossed the dice, are set to participate. I wish you all a little boost from lady luck herself.

"As for catching up on family business, I have a few announcements to make." Gerald Stewart pulled a slip of paper from his jacket pocket. "We have had seven new babies born to shop owners this year." He went on to name them, and encouraged each set of parents, in turn, to raise a hand and be recognized under a roaming spotlight.

"There are some farewells to mention." Gerald went on, announcing two deaths and several retirements.

"We also have some promotions to celebrate." He announced a boost for one of his trusted people, Jonathan Smithers, and for a woman who would soon be heading up his marketing department.

"Lastly, we have two surprising engagements," Gerald proclaimed. "The first is my old pal Willy Tritt, who after many years as a widower has beat me to the punch to find himself a new filly for his twilight years. And the second is formerly confirmed bachelor Michael Collins out of Chicago. Now I don't have to tell most of you that Michael is one of our few shop owners, male or female, who has managed to remain single. But he is also our youngest owner, so I've been patient."

As Michael raised his hand, the spotlight hit him and Krista. He beamed in pleasure to find Krista behaving comfortably in the pool of light, linking her arm in his, nodding to the crowd, accepting congratulations with the very essence of poise.

Krista could feel his pride washing over her and it made her feel remarkably content.

"If I missed any events, it is only because you all didn't report them to our fine newsletter," Gerald Stewart said in pointed closing. "So keep us in mind all year round. We want personal updates on everyone. It's what families do. Now I hope you all have a wonderful week of fun and relaxation. Don't any of you go losing your shorts at the craps tables. I believe in moderation in all things, expect, of course, in making our company a success. And it is each and every one of the franchise owners who make Decadent Delights a success.''

More applause exploded.

People began to move and mingle around Krista and Michael again. Suddenly a couple was planted directly in their space.

"Mikey!" the woman exclaimed from several feet away.

"Here come the Larkins," Michael cautioned. "Remember your topics of conversation. Weather, gambling, hotel."

"Norah." Michael allowed the older woman to seize him in a fierce embrace, then extended his hand to the man at her side. "Allan."

The couple abruptly focused on Krista, taking her in with bold inspection. Norah said, "So this is the luckiest girl on earth, second only to me!"

Chapter Seven

Krista surveyed the pair with interest. So these were the fabulous Larkins whom Michael raved about, these saviors who had given Michael his first job in a Decadent Delights shop in Chicago, mentored him into his own shop.

Both man and wife were about five foot five, plump and speaking a bit too loud. Allan's sandy hair was thinning on top. Norah's hair was a traditional hairdresser's cap of curls set in hairspray, colored a very pale yellow. Both appeared to be about fifty.

In a word, Krista would best describe them as robust.

In their favor, both were extremely well dressed, Allan in a black tuxedo and Norah in a slimming A-line dress of a heavy maroon jersey fabric that hung in elegant folds. Her emerald pendant and ring appeared to be quality jewelry.

"So this is Krista," Norah was saying.

Krista was unaccustomed to being embraced at business functions and tried not to wince in surprise as Norah gathered her in her arms. "We are so pleased to meet you, dear. Michael is like a son to us. We were never able to have our own, you see."

"Yes, congratulations," Allan added heartily. "About time our boy settled down."

"Now, Allan," Norah half scolded, "it was best for him to wait for the real thing. After all, with the value of the shop in the balance and all the stress that goes with running it, he has to get it right the first time. No, it would take a very unique lady to fill the shoes of Mrs. Michael Collins, one full of understanding, in it for the distance.''

The words of proud parents blinded by devotion. Krista glanced at Michael to find him locked in on her with perhaps the most poignant expression she ever seen on a man, full of need and hope. It was painfully clear that he wanted her to shine for these people.

''Well, Michael is a catch to be sure,'' Krista said playfully.

Michael balked but looked extremely pleased.

''So, how are things in Chicago?'' she asked.

The Larkins regarded one another with amusement. ''Haven't you told her anything about us, Mikey?''

''Of course I have,'' he said defensively.

''We've been in Vegas for three years,'' Allan explained.

Krista's brain absorbed the news. ''Oh. How convenient to be right on Gerald Stewart's doorstep,'' she declared with a broad smile.

Allan winked. ''Not a bad spot, eh, sitting on the big man's knee?''

Norah gave her husband's arm a swat. ''You are such a kidder, Al. Even when it comes to your own health.'' Her voice dropped in confidence as she addressed Krista. ''It's a weakness we don't advertise, but Allan has a bit of trouble with arthritis, in his hands.'' Krista's glance dropped to Allan's hands, which looked normal. ''Shooting pain almost paralyzed him in autumn, the last few years back in Chicago. By the time the first snow fell, he was in unbearable pain. It was the weather, you see, the nasty cold and dampness.''

Krista kept a benign face. ''How awful, for such a young man.''

Norah tittered. ''He's an old bear, really. Almost fifty-two. The doctor insisted that the midwestern climate was bound to be his hell from then on.''

Michael nodded sagely at Norah's diagnosis. "It only would have been a matter of time and Allan would've had to give up running the Chicago shop. There's so much hands-on work with the doughnut preparation, hauling and checking supplies. They appealed to Gerald Stewart himself and he granted them permission to open up a shop here, not far from his headquarters. We were all so grateful. The move to Vegas's arid climate certainly saved Gerald from an early retirement."

"Can't have him retiring," Norah squawked. "Underfoot on my home turf."

"No, dear, you prefer to be underfoot on my turf—at the shop."

"As if you could run the place without me, old bear." Norah smiled again. "So, Krista, have you set a wedding date?"

"Not yet," Michael said quickly.

Norah stomped a low-heeled pump. "Why ever not!"

"There are our schedules to consider," he fumbled.

"Do you have a career, Krista?" Allan asked.

Michael made a strangled sound that he disguised on a cough. "She's searching for options."

"I believe I've settled for the promotions game," Krista couldn't help announcing. "The creative challenges suit me perfectly."

Michael regarded her with perhaps his first hint of respect. Then proceeded to embellish the story. "She is doing very well with a Minneapolis agency, it's true. Has a delightful boss named Judy. They are always brainstorming on one project or another. Why, just the other night they had their heads together over a promo campaign for a local electronics store." He gave Krista's waist a squeeze. "Isn't that right, honey?"

"I was good, wasn't I, coming up with that robot?"

Norah was remarkably unimpressed. "Of course, you'll soon be devoting all your time to the doughnut shop."

Krista wondered if the older woman might be a bit

threatened by her having an identity separate from Michael's. "I suppose I may do that," she said slowly.

"What better way to strengthen your relationship than to stand behind your man a hundred percent."

There was no doubt as to whom Michael had fashioned his dream wife and idea of marriage after. She couldn't help wondering about his own parents, if they had had any influence on him.

Michael placed a kiss on Krista's head. "Naturally we have some issues to iron out still, but I can't imagine a wife who wouldn't support me wholeheartedly."

Norah tweaked his chin. "Of course you can't. There's no beating our system."

Fortunately for Krista, the matter was dropped. Conversation flowed on to lighter, more amusing issues. There was also a good amount of shoptalk, mostly concerning former customers in the Larkins' Chicago shop.

The banter eventually wound down. The Larkins sipped the last of their champagne under Michael's affectionate gaze. As they prepared to move on, Allan clapped Michael on the back. "We're having Gerald up to our suite for drinks later on, 'round midnight. You'll join us, won't you?"

Michael beamed like a child at Christmas. "Wouldn't miss it."

As the Larkins wandered off, Michael grasped her elbow. "Not a bad start, with your help."

"Thanks."

"Quick thinking with the responsible job. If I didn't know better, I'd have believed you are a part of Judy's operation."

"Double thanks."

Another compliment for Judy. How frustrating to field respect for her. How annoying that she cared what he thought! As much as she enjoyed being viewed the femme fatale, she missed being appreciated for her brains. It would be nice to receive both admiration and respect from a man like Michael.

After a few hours of socializing over dinner and dancing, Michael and Krista headed for the Larkins' suite, on the penthouse level. As they stood outside their door, Michael placed his hands on her shoulders—and tugged up the neckline of her dress.

"Excuse the fingers, but you are getting a little saggy."

"I am not getting saggy, mister." She quickly wrenched free in dismay.

"The dress," he quickly hissed, "I mean the dress."

It didn't matter what he meant. Her heart was beating fast and hard. It was all the fault of his kisses. The taste of his mouth on hers had rocked her unexpectedly hard. The very graze of his fingertips brought it all back. She rapped on the hotel door with her knuckles.

"Remember, keep a low profile."

"Yes, sir."

"And don't make so many funny faces."

"Try walking around in these shoes for five minutes, then we'll talk about funny faces."

A uniformed waiter escorted them inside. There proved to be two hotel employees in attendance, the waiter and a bartender. Soft music played in the background. The lights were soft, too, just bright enough to make out faces and objects.

There were perhaps a dozen people present. Norah, the perfect hostess, quickly took Michael and Krista in hand, intimating that they'd been included in an elite gathering of Decadent Delights executive material.

Norah, who plainly viewed her voice as a precious instrument to be enjoyed by all, sang out for attention. "I want you all to know Michael Collins and his lovely lady friend Krista." Amidst the blank stares she added, "Michael owns a shop. In Chicago."

Krista felt the reaction was at best patronizing. If any of

these guests had owned a shop before climbing the company ladder, they weren't going to brag about it.

Again she felt a twinge about the Larkins. Allan and the missus had to be hoping for a promotion to the executive level themselves, with this kind of schmoozing. And they were most likely on the cusp, judging from the number of higher-ups that they'd managed to draw. Not a bad long-range plan in itself. But she could think of no reason to keep it from Michael. If the arthritis story was a fake, they'd been keeping things from him for a long while. What was in it for them, except the obvious: to keep him at arm's length as one would a rival? Not a wicked thing in itself. But if he was regarded as a son, and they were reaping the rewards of his trust and devotion, it seemed to Krista a nasty game.

Michael touched her elbow. "I'll be right back. Allan wants to show me a belt buckle he bought at a pawn shop."

They'd been hours away from a window, as was common in casinos, so Krista was eager for a look outside. She wandered over to a wide glass pane for a view of the Strip. The night was inky black while stories below every color of the rainbow flashed or glimmered.

"Quite a scene, isn't it?"

The deep voice startled her. The powder-blue suit blinded her. "Oh, Mr. Stewart!"

"Didn't mean to startle you. Please call me Gerald."

"All right, Gerald, if you like."

His eyes twinkled merrily. "And your name is…"

"Krista Mattson, sir. You announced my engagement earlier to Michael Collins."

Another man soon joined them—a wiry man of about thirty-five with a lean handsome face, slicked brown hair and small wire-rimmed glasses. His stark black tuxedo was in direct counterpoint to Gerald's folksy getup. His eyes were also hard in a way that Gerald's were warm.

"Ah, Jon." Gerald smiled. "Jonathan Smithers is my right hand. Jon, this is Krista Mattson."

"Yes, I recognize her from the crowd as Michael Collins' fiancée."

Krista couldn't resist meeting Jonathan's cold observant eyes in kind. She knew his type, the detail man behind the man. He made it his business to know exactly who everyone was. She wondered how much of what Gerald knew of his own people was due to Jonathan's efforts.

"Are you from Chicago, as well?" Jonathan inquired politely.

"No, I live in Minneapolis," Krista replied evenly.

"This Michael is out of Chicago?" Gerald asked Jonathan.

This Michael? Krista tried to control her dismayed expression. Was it possible, with all Michael's aspirations, expectations and attention to this charade, Gerald wasn't aware of him?

"Our hosts, the Larkins, are out of Chicago, too," Gerald informed her jovially.

Krista moved in on the opening. "Michael got his start in their original shop, I understand."

"Oh, he's the prodigy, then." Gerald absorbed the news with interest.

Plainly, he didn't know Michael for dirt. This would have to be a grand-scale sales job, starting from the ground up. "That's right. He's certainly thrilled to be a part of the Decadent family. Running the shop is much of his life."

Gerald Stewart looked pleased. "How nice to hear."

"He's entered your contest, too."

"Has he?" The heavy brows jumped this time.

"Fully intends to win."

"I like that sort of ambition."

Without question, Michael would be crushed to learn the extent of Stewart's passivity concerning him. Krista winced, and it wasn't strictly the shoes this time.

"The Larkins are a fine couple, I must say," Gerald continued. "Stood out even before they moved here, always so attentive to personal remembrances. Too bad about

Allan's health trouble, forcing him to relocate out of his beloved neighborhood.''

"I imagine he and Norah have made themselves at home right here in Nevada."

"Yes, they have, in fact. Going way beyond the call of duty frequently. Taken this old widower under their wing, you might say, with their barbecues and cocktail parties and sightseeing excursions. Their request for a shop right in my territory has been of great benefit to me."

How odd that despite the coziness shared by Gerald and the Larkins, Michael apparently was never a topic of conversation!

"Has Allan's arthritis improved here?" she couldn't resist asking.

"Seems fit to me, all right. A real shame about that particular affliction, though, as I have some opportunities opening up very soon that probably won't suit him."

Opportunities? Krista grew alert. "So you have new plans within your organization?" she prompted. "How exciting."

Jonathan appeared nonplussed by the turn of subject. "This probably isn't the time or place to discuss such matters, sir."

Gerald chuckled, his brown pile rug bouncing on his head. "I do often throw caution to the wind when talking to a lovely woman."

"Mr. Smithers," she said sweetly. "Would you mind getting me a glass of mineral water, with a wedge of lemon?"

"Not at all," Gerald replied firmly for his assistant. "Thank you, Smithers."

Krista didn't miss the right-hand man's reservations at leaving them alone, but he had no choice. Presumably, Michael wouldn't want her to press too hard here. But he didn't have all the facts. Didn't know how capable she was, and didn't know the urgency of the situation. With some kind of expansion on the rise, it was crucial for Gerald

Stewart to have a clear picture of Michael Collins. She had to hurry, Smithers was pushing hard through the line at the portable bar.

"Your company stands as quite a success story," she ventured.

"Oh, my yes," Gerald enthused. "Nine hundred shops in twenty-seven states now. Quite an achievement for a man who started as an errand boy in his father's bakery."

"I can respect how you've managed to get your employees rallied round you like a huge family," she praised. *Even if you can't tell them apart.*

"Keeping the essence of family alive is mighty important to me," he said with a proud brace of his shoulders. "My wife Gloria's been gone five years now. All I have left of real kin is a brother in Kansas." Pain deepened the creases in his tanned face. "So the business has become my sole concern. It's a frustration sometimes, trying to keep my people straight—like your Michael, for instance—but damned if I don't try."

Her expression softened. Perhaps he was as sincere as his reputation suggested. That gave her hope that Michael still could somehow make an impression. It would take aggressive personal contact. Michael was on the right track in coming to conventions, entering this year's contest. But there was much work to be done if he wanted the chance at higher things—higher than a mere contest.

Suddenly Jonathan was back with her drink. And Michael was at her side, with an arm around her waist. "Hello, Mr. Stewart, Jonathan."

Smithers merely nodded, but Gerald Stewart extended his hand.

"It's Gerald to you, of course, Michael. Must say, your fiancée has been charming company."

Michael nodded. "She's been marveling at the weather here in your homctown."

"Has she?" He seemed surprised.

"I understand from Allan that temperatures have been mild, though a bit drier than usual."

Gerald winked at Krista. "We weren't discussing the weather, were we?"

"The hotel?"

"No."

"Gambling?"

Gerald chuckled. "Krista and I went straight beyond those clichés. She's wasted no time in singing out your praises. Telling me how much you enjoy your franchise."

"Really?"

"And I look forward to tasting your contest entry."

"Wonderful, sir."

Gerald put a hand on his shoulder. "How does it feel to be competing with the Larkins? Considering your relationship and all."

Michael was glowing. "Nice of you to remember."

"Of course I remember!"

"They are wonderful friends to me," Michael intoned. "I don't expect the contest to ruffle anyone too much, though."

"I had no idea the Larkins were entered in the contest, too," Krista said.

Gerald confirmed as much. "They're serious contenders. Norah's been teasing me to death about how great their entry is."

"She'll have some stiff competition from this fella, I can promise you," Krista assured heartily.

"That's fine," Gerald enthused, stepped away. "Good luck now."

Michael's face settled into a frown as he steered Krista off. "What have you to say for yourself, Simona?"

"Fair to partly cloudy?" she peeped.

LATER, BACK IN THEIR HOTEL SUITE...

"Ooh, Michael, that feels so good. Rub me right there with your thumb, just a little deeper..."

"I probably shouldn't be so attentive."

"You're the one who insisted I buy those death-trap shoes."

"Well, the glittery ones were all wrong."

"Tell that to my poor feet." With a groan Krista readjusted her lounging position on the sofa, wishing she hadn't let Judy talk her into bringing only her kimono for cover-up. No matter how she tugged at its hem, it kept sliding open on her thighs.

Seated at the end of the sofa with her sore pink tootsies in his lap, Michael seemed to be enjoying her writhing a little too much. He was at ease in a T-shirt and cotton sleep pants, his feet bare and white and pain-free.

"I think it's high time we review the evening," he said firmly.

"Seems a high price to pay for this massage."

"The best deal you can expect," he retorted.

Her mouth twitched in amusement. "Exactly what did I do wrong?"

"Let's start with the reception, that crack about the Larkins moving onto Gerald's doorstep."

"Well, they have done so."

"But you made it sound like a sneaky business maneuver, when the move was for health reasons."

"You must admit, Allan's hands don't look arthritic."

"It's all too real, believe me. I'll never forget the traumatic phone call from a very distraught Norah. To save my feelings, they'd withheld telling me until the move to Vegas was set with Gerald."

Business sharks frequently kept their deals under wraps until the last minute, she thought. "What did they want of you when they did finally call?"

"They needed me to help with the transition from Illinois to Nevada. I had to leave my own shop with my assistants to help them prepare for the move. I made some big sacrifices to help them relocate. But I wanted to do it. Repay them for helping me out. Wouldn't you do the same for someone you cared about? In a good cause?"

How could she deny it, considering this kettle of soup the aunts had pushed her into? "Been there, done that," she admitted.

He beamed with a devotion that made her heart twist in envy. "The Larkins do try especially hard with Gerald. But the personal touch is a very effective and common business tactic. Don't expect you to fully understand having no real competition with your column. You just receive letters, sift through them, and fire off glib replies from the safety of your office. Those of us within a system full of people have to deal with numerous obstacles in order to stand out, make progress."

How Krista longed to discuss these matters under her own efficient colors. Instead she settled for the next best thing, a petty retort. "Everybody understands the art of sucking up to the boss."

"My life is so separate from the Larkins these days, I prefer to simply relax and enjoy their company when I do see them."

"Regardless, you're bonded in some high-stakes competition."

"Yes. But at worst they are my friendly rivals. I should know."

Krista realized the Larkins were a sensitive issue. And she probably had no right to cast doubts about his friends. At least not without just cause. "If they are half as wonderful as you say, I'm sure all is well."

"Just be good to them. As much as I cherish my business, my friendship with them is of the utmost importance."

"Message received."

"As for the party in the Larkins suite—"

"I know what you're going to say," she cut in. "But Gerald Stewart lives here, Michael. He's not interested in discussing the local weather."

"So of all possible topics, you chose to drill deeply into my business."

"You should be on your knees, thanking me for getting out the drill."

"For Pete's sake, why?"

She didn't have the heart to tell him that she was responsible for refreshing Gerald's failing memory on the subject that Michael existed. "Because I found out something useful."

He squeezed her feet a bit too hard, causing her to yelp. "What!"

"Gerald is planning some kind of expansion."

"Really?" His brows settled into a frown. "Funny I never heard a rumbling. You sure?"

"Positive. Must still be at the hush-hush stage, because Jon Smithers cut him off."

"Perhaps you misunderstood."

"No!"

"Even so, I don't like to think of you gleaning such information. Not when you routinely put one of *these* in your mouth column after column."

She was affronted to see he was holding up her foot.

"Still, what's done is done." He continued his massage, growing pensive. "If this news is true, it must be hot off the presses. There hasn't been the slightest rumor." He gazed upon her with wonder and irritation. "Amazing, of all the employees surrounding him, he chooses to confide in you."

She fluttered a hand. "My loveliness was mentioned as a distraction."

"You are lovely," he conceded.

"I am?"

"As if you don't know it."

Krista's heart quickened. She felt like Cinderella as this man surveyed her new dazzling image with longing. She couldn't help thinking once again that he was very much like the prince of her dreams—handsome, successful, dead-bang sure of himself. It was a fairy-tale moment, without doubt, right down to placing her foot in the prince's waiting hand.

His waiting hand was presently on the move, over her ankle to her calf with a massaging glide. Only to be interrupted by the ringing of the telephone. Reluctantly, he leaned back to the end table to reach for the receiver.

"Hello, Norah." His body language changed abruptly. Krista nearly bounced off the sofa as he sat upright. "No, we're still up. Krista's feet are sore from tight shoes. Yes, they looked spectacular with her dress. Got them here in one of the shops. I don't recall the name of the place—she'll know."

She socked him in the arm, mouthing, *I don't want her to have the same shoes.*

His blank expression suggested he didn't see why. "You'd probably find them just as uncomfortable, Norah," he offered lamely. "Oh. Maybe..."

"What?" Krista whispered, clinging to his arm.

He continued the conversation, trying unsuccessfully to shake her off. "Really?" he eventually said. "Hang on a minute." He cupped a hand over the mouthpiece. "I don't know what to do about this. Norah intends to have some of the wives to her house for lunch tomorrow. Wants you to come."

"Is that necessary?"

"She does head up a small clique, makes a point of getting the women together in some way at every convention."

Norah *would* cover every conceivable networking angle, thought Krista.

"I'll understand if you don't want to...."

But his eyes told a different story. And Krista knew it would look mighty strange if Michael's devoted fiancée passed up time with his surrogate mother. With misgivings, she agreed.

"She'd love to. Great. Sure, I'll tell her." Michael hung

up. "She will come for you in the morning around eleven-thirty. Plans to fit all of you into her new Cadillac."

Krista folded her arms over her gaping robe. "How cozy."

"Oh, and she says to dress casually."

"What was the verdict on my shoes?"

"She has to have them." He touched her chin as it fell. "Couldn't you take that as a compliment?"

"I'd rather she find her own shoes."

"I really don't see the difference."

"Because you are a man content to wear a red uniform shirt day after day!" She made a sputtering sound. "It's a girl thing, Michael. The quest for uniqueness."

"You are unique, I promise you."

She couldn't help throwing him an appreciative look.

"You did hear me try to stop her," he offered in solace. "Told her you found them a tight fit."

"How did she respond to that?"

He hesitated. "Says her feet are bound to be smaller than yours."

"The smug old operator!"

"You probably won't ever wear yours again. So what does it matter?"

"Of course I'll wear them again! I love them!"

"After tonight's agony, you'd really wear them again?"

"That's right."

"So, this foot rub wasn't as necessary as you made out."

"As if I'd turn down the offer. My first, by the way."

"And my last. You con!"

Krista popped up from the sofa in a huff. "I'm a con because you've made me one!"

"Calm down."

"Maybe I should rethink this lunch tomorrow."

He slapped his thigh. "Oh, c'mon."

"Considering all your insults—and Norah's—I think I deserve a treat."

He sighed hard, leaning forward on the cushion. "Okay, what are your terms?"

She lifted her nose in the air. "I am ordering something from room service. My favorite late-night snack."

"I can only imagine what the temptress Simona craves at night."

Her face glowed with anticipation. "Fresh fruit, crackers and milk."

He was delightedly surprised. "After a long day that's my favorite, too."

Once they ordered and shared the feast, they parted company for the night. Michael put his hands on her shoulders, kissed her forehead. "Thanks for today."

"You are very welcome."

"And thanks in advance for your stint tomorrow."

"Don't close the books on that tab yet. You still may owe me."

"Will you at least try to like Norah?"

"If she tries to compare our feet—"

"She won't. Please try and find the good in her? It would make me very happy if we could all get along." He skimmed her cheek with a finger. "We're halfway there, really. I like you, you like me, I like Norah, Norah likes me."

The very idea that he wanted her to share his feelings for another person brought them into new personal territory, more intimate than physical contact. And made her heart skip in delight. "I'll give it a shot," she promised softly. "Maybe in return, you can relax, have more faith in me."

"I am trying. But your signals are at best, mixed."

She rolled her eyes. "I think it's time to say good-night, Doughman."

"Good night to you, Simona."

She couldn't help but be surprised at how interesting this trip was turning out to be. The convention was full of intrigue and challenge. As Michael purported, there were measurable gains to be made on-site for an ambitious DD shop owner. How quickly she, the cautious career woman, had been pulled into his world, a part of his schemes. How very much she was enjoying it all.

Chapter Eight

Krista was lingering over coffee in the suite late the following morning, when there was a knock on the door. A look through the peephole confirmed that it was Norah Larkin. She was early. By a whole half hour.

Why do people do that? Krista wondered. Remembering how much her cooperation meant to Michael, she invited Norah inside with a broad smile.

Norah breezed past her with a "Good morning, Krissy."

Krista had never been addressed by that particular nickname. It didn't suit her at all. But then, in her opinion, Mikey didn't suit Michael, either. So no matter how good their intentions, apparently the Larkins didn't have a knack for nicks.

"I wasn't expecting you until eleven-thirty."

"That's the peril of making plans through a man. All the DD wives are meeting me in the lobby then. But it's different for us, of course."

"Because of the shoes?" she guessed.

Norah erupted in laughter. "I would like you to point out the shop that carries them. But you are our Mikey's fiancée. You'll be getting very special treatment from me always."

Krista allowed her reserve to melt a bit. "I'll just go get my purse."

Norah made a sound that made Krista pause in the bedroom doorway. "You aren't wearing that outfit, are you?"

Krista gazed down at her red shorts and striped knit top. "You said casual."

"Again, the male translation is at work here. I said informal."

"Oh?"

Norah gestured to her own outfit of lavender slacks and shirt. "All the women will be in slacks and a higher end blouse."

Krista wasn't into polyester in particular, but had a full appreciation for her message. "I'll find something else."

The change was quick. She'd done some ironing this morning and had her navy pants and white cotton shirt within reach.

Krista returned to the living area with a word of thanks on her lips. She paused in midsentence, however, when she came upon Norah at the writing desk, her hands on Michael's briefcase.

"We gave Michael this case for his birthday years back," Norah explained. "Always kept his important possessions in it. I'm glad to see he's taking good care of it."

"It is a nice one," Krista agreed.

"Allan prefers this key model over the combination style. He's always been more apt to forget his combination than lose a key."

It seemed unnecessary to explain why they'd chosen the key model versus combination model. A cynic might wonder if the Larkins had kept a key to the case. It was a trick worthy of a snoop of a parent.

But it wouldn't do to be so suspicious, not if she was going to please Michael by bonding with Norah. She would try hard, beginning with a trip down to the shoe store.

A small group of women, four in number, awaited them in the lobby. To Krista's pleasure, Beth Norquist was among them. Norah, high on her shoe purchase, introduced Krista to the others. Norah had indeed steered Krista correctly on fashion. The group as a whole, despite their range in age and body type, they were all dressed well enough for a luncheon in any better restaurant.

Norah's prized pale-pink Cadillac awaited them on the hotel's circular drive—most likely thanks to a handsome tip Norah passed along to the valet. The ladies squeezed inside, allowing Norah her bragging rights on the vehicle, but teasing her about how well their Vegas franchise must be doing.

Norah merged onto the strip, plowing through the congestion of both car and pedestrian traffic. Krista was positioned at the front passenger door and gazed out the window at the dazzle of hotels with their statues and fountains, one building grander than the next. Krista had always sought quieter spots for the brief vacations she allowed herself. Now she felt she'd been missing out on a fascinating getaway.

The road trip proved a verbal free-for-all. As Krista expected, these women knew each other rather well and played catch-up with a sense of humor. This crowd was quite separate from the more guarded executive lot at last night's cocktail party. Their husbands were on Michael's level, owners of Decadent Delights shops. Krista noted with interest that Norah fit in with their league as comfortably as she had with the executives. But she definitely had a different face on today, far less refined in manner and dress—even her grammar slipped as it would among casual friends. Without doubt, she knew how to cover her bases with skill.

Before long the Cadillac was rolling along I–15, into a world far from the glitz of the Strip, a residential area of well-kept houses. The Larkin house, like many others on the block, was a sprawling ranch-style structure with a high fence enclosing the backyard. Unlike Minnesota, which was currently enjoying crisp September weather, Vegas, with its flat sandy landscape, was simmering in the sunshine like a huge sizzling griddle. It was no wonder air conditioners whirred in a constant hum.

The interior of the home proved breathtakingly beautiful. The floor plan was an open style with cream-colored plastered walls, honey-toned wood, beamed ceilings and tiled floors scattered with rugs. The living room was especially spectacular with a stone fireplace and a variety of southwestern art pieces on the walls and various stands.

Through glass doors overlooking the fenced-in backyard Krista found a huge stone patio with outdoor furniture and a swimming pool with two small cabanas.

The Larkins clearly were making money.

The crowd was starting down a hallway beyond the living room, so Krista quickly fell into line. They ended up in what Norah referred to as the library. True, many shelves boasted many books. But it was more of a shrine. To the Decadent Delights empire.

The women sauntered around the room, making appropriate noises about Allan's achievements. The walls were covered with frames of every conceivable size and kind, their contents pressed under polished glass: certificates linking Allan to a number of organizations, from the boosters to the Red Cross to the fire department; notes of gratitude from patrons; honorary diplomas from a number of Chicago schools. There was also an extensive display of photographs chronicling the Larkins and their shop over the years, too dense to absorb with a single glance. All in all, a very impressive collage.

But nowhere did Krista glimpse Norah the woman. Not one certificate or photo or note had her separate stamp on it. Furthermore, there wasn't a trace of a personal project in sight. No needlepoint in progress, no half-solved puzzle, no abandoned gardening glove, no stray golf tee.

Krista's earlier fears were confirmed. Michael had chosen the most narrow-minded model for his dream wife.

"So what do you think?" Norah asked, jolting Krista from her thoughts.

"Very nice."

"This is my whole life," she announced proudly with wide-spread arms. "Making a go of the shop, encouraging Allan to be his very best."

"I believe you've succeeded," Krista said honestly.

"Have you seen the photos of Michael?"

Suddenly Norah had Krista's interest. She led her back to one of the larger photo displays and pointed to the grainiest of the bunch, a small square one showing a gangly teenage Michael standing outside a Decadent Delights shop, wearing a bright-red DD polo shirt. His shoulders were sturdy and straight, but he had a spindly look about him, as if he needed a decent meal. By the cock of his chin, Krista guessed his body weight matched his pride.

"That's his first day of work with us."

"And you thought to take a picture?"

"Oh, my no. He was just another kid, then. His mother took that shot with a crummy little camera. The most attention she ever paid him, is my guess. She was thrilled he was going to be bringing home an income."

Krista's face fell.

"Surely you know about her."

"Not much," Krista said vaguely.

"Mikey's not one to complain, that's so. But you have a right to know things, now that you're engaged to him. Barb Collins was a real piece of work. An alcoholic uncertain of who she slept with at times. Never even knew for sure who fathered Mikey. She clung to him when sober and berated him when drunk. Came into the shop on occasion looking for Mikey. Made a stinkin' fool of herself every time. Mikey took to hiding at the sight of her. To this day he doesn't know how many times I slipped her a twenty and a sack of Lemon Glaze Ices just to get rid of her."

"You speak of her in the past tense."

"Oh, she's dead all right," Norah confirmed. "Her liver finally gave out. Drank like a fish until the end, hoping for a liver transplant. But they don't keep you on the list if you continue to booze it up. So in a way, she never even gave herself a break.''

Krista suspected that Michael knew full well about the cash and doughnut bribes supplied by Norah, and probably many other small kindnesses. It went far in explaining his devotion to the Larkins.

The photos bearing Michael's image were arranged neatly, highlighting events in his life in relation to the Larkins. Norah confirmed that he quickly became part of the family, as close to a son as they'd ever had. ''Yupped on Allan's heels like a desperate puppy, taking the business straight to heart.''

It was no wonder Michael was so anxious to be a part of their world, with a dysfunctional mother and no clue to his father's identity. Krista's heart ached for him as she imagined the needy child he must have been, and as she thought of her safe childhood in the hands of her father and aunts. Making an effort to control her emotions, she gestured to the other pictures of the shop. ''I've noticed Randy Norquist in a lot of these shots, as well.''

''Oh, yes. Our Randy. He had a fine stable family, so there was a difference in how much time he spent around us. Still, a credit to the business and our DD brood.''

Krista pointed to a photo of Michael that was perhaps five years old. ''Here's one with the briefcase you gave him.''

''Ah, the briefcase,'' Beth Norquist remarked, sidling up to them. ''Randy still has the one you gave him, too, the day he quit to go away to college. Still hoards all his stuff in it. I imagine Michael still keeps treasures inside his, as well.''

''I'm sure he does,'' Norah said proudly. ''Saw it just this morning in his suite. Quality will tell. The case looks brand-new even now.''

''So does Randy's,'' Beth said. ''Though I can't tell you

how many keys he's lost,'' she confided to Krista, who smiled in understanding.

''I've been known to misplace a thing or two myself.''

''Dear, do you want yet another of Allan's keys?'' Norah chortled.

Beth bit her lip as if summoning tolerance. ''No, Norah. I actually keep one on my key chain now. He is better, since Katy was born. Now he knows I have another baby to look after.''

''We tried to keep him straight.'' Norah rolled her eyes. ''Though the gloves he lost during many a long Chicago winter would've supplied a small school! Not that we haven't always been proud of Randy,'' Norah added. ''Just as proud as we are of Mikey.''

Beth appeared amused. ''With all of your phone calls and e-mails full of questions and advice, we've never felt neglected.''

''How time flies—both boys have their own shops now. Must say, the fellows are more successful than we ever expected.''

''Between their shops, they do have downtown Chicago covered,'' Beth said, then added abruptly, ''Not that there wasn't always room for Allan's shop, as well.''

Norah's smile was frozen. ''Of course there was room! We were doing just fine with our customers. If not for Al's arthritis…''

Krista moved swiftly to calm the rough waters. ''Michael's and Randy's success makes you the biggest kind of success.''

The older woman glowed at the thought. ''We did teach them the value of hard work. Neither Randy nor Mikey ever let us down in that regard. Still, I miss the old days when they were young and eager and reliant on us.'' She took a gallant breath. ''But we must carry on. Michael will, at last, have a suitable wife in you, as Randy has in Beth, a wife who fully understands her role in the Decadent Delights operation.''

The woman was nothing less than a steamroller in her opinions. Krista struggled to be discreet. "I can see how valuable you've been to Allan."

"I could have had a job in promotions like you, maybe— if I had wanted to."

"I'm sure—"

"But it isn't a good idea. Our men need our whole-hearted support." With that said, Norah was on the march, beckoning the group through the door, announcing it was lunchtime.

Krista began to follow, only to feel a tug on her arm. Beth Norquist was detaining her with a whisper.

"Hey, just want to make sure you aren't shell-shocked. You know, by the Larkin sanctuary here."

Krista betrayed her gratitude with a smile. "It is sort of suffocating."

"So is Norah's spiel. We girls all have heard it as we prepared to walk down the aisle. At the first scent of an engagement, Norah was right at it, trying to convert the bride into a mini version of herself. No one's really ever taken her obsessive dedication to heart. We love the business, it's true. But we all have outside interests to balance our lives."

"Anyone with a separate career?"

"Not anymore. Between raising children and helping at the shop, there isn't time or inclination to branch out. I was Randy's bookkeeper when we first began to date, so I'm a natural around the shop. Even now I enjoy the job, and it saves money. Our daughter Katy has developed a breathing disorder and our insurance doesn't cover all the drugs and doctors' visits."

"I had no idea."

"We'd rather the crowd doesn't know things are tight. We have our pride. I only mention it now because I figured Michael had already given you an inkling as to how things are, being he's Katy's godfather."

Krista was sure he would've gotten around to mentioning

the Norquist's child, in time. To compensate, she asked to see a photo of Katy.

"I have some at the hotel. I'll show you later."

"If there is anything I can do to help you…"

"We get by. And who knows, maybe we'll win this year's contest. Or at least come in as a runner-up."

Krista couldn't resist offering her a confidence in return. "My biggest worry of the moment is that Norah is the kind of woman Michael wants."

"We've noticed, Randy and I especially, being right in town with him. We've done as much as possible to set him straight, setting him up with all sorts of women. But in his defense, it's hard to find true love when you're working 24/7 to keep your shop afloat. And he's more vulnerable to Norah than the rest were. Her being his mother figure."

Beth gave Krista's arm a squeeze. "You won't regret hitching up with Michael. You will soon be part of the DD world. It's really very exciting. If you really love him, you can work this two-career thing out, convince him that Norah's thinking is horse-and-buggy out of date."

If she loved him. Darn if Krista wasn't beginning to think she might.

There was some commotion in the dining room as the women began to seat themselves at the large mission table. Accustomed to playing the name game in her business, Krista had them all down pat by now with her own identification system. There was Beth, of course. Also young Lucy from Florida, married to an older divorcee with teenagers. Laurie from California attended Berkeley. Amanda with the soft drawl hailed from North Carolina.

As they dined on Waldorf salad and iced tea, topics of discussion varied from cold medicine to television's *Frasier.* As Beth had intimated, interests were diverse, apart from the shop; bowling, skiing, church work, jogging, dancing and swimming were among the activities mentioned.

Krista's own meager hobbies of scrapbooking and softball were delved into with a smattering of questions. Polite queries about her job followed. She tried to keep her answers brief, so Michael wouldn't find himself too deeply trapped at a later point.

The Decadent Delights empire was not mentioned once. As Michael had cautioned her, there appeared to be an unspoken agreement on the subject.

No sooner had Krista recalled this than a dessert platter arrived via Norah's uniformed server. Under a napkin that Norah whisked away with a flourish sat a pyramid of sugar-coated orange doughnuts.

Doughnuts for dessert? Murmurs of surprise, along with groans, filled the air.

"This isn't just any doughnut," Norah was swift to explain.

"Is it your entry?" Laurie asked eagerly.

Krista noted a change in the atmosphere. The subject of doughnuts was suddenly fair game. A bright eager energy took over the table.

"Of course it isn't our entry," Norah brayed. "This is Gerald Stewart's first doughnut. The doughnut that started the whole empire. The flavor's been retired for years. But Gerald was kind enough to give me the recipe for Christmas last year. I thought you might enjoy tasting it."

"I bet you enjoyed making them," Beth teased.

"Naturally I did! The art of the doughnut is a religion." Delving into the stack of dessert plates delivered to her elbow, she used a tong to place a doughnut on each plate and hand them around the table.

Krista bit into hers with appreciation. The taste was heavenly. "Why did Gerald choose to retire this recipe?"

"His late wife Gloria tired of them some years back and asked him to do so," Norah replied. "I believe the flavor reminded her of their struggling years and she wanted to put the past behind her. Gerald never would have denied Gloria anything."

"Wouldn't it be a thrill to win that contest, all the fame

and money?'' Laurie said on a sigh. ''We were so close last time, with the logo competition.''

''C'mon, Ms. Berkeley graduate,'' Lucy argued with a grin. ''Your entry was some sort of hieroglyphic nobody aside from the world's dusty old professors could read.''

Laurie sniffed. ''Gerald Stewart has been to Egypt and completely understood the theme.''

''Our image was quite effective, too,'' Amanda put in. ''Gerald himself was very impressed with the doughnut-juggling clown.''

''I'd like to see all your logos,'' Krista announced. Broad smiles reflected back at her.

''That would be fun, showing them to someone in promotions,'' Lucy decided. ''Krista can give us her professional opinion.''

''Norah,'' Beth said, ''get us some pens. Felt tip, if you have them.''

Norah wore the grumpy expression of a hostess who has perhaps lost control of her table. ''What ever will you write on?''

''It doesn't matter.'' Impulsively Beth picked up the large square paper napkin from her lap. ''Bring a few more of these.''

''I'd love to see your logo, too, Norah, of course,'' Krista coaxed.

''Very well.'' The woman rose and lumbered off.

Beth leaned over the table to whisper, ''See, you're already showing her you've got a backbone. She'll soon realize you aren't putty.''

The women spent the next twenty minutes sipping coffee and sketching their logos with felt-tip pens.

''Who did win the contest?'' Krista asked, stirring some cream into her cup.

''Haven't you seen the logo?'' Lucy asked. ''It must be all over Michael's shop—even the rest room doors.''

''I haven't been to his shop or any other,'' she confessed. ''I'm from Minneapolis. Gerald's chain hasn't quite reached us yet." To her relief they all seemed to accept this edited version of the truth.

Norah tapped her temple with a finger. "The winner was some diabolical genius from Houston who thought to put Gerald's picture in the center of a doughnut, pompadour wig and all."

A round of laughter filled the air.

"It was quite brilliant," Beth agreed, "as Gerald is so very fond of his own image."

Once the sketches were finished, they were passed to Krista. There was Amanda's juggler, Laurie's hieroglyphic, Beth's picnic basket, Lucy's oven, and Norah's bakery case. Naturally, they were rough copies, but in her opinion, all original and well thought out. She was lavish in her praise, but did take the time to offer tips on making the logos more effective—in case DD ever found itself in need of another.

They all expressed gratitude for her input.

Krista felt she was the one learning the most, however. Norah's narrow-minded devotion to her husband's life was exceptional. These women, who had chosen to partner with their husbands, were bright and ambitious, leading rich full lives. Leaving Krista to believe there had to be great satisfaction in doing so. Never once in her adult career had she thought of participating in something outside her own zone of expertise.

"Now it's your turn," Beth encouraged.

Krista was startled to realize Beth was addressing her.

"Go ahead and make a logo of your own," Amanda pressed. "Unless, of course, you think Gerald's mug rightfully belongs in that doughnut hole."

"Actually, his mug should be on the logo," Krista told them. "He has such a wonderful reputation. But I do have an alteration in mind."

Norah swiftly held a pen and napkin under her nose. It was their turn to enjoy coffee while Krista sketched.

Krista was always confident in her work, but when she

finished, felt a slight twinge of insecurity as she held up her sketch for perusal. With neat practiced strokes she'd created a logo with Gerald's face inside a store window versus a doughnut hole. The biggest change, however, was the loss of his toupee. She didn't know the shape of his head, of course, but it was now hairless on top.

The table grew silent. Krista sensed that perhaps they felt upstaged. "Keep in mind, this sort of thing is my business."

"Gerald would've hated it," Norah declared bluntly. "Nothing personal, Krissy, but anything short of his exact self-image wouldn't cut it. I kick myself nearly every day for not realizing it before the Texan."

Murmurs suggested everyone agreed with Norah on all counts.

"One consolation is that there is another contest in motion this year," Krista pointed out. "More cash prizes."

Norah happily agreed. "The prize for the logo was only twenty grand. For this doughnut flavor competition there's a lot more at stake—a hundred grand and nationwide fame for the winner, fifty grand each for the two runners-up."

"Truth be known," Lucy said, "I think our Butterscotch Sunny has a great chance of taking some honor."

Laurie gasped. "Lucy! You know Kyle would have a fit if he heard you divulge the name of your entry."

Beth watched Lucy whiten. "Oh, c'mon, Luce, it's only us."

Lucy's fist rapped the yellow tablecloth. "Kyle will kill me."

"Not if we all confess the name of our doughnut entry," Beth decided. "Then we'll all be even. Okay, everyone? I'll start. The Norquist entry is called Cinnamon Spice."

"Ours is Vanilla Scoop," Amanda reported.

Laurie sighed and gave in. "Ours is Burnt Brown Sugar."

"I don't like this sort of pressure," Norah claimed. "But

for the good of the sisterhood, I'll tell. Our entry is Norry's Cherry Chip Glory.''

Krista wondered if she was the only one who noted the Larkins had deliberately combined Norah's name with that of Gerald's late wife. Perhaps it was Krista's promotions expertise that gave her the edge on that one.

Presently, they were all waiting expectantly to hear the name of Michael's doughnut. ''Oh. My turn.'' Krista swallowed hard. ''To tell you the truth, I have no idea.''

Moans of disappointment, maybe even disbelief, filled the air. ''No, honestly. Michael hasn't told me a thing.''

''But you are engaged.''

''This must be consuming his life.''

''What do you two talk about?''

Krista hesitated. ''Well, he's taken quite an interest in my shoes.'' To her relief, laughter broke out around the table.

The party extended into the afternoon. Moving outside to the pool, everyone splashed about in borrowed swimsuits from the Larkins' vast collection.

The atmosphere was quiet later as Norah's pink Cadillac retraced the route to the hotel. Krista used the time to think. The Larkins did truly care for Michael. And plainly, he owed them for pulling him up to a higher status. But she guessed that he had already paid them back over and over again for their kindnesses, dating back to his teenage years at the shop. Knowing him as she did, she imagined him eager and helpful always.

What mattered most was today, his future. Continuing to use the Larkins as role models was proving a detriment. Understandably they stood for continuity, security. But it was time for him to move on, build his own unique niche.

Michael needed a woman just like her, Krista decided.

Perhaps even Krista herself.

Beth's encouragement, today's group acceptance, went far toward bringing the idea closer to reality. But was it possible to make him see their compatibility, when she was lying about who she really was? Could he accept her despite her deception? And if she had to show him the difficult truth about the Larkins, could he ever forgive her that?

Chapter Nine

Convention activities broke off about three that afternoon. Randy Norquist caught up with Michael as he poured a glass of water from the table at the rear of the conference room.

"Saw you come in about forty minutes into the presentation," Randy said, shifting his briefcase, identical to the one Michael carried, from one hand to another.

"I was in a marketing workshop but couldn't resist getting a look at the new cash registers Gerald's come across."

"They're technical wonders, aren't they?"

Michael nodded. "I may have to invest in a couple. How about you?" The moment Randy's expression fell, he knew he'd made a mistake.

"You know I can't spare the money right now. Not with Katy's health."

Michael was appropriately rueful. "Has she taken a turn for the worse?"

"She's no worse than when you saw her Labor Day weekend. But the doc is keeping close tabs on her and it's costing me."

"My offer to help stands—"

"I know." Randy's tone was abrupt. "I do appreciate the offer. Every time you make it. But I can take care of my family."

"Have you discussed my offer with Beth?"

"No!"

"Because she might take me up on it," Michael predicted dryly.

"Don't even go there, buddy."

"Okay, okay. Pride is a good thing, but should be taken only so far…"

"With any luck we'll win this contest," Randy said hopefully. "A hundred grand and the fame that will come from being the recipe king."

Michael wanted the win so much himself that he declined comment. He'd much prefer loaning his friend the cash to giving up the joy of winning. There was silence as he sipped his water. Finally he said, "Wonder if the women are back from Norah's yet."

"Allan called home about an hour ago and they were swimming. Krista much of a swimmer?"

The question made him squirm a little. "I'm not really sure."

"I suppose in the rush of switching fiancées, some details got lost." Randy took the glass of water from his tense friend's hand. "C'mon, let's go find something tastier to drink."

They ended up in one of the hotel's three casinos, a center of action, noise and dim lighting. Roulette, craps and blackjack tables were clustered around the vast room, as well as row upon row of slot machines blinking and clanking as gamblers pulled arms and cheered on the spinning reels.

The men settled in at a bar for Manhattans.

"Maybe we should have changed clothes," Michael said. "We look like twins with our cases, dressed in our red Decadent Delights polos."

"Ah, but if Gerald sees the shirts, he'll be so gratified."

"You never stop angling." Michael rested both arms on the bar and stretched his spine. Unaccustomed to the sitting these conventions required, he always grew restless. He was feeling another discomfort, as well, over the lie he was living with Krista. He certainly was in no position to chide his friend for angling for the boss's favor. He was just as bad, toting along a fake fiancée for the express purpose of pleasing Gerald Stewart. He had considered telling Randy the truth from the get-go, but only briefly. They were close friends. But in a company contest, it was every man for himself.

Randy was perusing the room. "Don't look now, but we're in the sights of two very eager females. Who knows what sin they might have in store for us."

Michael stared at Randy Norquist in surprise. "That's no way for a family man to talk."

"Humor me. Take a look."

Michael glanced over his shoulder. Rather than a pair of babes on the prowl, he found women in their sixties, a petite blonde and a more formidable type with a cap of gray curls. Both were dressed in shiny nylon jogging suits, bright in color, the blonde's suit predominantly pink and the other's mostly blue. "I don't think we're in any danger of losing our wallets or our shorts to them." With a chuckle he turned back to his drink.

Randy pounced on him again in short order. "So, my man, how is it that in place of skinny whiner Colleen, you have an angel on your arm?"

Michael gave him a sidelong glare.

"So that *was* her name. I thought so. Colleen McManus. Good old fiancée number one."

"She's history, Randy."

"That was only two months ago. What happened to her?"

"Don't make a case out of it. You only met her once."

Randy's jaw was set stubbornly. "Just three weeks ago, at my Labor Day barbecue, you said Colleen was fine. Colleen McManus was fine."

Michael was now as tense as a tiger. If only Randy had never laid eyes on Irritated In Illinois. Somehow, he had to satisfy his friend's curiosity, put Colleen behind them for good.

The two older women had at some point eased up on bar stools beside Michael, but he didn't pay any attention. "Colleen was fine—is fine."

"Was she gone by Labor Day?"

"Things were rocky by then," Michael said distantly. "I wasn't ready to talk about it."

"Beth and I figured you came alone that day because it was a potluck and Colleen didn't want to deal with handling a share of the food."

"Her obsession with starvation was embarrassing at times."

Randy nodded. "Gerald would never have accepted that skeleton in the long run, his whole life centering around the joys of fat and carbs."

Michael was resigned. "I know. When I began to date Colleen, I didn't realize her eating problem was so serious. A lot of women do pick at their food. I was focused on other pluses, her vitality, her energy. Coupled with the fact that she had no solid career plans as yet, she seemed a likely candidate to fill the shoes of Mrs. Delectable Delights."

"Don't look so glum about the mistake. You saw the best in her."

"Of course I did! But as it turns out, she had no interest in even checking out my workplace, giving it a shot. All she did was whine about my long hours." He waved a dismissive hand.

"Well, she's missing out on a great guy."

"Is she?" The aging blonde at his elbow intruded with a flutter of mascara-coated lashes.

"Yes!" Randy assured.

"Can you dance?"

Michael was startled. "I guess. A little bit…"

"Popular with your peers?"

"Back in high school he was prom king!" Randy tossed in.

"But you work too hard?"

"Maybe a little too hard," Randy replied. "He learned the work ethic early because he had to support his mother. But get him going and he's the life of the party."

"This Colleen may have had you all wrong, then," the larger woman surmised. "She didn't give you a proper chance to prove yourself."

"No, she didn't. Ma'am." Michael's impatience with this unexpected interference was growing evident. "But I jumped to some assumptions myself, figured with a little push she could see my vision. Turned out she had no career plans because she preferred to play, exclusively and indefinitely. Her charms, her clothes, even her starvation, were all signs that she was stuck in the teenage groove. She wasn't ready to grow up and settle down."

"You paint a vivid and stark picture of her."

"I paint a gray picture of her," he corrected. "The world is shades of gray. And it wasn't entirely her fault. For my part, I was so anxious to marry, I pretended she was something she wasn't."

"We can all make mistakes in judging people," the same woman grumbled not too happily.

The blonde patted Michael's hand. "Plainly, all you want is to settle down with a nice caring girl. A fine goal."

The women beside him were making clucking sounds. Embarrassed by the admissions he had just made to the strangers, he glanced at them sharply. "Would you ladies mind..." He paused in midgrowl. How could he rebuff them when their eyes were misty in sympathy? "Would you ladies mind...a drink?" he offered lamely.

"We haven't even been formally introduced," the larger one demurred.

"I'm Rachel and this is my sister Beverly," the blonde swiftly supplied. "And I'd like a martini. Two olives."

Beverly's ample bosom rose and fell as she frowned

upon her flashier companion. "I wouldn't mind a gin and tonic. No ice."

"Nice to get the amenities out of the way so smoothly," Michael said with a tinge of humor, hailing the bartender.

Minutes later, with drinks in hand, Michael offered them a toast. "To ladies who possess both beauty and experience, and who know better than to mess with a man's heart."

The sisters blushed, appearing uncomfortable with his praise.

"Without doubt, you are better off without this Colleen," Rachel stated.

Michael shrugged. "I do feel sorry for her, though. She will probably continue to stumble around. Doesn't even have the common sense to discuss her problems openly, at the source." He was aware of three sets of eyes trained on him. "Instead of giving me a chance to work things through with her, she actually went to a third party for advice. A very nosy third party who, without any insight, whacked off my—uh, pride."

The ladies inhaled air and liquor. Randy picked up the gap. "Don't worry about this fella. Since his breakup, he has hooked up with the loveliest girl you can imagine. Don't understand how he did it so quickly, though."

"It wasn't that fast."

"Sure it was." Randy raked his hand through his hair. "Why, when you sent in the news of your engagement to the DD newsletter, it was in reference to Colleen. Had to be."

"Yes—"

Randy leaned over the bar. "There, you see, ladies? Fast."

"So you're happy now?" Beverly prompted.

"It does seem the luckiest find of my life," Michael stated, a bit amazed at his gusto. "She is everything a man could want. Lovely, charming, sweet. A little bossy and chatty, maybe. A little too interested in my business affairs.''

"But surely you want someone interested in your affairs," Beverly countered.

"Someone qualified," Rachel added.

"She's a bit wild for me," he admitted. "It takes some getting used to." He turned to Randy. "Do you know she had the nerve to take a poke at the Larkins for moving into Gerald's territory?"

To Michael's surprise, Randy chuckled. "Bravo. About time someone publicly pointed out the obvious."

"So she did a good thing?" asked Beverly.

"She did a very good thing." Randy pushed a bowl of nuts at the women. "Michael and I have always been a bit too fond of the Larkins because they gave us our start in the business. But it doesn't hurt to watch one's business rivals closely, no matter what the bond."

Rachel took the reading glasses dangling from a chain and slipped them onto her nose. Squinting, she read the fine print on his name tag. "Sister, this is our Michael! Our Michael Collins!"

Beverly pounded the bar with a formidable fist. "Why, I never."

"We've been looking for you all day long, dear. Reading tag after tag on red polo shirts until we're dizzy." She lolled her head in exhaustion.

"You enjoyed the hunt, Rachel," Beverly sniped. "Got three propositions in the bargain."

"Four if you count the man with his wife," Rachel tittered.

"Who are you ladies?" Michael finally demanded.

"We are Krista's aunts," Rachel gushed. "Rachel and Beverly Mattson. Surely she's mentioned us? Her father is our brother, we're her only relatives in Minnesota?"

"We're here on a package deal. Four full days of fun in the sun."

A smile froze on Michael's face.

"You mean to say Krista hasn't introduced you yet?" Randy asked.

That would seem weird in a genuine engagement, Michael realized. "Beverly, you did phone her once when we were together," he said, desperately referring to one of the calls during their clash at the newspaper.

"Yes, I do remember," Beverly said, looking a bit startled.

"You called about a recipe."

"Ah, I expect I did."

"It's good to know Krista is such a good cook. That people call her about recipes."

The aunts gaped.

Beverly was the first to recover, going on to make what appeared to be a painful confession to Randy. "It isn't unusual that Krista might hold back on introductions. She is sometimes self-conscious about our interference. We are hopeless snoops, you see. But we have so much love to give."

They were mighty good snoops, Michael decided. Look at the way they'd tracked him down, the info they'd just gleaned from him. Exactly how much did they know of the fake engagement? Did they understand the charade? The fact that no one must know Krista was columnist Simona?

Suddenly it seemed imperative to get rid of his friend to give some and pin down their exact intentions. "Randy, would you mind if I spent some time with Krista's relatives?"

Randy took the request with grace, popping a last pretzel into his mouth. "Nice to meet you, ladies."

"Don't bother with that," Michael said as Randy reached for his wallet. "I'll pick up the tab."

Randy nodded and was gone. With a blink Beverly had moved around Michael to take Randy's vacated stool. Suddenly he was neatly pinned between the sisters.

"I think we need another round," Rachel decided.

Michael hailed the waiter. "So what exactly brings the

two of you here on our heels? Seems a lot of trouble, even for the average snoop.''

The women exchanged a mischievous look.

''Your charade is just too exciting.''

''And, well, we thought maybe we could be of assistance. You know, offering extra cover.''

He was aghast. ''You know the whole story?''

Rachel clasped her rouged cheeks. ''Truly exciting. Truly.''

''So is Krista doing a good job?'' Beverly asked bluntly. ''I have no complaints.''

''Super. Then, you won't be suing over Simona's advice, after all?''

''Not if things proceed as planned,'' he answered slowly.

''As angry as you may be with Simona's advice, you must admit she has gone out of her way to rectify the situation. Her presence here is a real sign of caring, a determination to set things right. As a fairy godmother might.''

''I'm not the vindictive kind. All I want is help out of this mess.''

Their drinks arrived. Beverly dabbed a cocktail napkin to her mouth. ''So are you serious about your feelings for Krista? Or is it part of the act?''

Michael had reached his limit. ''This is getting way too personal.''

''But you've been discussing your romantic feelings in a public lounge.''

''I was confiding in my good friend. You chose to join in.''

''And you kept right on talking.''

''Because I mistook you for strangers! Everybody confides in snoopy strangers once in a while.'' His voice grew hushed and desperate. ''You aren't supposed to end up participating.''

''You can't expect less of good fairy godmothers.''

Michael frowned. ''I thought you said Simona was the fairy godmother, Rachel.''

Beverly's eyes flashed daggers at her sister.

"We're all here to help like fairies," Rachel said sweetly.

"I'd rather not discuss my feelings for Krista yet," he stated evenly. "We are still sorting things out. The charade is our immediate concern."

Rachel's eyes grew huge. "Oh, we won't spoil things."

"Can I have that in writing?"

"So, where is Krista? We've been calling your suite all day."

"She is lunching with some of the other wives here at the convention. Many of them are very friendly."

"Oh, how nice," Rachel gushed. "Krista doesn't have near enough friends."

"I imagined Simona with an address book full of friends."

Beverly pointed to the olives in her sister's glass and advised her to eat one. "The persona of Simona is quite dazzling. And justifiably so. Her column has a huge following. But it is hard to make true friends when one is a special celebrity. All in all, Krista spends way too much time and energy on her career."

"Speaking of careers. I don't want anyone to know Krista is behind the "Simona Says" column. There's little chance that anyone would connect me to the Doughman query, but steering clear of the entire column seemed best. Besides, no one would ever believe I'd marry the source of that dippy advice." He noted the ladies' faces pruned at his criticism and couldn't help thinking maybe they were a bit too close to Krista and her career. "In any case, Krista's been kind enough to choose a more suitable career for appearances. She's claiming to be a consultant for Bigtime Promotions. Please, if put on the spot, don't forget that detail."

The aunts exchanged an inscrutable look. "No problem."

"Good. You know, when all of this is over, you might

want to steer her to a more stable lifestyle, like that of Judy Phillips.''

"You've met Judy?''

"Yes. Now, there's a woman with her act together.''

"If it turns out you and Krista, well—'' Rachel tipped her blond head back and forth coyly ''—end up infatuated, I wouldn't worry about her being too wild for you. It's my guess she could learn to appreciate the tamer comforts of a settled relationship.''

Perhaps they were right. He wanted to believe they were.

Beverly rubbed her hands together gleefully. "I am so glad we've had the chance to talk things through. All that's left really, is the subject of your super-secret doughnut.''

"My what!''

"Your doughnut, dear. Tell us the flavor, whether it's baked or fried.''

He regarded them in tight-lipped silence.

"It's all right,'' Beverly assured gravely. "We consider ourselves an integral part of the Collins team now.''

Suddenly he was an entire team! The Mattson women were infiltrating on all levels. How much he could handle was something to be seen. Looking around he said, "Be that as it may, about the team, I am not comfortable discussing my doughnut.''

Rachel tweaked his cheek. "You're feeling shy.''

"It isn't that. Contestants aren't discussing their entries. Period.''

"Perhaps tomorrow, then.''

They blissfully ignored his continuing protests as they slid off their stools and smoothed their bright nylon suits. "Be sure to tell Krista we are looking for her.''

"That I will do, ladies. I promise you.''

Chapter Ten

Michael was half dozing on the sofa, watching a movie, when Krista returned to the hotel suite around six. He cracked open an eye to survey her. "How did things go?"

"Wonderful! Mostly. But you did let me down. Boy, oh boy." She paced in front of the television, arms folded across her chest.

Michael raised up to a lounging position in heightened alert. "Explain."

"Everybody was bonding, sharing, and there I was—on the outs."

"Why?"

"Because I didn't know the flavor of your doughnut, that's why!"

He was aghast. "Contest entries are always a private matter."

"You wish."

"They discussed the actual flavors?"

"Yes!"

"They asked you specifically about my flavor?"

"Yes, yes, yes!" Her arms flew dramatically. "Went right around the table naming off their entries. Finally they landed on little ol' me, then sat, waiting. And I had no answer to give. Can you imagine the shame? Here I am, your fiancée, with no clue to your contest entry."

He shook his head with a sardonic smile. "Apparently,

none of the women should've been trusted with the information.''

She raised a stifling palm. ''Don't even try to apologize for your thoughtlessness—for sending me blind into that trap.''

He was astonished by her stance. ''No way would I have thought to prep you. Never in my wildest imagination did I expect entries to be discussed openly.''

''The worst part was, they didn't believe I didn't know—at least, not at first. Oh, eventually I managed to save myself with some fast talking, but it did seem mighty fishy on the face of it, that, after listening to their secrets, I was refusing to share. So what *is* your flavor?'' Rounding the coffee table she shoved his legs off the last sofa cushion to make room for herself, causing him to yelp in protest.

''You expect me to tell you now?''

''I most certainly do. My curiosity is bursting at the scams.'' She paused, then added in a small voice, ''Weren't you ever planning to tell me?''

''Wasn't sure you cared.''

''Didn't know how much I cared. Until today.'' She shook a finger at him. ''It's all your own fault I'm getting in so deep, am hopelessly intrigued.''

He couldn't conceal his pleasure over her enthusiasm. ''I suppose everyone will expect my fiancée to lend a hand in the kitchen during the test runs on the recipe—''

''As they should. We are partners!''

''I do want to be partners.''

''Then, prove it. Take me into your confidence—into your kitchen!''

His gray eyes sparkled with new curiosity. ''Let's begin with you telling me the names of their entries. If you remember any of them.''

Looking rather proud, she began reciting the list, ticking the information off on her fingers.

''What about the Larkins?'' Michael asked before she could finish.

"The Larkins are the most ambitious, calling their entry Norry's Cherry Chip Glory. Get it? Her name linked with Gerald's late wife's name? Clever, with Gerald Stewart the deciding judge."

"Yes. A panel of chefs from the outside will score the doughnuts, whittle the finalists to three. Then Gerald will choose a winner and two runners-up."

"So what is our entry called, Michael?"

Our entry. He smiled involuntarily at her new matter-of-fact claim. His heart skipped under her zesty gaze. No real fiancée could show more genuine interest in his aspirations. This was all he wanted, the chance to conspire with a special someone. "It's called Pineapple Upside-Down Doughnut."

"Hey, I like it."

"I've been determined to keep it a secret for months, you see, because the name gives away so much, suggests that it is like a pineapple upside-down cake. While most entries will be fried, mine will be baked. I'm constructing each doughnut like a mini-cake, with crushed pineapple and chopped maraschino cherries atop a layer of cake. It's a very unique idea that I didn't want to share."

"Do you really think one of the group would have tried to copy your idea, given the chance?"

"Unfortunately, I am a likely target. Besides my years in the doughnut business, I have a culinary background. And I am known for making creative desserts. It might have been tempting for someone to try a knockoff."

"Surely it is all right at this point for other contestants to know of your recipe."

"I suppose it can't do any harm now, but I still don't like it, the way things are being discussed among the wives. Prying always leads to trouble."

"What shall I say the next time I'm asked?"

"They will wonder why I never told you, I guess." He was thoughtful for quite some time. "Seems the only way to explain my secrecy, to keep you in good standing with the wives, is to claim I was keeping the doughnut a surprise because it is named after you. The Larkins are pulling a name stunt, with the Norry Glory business. If asked,'' he finally said, ''you will say it's called Kris Pineapple Kringle.''

''If you win, I will be sort of famous.'' She smiled, as if savoring the idea.

''Still can't believe the wives dared cross that line...''

''Maybe such talks are common,'' she theorized. ''If you've never had a lady on the inside, you wouldn't know for sure.''

''I never have. So it is possible. Remember who started the whole confession jag?''

''Norah. She brought out doughnuts made with Gerald's first recipe. Someone asked if it was her entry, and the subject was ripped wide open.''

Michael basked in the fond memory. ''The Orange Blossom Special. They were delicious. Norah probably was more intent on bragging that she had the prized recipe than she was on sizing up the competition.''

''Maybe.''

''You promised to give Norah a break.''

''I have kept that promise. But she did initiate talk of the contest. And she was handling your briefcase this morning here in the suite.''

''She have a reason?''

''An excuse of sorts. Said she was admiring the way you and Randy have taken good care of her gift.''

''Maybe she was doing just that.''

''Possibly. She's a pain with her tunnel vision on marriage and the shop. But she appears to care for you very much. Wanted to make sure I know it, too.''

He grew worried. ''Exactly what did she do to instill this new faith?''

''She took me aside before lunch to show me some old photos of you, talk about your start in the business.''

''I see.''

"She told me about your family life, too. I'm sorry your mother had…troubles."

"Yes." His mouth tightened further. But she didn't seem to notice.

"I can see how Norah would emerge as a mother figure. I can also imagine that the reason you want to mold a wife, pull her in close, is so you can feel secure, in control, unlikely to be abandoned again."

"Dammit, Krista! Haven't you gotten me into enough trouble with your pop analysis?"

"Sorry. I'm just relating everything as it happened." She paused, plainly collecting herself. "I don't mean to intrude on any touchy territory."

"Of course you don't." He relented. "I shouldn't be snapping at you." He clasped his hands between his knees. "It's just that Norah has told you things I rarely talk about. I can date a woman for months without ever revealing so much."

"You can trust me with your secrets, Michael. I promise."

He lifted his eyes to her tender face and instinctively felt a warm reassurance. "Okay. Now, let's get back to the luncheon," he said brusquely. "The doughnut flavors were discussed. Then what happened?"

"That is when I really began to shine for you," she reported. "I felt obligated to somehow clear away the tension over the flavor snafu. Someone had mentioned the last convention's logo contest. So I fed off of that, encouraged all of them to sketch their entries on napkins for me. Must say, they appreciated my critiques."

"Your critiques?"

"They see me as a promotions specialist, remember? And I do help Judy out enough to know things. Anyway, they were so impressed with my tips, they urged me to sketch my own logo. So I did. I may be prejudiced but I like it better than the company's present choice."

He thrust out a demanding hand. "I'd like to see your logo."

She grew helpless. "I'd like to show it to you. Unfortunately it disappeared off the table before I could slip it into my purse."

He grew wary. "Everybody's napkin disappear?"

"Who knows? The server was clearing plates at the time, so I figure she took it away."

"Did you actually say you thought your logo was superior to the winning logo that graces every store in the nation?"

She beamed. "Everybody said so."

"Exactly how did you improve upon our company's image?"

"I merely removed a certain eyesore."

"Gerald Stewart's likeness?"

"No, I simply lifted his toupee. Not that I have seen him in his domed glory, but I have a general idea of what he must look like. Must say, my rendition brought the house down."

"Just out of curiosity, did you pause for even a second before your hand flew over the napkin to think about possible consequences?"

"Just the opposite," she confided blissfully. "The idea just flowed."

"Stop now to consider what will happen if that logo has fallen into the wrong hands."

"What do you mean?"

"Hands that might turn the napkin over to Gerald Stewart himself. Think of how the vain Gerald might react to the comical sketch. He might consider it a personal and unforgivable blow."

"It was such a lighthearted luncheon. Between the girls."

"All it takes is one person to break a bond of secrecy."

"Poking into recipes for a leg up is one thing. But do

you really think someone would risk damaging your relationship with Gerald beyond repair?''

"It is possible."

"I hope not. Despite the competition, I like all those women.''

"I am thrilled that you do. Most of the time, it makes for a great working relationship. But with rivalry this keen, it doesn't help to put this kind of inflammatory temptation in front of a desperate competitor.''

"Who's desperate enough to run to him with my napkin?''

"I don't know. Just as people don't know how desperate I am, coercing you along for the ride as my bride-to-be.''

"Guess I got carried away, grandstanding for the girls. Please don't be angry, Michael.''

"I'm more frustrated than anything else,'' he confessed. "One minute you're the coy advice guru, the next my confidante, the next an adwoman.''

"I sound truly fascinating,'' she teased.

"True, but I'm far more comfortable with a person once I've figured them out.''

"I can understand that—''

"You understand that, too?''

She pressed her lips together, as if finally reaching her comeback limit.

Clearly, she meant well, was trying so hard to help him. Sitting up, he touched the loose, damp tendrils on her shoulders with an expression of regret. "All I know for sure at this point is that I want to know you better. A lot better. Realized as much when I didn't even know if you could swim.''

"How does that fit in?''

"Just a funny little moment I had with Randy. He reported there was some swimming going on at Norah's and he wondered if you swim. Suddenly I really wanted to know if you do.''

She smiled. "That is so sweet, Michael. As it happens, I do a lot of swimming at home. Laps at the YWCA."

"Well, I like it, too. Swim at my club."

"Maybe sometime we can swim together."

He paused to imagine such a sometime—frolicking in the water with his own sexy mermaid. Then he remembered the issue that had kept him distracted from the television for the past hour, the aunts. After the shocks she'd reeled him he couldn't resist turnabout. With a benign smile he said, "We could even make it a family affair if you like, you and me and Beverly and Rachel."

She gaped at him. "My aunts call or something?"

"They're here. Tracked me down in the casino."

"Well, they would be in the casino, being big gamblers back home at the Indian-run places," she said gaily. "Mystic Lake, Turtle Lake, Hinkley—they hit them all."

"They outright admitted they are here to snoop."

Her affectionate tone was strained. "Why, the old dears."

"They've been trying to find us all day, calling this suite, bobbing for name tags on polo shirts."

"How much do they admit to? To knowing, I mean," she stammered.

"You're fully aware that they know the whole shebang! The fact that I am your column's Doughman, that you have offered to fix my broken engagement by posing as my fiancée. Did you really have to tell all, Krista?"

"I didn't mean for the whole story to pop out. But I had to tell them I'd be out of town or they'd have worried."

"As things stand, I believe they are more curious than worried. And possess unusually strong opinions on my whole dilemma. I can see where you got your sly edge for the advice column."

She averted her gaze. "The Mattson women have many talents."

"No doubt!" He clasped his hands together, carefully choosing his words so as not to offend. "Don't get me wrong. I like your aunts. They are fun. But they are also impetuous and invasive. Traits that make me very nervous.'' He went on to explain everything, including Randy's interest.

"My aunts' only sin is loving me too much,'' she assured hurriedly.

"I believe it, as their present mission appears to be far more complex than steering you clear of a lawsuit. I believe they'd like to marry you off.''

"What!''

"To me, of course.''

"What!'' Her shriek stung his ears.

"It hasn't taken them long to get caught up in the romantic angle of our trip, to imagine we could be real together. If I do say so myself, I think I passed their screening.''

"This is crazy. You should be outraged, rather than wearing that moony grin.''

His amusement deepened. "I am flattered that they think I am worthy of their precious niece. I sense they have high standards.''

"The nerve, sharing all that with you.''

"Seems only fair, as you've discussed everything about me.''

"The interfering old ducks. I will definitely have a talk with them. ASAP.''

"Seems best. But be gentle in relaying my views. Under other circumstances, I would love to spend more time with them. It's just this production, with all its complexities, doesn't need two more bit players.''

"I heartily agree. It is imperative that they leave town immediately.''

She reached back to the house phone of the end table. "Have you their room number?'' Michael provided the number and she gave them a ring. Unfortunately, no one answered. "Now what?''

"You could try and hunt them down," he suggested anxiously.

"This hotel has three casinos."

"They found me in Sultan's Fancy on the main level."

"Okay, I'll go have a look. Remember what they were wearing?"

He described their nylon running suits.

"I will call you when it's over."

"You sound as though you're going down there to execute them."

She raised a halfhearted protest. "No, of course not."

"But you look as if you wish…"

"It's a matter of wearing this very look, of being firm, of not letting them mold me like Play-Doh."

Michael flinched as the door slammed behind her. Apparently, the aunts had a history of pushing her into some very tight corners. How did the two sweet old things ever manage it? Maybe they could give him lessons.

A QUICK RUN THROUGH THE ROWS of slots in Sultan's Fancy paid off for Krista. As she predicted, the aunts were belly up to adjoining progressive machines, a bucket of coins between them, their eyes glued to the spinning reels of bars, bells and fruit.

"Are we winning?" Krista asked, placing a hand on Beverly's beefy back and one atop Rachel's delicate shoulder.

"Breakin' even," Beverly replied matter-of-factly over her shoulder. "So you finally got our message, then?"

"I got it, all right. Straight from Doughman himself. How could you approach him that way? It's amazing he wasn't more suspicious. You aren't even supposed to know what he looks like!"

"We handled it real smooth," Rachel insisted, yanking down the arm on her machine. Hitting a run of cherries, she watched coins tumble into the payoff return. With a squeal she scooped them into her plastic money cup.

Beverly watched the win with envy. "We're in no danger of being unmasked, as that man's every wheel is already spinning in another direction. Now, let's have a look at you."

Keeping a body block on their machines, the aunts stopped play long enough to turn to survey their niece.

"My, don't you look relaxed," Beverly boomed. "Nothing like the driven executive we know."

"Your complexion is so pink," Rachel cooed. "I'd swear you were having good sex."

The implication hung between them for a good thirty seconds, during which time Krista's complexion grew five shades darker. "I am not—" She stopped, realizing she was about to play right into their web. Given the chance, they'd take back control of the whole charade. That wouldn't be fair, as she was handling things quite efficiently. "I am not here to answer questions," she went on to say. "I'm here to ask them."

Beverly tsked. "Of course you wonder why we're here."

"We got to wondering whether Doughman deserved our published flogging, after all," Rachel said reluctantly, staring at her coin cup.

Beverly took up the slack. "Not that we are apologizing outright, mind you. Simona must never be chicken-hearted in her advice. Still, we do like to be accurate. Once you got involved with him, started enjoying yourself, doubts set in. Would a genuine dud have so readily agreed to the masquerade we invented? Would he possess the daring and confidence to pull it off? Well, we saw no alternative but to follow you here, see if, in fact, we had screwed up by condemning this man as a hopeless bore."

Suddenly Krista recognized the chance to nail down a rare and most welcome admission of error on their part. "So are you telling me that you've actually come to see your judgment was wrong?"

"My, yes!" Rachel gushed. "Michael's risen from dud to dish in record time."

Beverly agreed, though dispassionately. "He is quite charming, it's true."

"I tried to tell you so back home," Krista chided.

"Don't get all high and mighty on us, though," Beverly cautioned. "We still feel our advice to Irritated In Illinois was valid. We may have misjudged Michael's personality, but not the doomed relationship. It was a mismatch if ever there was one. Having drinks with Michael set a lot of things straight. He believes, rightfully so, that his fiancée was probably only looking for an excuse to break up with him because she was completely unprepared for marriage. For his part, he realizes he pushed her too hard, expected too much. All in all, blame was distributed quite evenly. Bottom line—Simona's advice was for the better good."

Krista's retort was dry. "Okay, you saved Michael from a bad marriage. But let's not overlook the fact that a frank talk with him up front, without involving me, probably would've had the same effect."

"Oh, but then he wouldn't have had a nice girl to bring to the convention," Rachel said. "And you wouldn't have met a suitable man or taken this vacation. A vacation you sorely needed. It's been a while since you broke from routine."

Beverly's smile was smug. "Our scheme is the closest you've come to real romance in ages. This Michael character is ripe for the picking and it's plain he's interested in you."

"And obviously you feel the heat," Rachel said, "in your own repressed and cautious way. Even if you haven't managed to consummate your relationship yet, you have never looked prettier, more content."

"We feel so strongly about our goodwill that we are willing to confess everything to Michael this very minute," Beverly proclaimed bravely.

"What!"

"It's high time he discovers with whom he is dealing—

a talented fellow member of the executive stress club. It's bound to speed up the courtship.''

Krista pressed fingers to her temples as if warding off a migraine. ''No, no.''

The aunts were at this point justifiably confused. Here was the opportunity she'd been longing for, to reveal herself as a lucid woman with a solid career. But a sudden unexpected gut instinct held her back.

''This is not the time for a confession. Michael's under enough strain right now, plotting contest strategy with the reality we've fed him. It would be a disservice to rock the boat. He'd be angry about the lies and might, in a burst of pride, send me away. That in turn could upset him enough to cause him to blow the contest. Even perhaps put you back on the line for a lawsuit.''

''He likes us too much now ever to sue,'' Beverly said confidently.

Rachel also took the peril in stride, tweaking Krista's cheek. ''Understandably you want to get him into the sack before confessing your sins. It's every woman's prerogative to cloud a man's brain with desire.''

''Ooh, you two will never understand the art of the deal.''

After turning in their coins for dollar bills, the aunts wandered out to the lobby with their niece. Along the way Krista prepared to explain why they might consider cutting short their four-day trip. But the words didn't come easily. They were so excited about finally making it to the gambling capital of the nation, about seeing their precious niece looking so relaxed. And a part of Krista was happy they finally appreciated Michael's magnetism.

Still, they were so unpredictable and had no real purpose here beyond a relative's snooping privileges.

''Have you considered how you will spend the next few days?'' Krista prompted, steering them to a fountain, beside which was a gilded bench padded with a gold-colored cushion. It sat only two, so Krista remained standing. "If you stay on, that is?"

"There are so many things to see and do. Or we may just hang around right here in this hotel." Rachel gave the lobby an airy perusal. "It depends upon how interesting the convention is."

"You two aren't conventioneers. You need a badge to enter any of the activities. Even I don't have a badge."

"Am I to understand that you would prefer we leave town altogether?" Beverly asked abruptly. "When we've already paid in full for a four-day package of glamour and fun in the desert sun?"

Krista withered a bit under her hefty aunt's stare. "You could come back another time."

Rachel pressed a hand to her heart. "Is that what you want?"

"We do already have our hands full." She watched the aunts exchange glances. "One slip-up by you and the whole scheme might fall apart. Would you like that responsibility?"

The two ruffled hens locked eyes. "I suppose we could cooperate," Beverly finally grumbled. "If you see it as totally necessary..."

In her joy Krista took an involuntary step back, jostling into a sturdy frame. She whirled around to find Gerald Stewart standing behind her. He was dressed in a plaid western-style yoked shirt and tan jeans. Toupee glued in place.

"Hello, there,...missy."

"Krista Mattson, Mr. Stewart. Michael Collins's fiancée."

"Dear child, I know that," he lied smoothly. "Do call me Gerald." He was looking over her shoulder now. At her aunts. "Who are your lovely companions?"

Krista should have expected it. Rachel's golden hair and vivid makeup and pound of bangles rarely escaped the attention of the average middle-aged man. Not to mention her voice that rang like a beckoning bell, or her petite figure, set to advantage even in her loose nylon suit. The doctor had told her to stop crossing her legs in order to relieve chronic back pain, but Rachel couldn't bring herself to sacrifice the provocative pose.

Krista made introductions, sensing that Gerald Stewart was at his most attentive.

"Just arrived, eh? All the way from Minneapolis." He surveyed the bench the aunts sat upon as he might a case of his own tempting doughnuts.

"A four-day package deal," Rachel cooed. "Here to support our Michael."

Our Michael. Krista thought the coo was overdone, but Gerald seemed all the more pleased.

"That's the spirit," he said. "My kind of family loyalty."

"There's not much my sister and I wouldn't do to keep the Mattson machinery in running order."

Beverly's claim made Gerald's whole tanned face crinkle in pleasure. "Can't be too serious a mission, here at my lively convention, surrounded by so many games of chance." With that he hazarded a wink.

"We've never seen such a spectacle as the Vegas Strip. We can only imagine how it dazzles after dark."

Krista tensed in the brief silence to follow. Rachel had cast her line on the Stewart waters, struck in her trademark damsel pose.

Gerald swallowed the bait in a single gulp. "I would be honored to treat you to a stellar night of excitement."

Beverly's ample bosom lifted in a sigh. "We're not sure we're available."

"Why ever not?"

"Because we may have to leave," she said with a pat to her gray head. "Due to an unexpected…glitch in our plans."

Both aunts leveled Krista with an accusatory look.

Krista, who had moments ago felt so in control, now felt her expression go blank.

"Can't be anything too serious. It would be a shame to break up our little group." He smiled upon Krista. "Naturally I am including you and Michael in my invitation. Surely you can take care of any glitches these ladies have."

"Do you think you can, Krista?" Rachel peeped.

Krista was caught off balance by this development. But its value was not lost on her. A night on the town with Gerald would be a splendid opportunity for Michael to step forward, perhaps finally make an impression on Gerald. The price paid would be the aunts' uncertain company.

Here she was, facing another hurdle that would affect Michael. Another he'd rather address himself, no doubt. But he wasn't here. Whether he could appreciate it or not, she was an executive with all the cunning he himself possessed, and she was perfectly capable of making this move on the game board. Truth be told, there was only one reasonable move to make.

"Of course the aunts will stay on. I shall speak to the reservations desk about your room mix-up right away," Krista improvised. "We'd all be happy to join you, Gerald."

He smiled broadly. "We'll meet here in the lobby round six-thirty."

"Now, Gerald, you must tell us all about this business of yours." Rachel rose in a fluid motion to take over, pulling Gerald Stewart down on the bench, sandwiching him between Beverly and herself. "We adore doughnuts, no two ways about it."

Krista stood by dazedly, aware that she had been ruthlessly cut from the conversation. There seemed no choice but to exit.

MICHAEL WAS WAITING for Krista in the suite. She realized she was catching him in midpace near the sun-drenched patio doors. All at once he looked tense and so very happy to see her, as only a co-conspirator can.

"How did it go?"

She took a deep breath. "I think I need a drink."

He followed her to the wet bar. "Do you have good news or bad news?"

She unscrewed the cap of some ginger ale and took a gulp. "My news is up for interpretation."

"What does that mean?"

"They agreed to leave, if that's what we really wanted."

He watched her warily. "That sounds like good news."

"But while we were in the lobby discussing this good news, Mr. Stewart came ambling by."

"Did you speak to him?"

"I spoke to him," she said heartily.

"Did he ask about me?"

She set down the bottle. "We sure talked about you, oh boy."

He grasped her arms. "And…"

"The result was a dinner invitation for tonight."

"Us? With Gerald?" His voice surged with joy and he twirled her around.

Krista hadn't been twirled by a male in twenty years, since kindergarten. Once she grew older, boys found her too imposing to handle. But not so here and now in the role of Simona. Michael spun round and round, sharing the victory with a laugh. It felt marvelous and freeing, nothing like the way she felt in her Ms. Big persona—the one she'd inadvertently carved in stone back at the office.

He finally put her down, tapped her nose and asked for details.

Her voice was breathless. "We're to meet him downstairs around six-thirty. Nothing was mentioned about dress. No doubt we'll be safe with semiformal wear. Something suitable for a floor show."

"That was an inspired maneuver, I must say. You were

really on the ball, the way you juggled him and your aunts in a matter of an hour.''

''All in a day's work.''

He gave her a lip-smack on the mouth, which swiftly deepened to a sweet lingering kiss. They broke apart, mildly self-conscious, slightly shaken by the small current running between them. He was the first to recover. ''I don't understand how you could have worried that I would see this as bad news.''

She lifted her eyes to his hesitantly. ''The aunts had agreed to leave, before Gerald came along with his dinner invitation. But now all that has changed.''

''Are you saying he included them in the invitation?''

''Yes.''

''And they accepted.''

''Right again.''

''Gerald is always the gentleman.''

''He was most insistent. The three of them clicked, partly, I imagine because they are so close in age.''

''Well, Rachel is a bit of eye candy, I imagine, for the older male.''

''So, are you fine with it?''

''Honestly, no. They—they say all sorts of stuff! It's one thing for doting aunts to run some interference, but this pair takes a linebacker approach to the game.''

''I'm sure they will be on their best behavior in front of Gerald. They like you and understand his importance to you.''

He regarded her with boyish hope. ''Any chance they might leave tomorrow?''

Krista remained sympathetic. ''Gerald might think we're mistreating them if they do. He knows they intend to stay for four days. Hinted that he plans to keep an eye on them.''

''He actually went so far as to say that?''

''Afraid so.''

Michael sighed resignedly. "Guess I have no choice but to play this out Gerald's way."

"Look on the bright side, you now have the opportunity to engage Gerald in a little one-on-one conversation away from all other distractions."

"I do, thanks to you. I am very proud of you, Krista. An opportunity fell into your hands and you handled it with the cunning and diplomacy of an executive."

"I always say we make our own luck."

"So do I. Still, I can't help but feel that maybe some of the Vegas charm may be rubbing off on me. Have you considered the lucky twist of fate that put you in the right place at the right time to connect with Gerald?"

Krista was noncommittal, thinking of a string of ironic twists of fate instead. After forcing Krista to play Simona against her better judgment, the aunts were now feeling a rare wave of remorse, wanted to fess up to being Simona. And despite Michael's devotion to Decadent Delights, its corporate owner didn't know him for dirt. This would most likely change due to the two nosy women that Michael desperately hoped to shoo away.

A part of her hated keeping him in the dark, the part that hoped they might have a future. After all, good relationships were built on a foundation of trust. But then again, it did seem wrong to make him stumble over dodgy facts when he was on a winning streak. If he were any more pumped up for the contest, she'd have to tie a string around his neck to keep him from floating off.

Chapter Eleven

Krista emerged from her bedroom at six-fifteen, dressed in a pale-blue knit dress that gently clung to her curves. Her jet hair was loose and flowing, without the wild Simona ripples. Her makeup was subtle with just an extra flash of green eye shadow. Silver jewelry adorned her hands and throat.

Michael was appreciative. Being a Taurus didn't seem an issue this round. "You look gorgeous."

"Thank you, sir." She inspected his off-white linen jacket and navy slacks, moving closer to smooth the collar of his light blue cotton shirt. "You look pretty gorgeous yourself."

"Hope we've dressed well. To Gerald's taste."

"Relax, Michael. Gerald has no taste."

He exhaled. "You're right. It's getting tougher to defend that colorful western wear the more I see of it. And that rug on his head is a sight. Not that you should've sketched him topless on that napkin. If a man doesn't want to come out of the bald closet, it is his right."

She patted his cheek. "I wish you'd stop worrying about that napkin."

"At least you didn't sign it. Did you?"

"So what if I did?"

He took her by the arm and steered her to the door. "C'mon, we're going to be late."

Gerald Stewart and the aunts were waiting in the lavish lobby near one of the fountains. Gerald was wearing a gray suit with a red shirt and figured string tie, toupee puffed to attention. Beverly's gray hair was curled tight against her head. She was dressed in a dark-green sheath that concealed her stomach. Rachel's blond ringlets were fluffed around her chin. She wore a flouncy gold lamé dress short enough to show off firm thighs encased in black stockings.

Michael grasped Krista's arm at the sight of them. "Good lord, Rachel and Gerald would be a mini carnival if they stood side by side. Beverly is nothing short of color relief, standing between them as she is."

Krista figured the positioning was no accident. Rachel was such a flirt, and it would be like Beverly to keep their trio platonic.

Gerald welcomed them to their group. "Here they are," he proclaimed. "We're going to the hottest show in town," he announced, hustling them all to the door. "*Siegfried and Roy* at the Mirage."

A white limousine awaited them at the entrance. Gerald pushed aside the driver—his full-time employee, as it turned out—to help the ladies into the back. He then climbed aboard, leaving Michael to fend for himself.

The interior smelled of cigar smoke, which worsened when Gerald lit up a Cuban. He puffed contentedly as the car rolled through the gaily lit night, remarking that it was a relief to once again smell subtle perfume intermingling with his smoke. It was Krista's Chanel, but the aunts kept mum about it.

Unusually demure under the mogul's gaze, Beverly commented on the show tickets. "A hundred dollars a pop seems a foolish extravagance."

"I can well afford it," Gerald assured her gently.

"Especially as there is no meal included."

Rachel elbowed her sister sharply. Gerald didn't notice, however, as he threw back his head, roaring with laughter. "We will have a late supper. Anything you like, Beverly."

"She had some cheese and crackers up in the suite, Gerald," Rachel reported. "Don't mind her."

"Don't mind *her*," Beverly scoffed in return fire.

Gerald leaned forward sagely. "I intend to mind you both very carefully. Mind all of you," he added, as if in afterthought.

Krista wondered if Michael had any inkling as yet to the amorous older man's motives. After years stuck on the business fast track, Michael seemed pathetically oblivious to the wiles that went on around him. Judging by his broad smile, she figured his being Gerald's afterthought suited him pretty damn well for the time being.

The Mirage was set apart on the Strip by its fifty-five-foot volcano. Gerald halted the party outside the entrance to watch it erupt on the half hour.

The interior proved to be a tropical haven with lush greenery and polished bamboo. The group stood taking in the atrium rain forest while Gerald explained that it was the hub leading to all areas of the hotel.

Spotting a gigantic aquarium behind the front desk, Krista distracted the aunts in an effort to give Michael a moment alone with Gerald. But it didn't work. Gerald followed, eager to point out the tropical fish in the tank, as well as stingrays and smaller sharks.

The *Siegfried and Roy* production proved to be on a grand scale, with state-of-the-art lighting, sound and special effects. Dancers and acrobats supported the magicians, as did a fire-breathing dragon, white tigers and an elephant that magically disappeared during the act.

Afterward, Gerald led them to the hotel's Samba Grill. Ushering them inside he explained that it was a newer place, and, for Beverly's benefit, added that it charged moderate prices. When Beverly looked flustered, Gerald moved in to give her a fond peck on the cheek.

The eatery had a Brazilian theme, and was decorated in vibrant colors. Gerald was known by the staff and was led back to a spacious table in a corner.

Michael opened his menu, then looked over at Gerald, seated across from him. "Maybe you can make some recommendations."

Gerald turned to the waitress and ordered a variety of appetizers, coconut prawns and duck tamales among them. Everyone expressed appreciation for his offer of drinks. Michael showed off by remembering that Rachel enjoyed a martini with two olives and Beverly a gin and tonic, no ice.

Once the drinks arrived, Michael politely steered the conversation away from Beverly's knitting club to the convention's contest.

Gerald responded eagerly. "Wait until you see the contest area in the basement of our hotel. There are deluxe stations set up for the bake-off, with convenience in mind, not to mention privacy. Everyone has a right to his or her own space. No room for chatter among contestants in a race, I always say."

Michael gave Krista an I-told-you-so look before turning back to Gerald. "I've heard about state-of-the-art ovens you've shipped in. Been looking forward to having a look. As you know, however, the area has been off-limits to contestants thus far."

"True. Practice sessions start tomorrow morning. Suppose we could have a look tonight, if you like." Gerald then glanced at the aunts. "You ladies cook?"

"We get along," Beverly assured.

Michael smiled. "That's an understatement, if you're half the cook Krista is."

Krista shifted uneasily on her chair. "Oh, Rachel and Beverly are just as good as I," she assured.

"We sure are," Beverly agreed.

"As it is, we are simply too busy with our job to spend a lot of time in the kitchen," Rachel said with a small hiccup.

Gerald rested an elbow on the table, leaning forward with interest. "What job is that?"

"Public relations, mostly," Beverly hedged. "Nothing official. We help people around the community in various ways."

Rachel laid a bangled arm on Gerald's hand, her voice sweet as honey. "We love helping people. Especially old people. It's our duty."

Beverly humphed. "You sound like a beauty queen contestant with that line. We *are* old people. Helping all kinds of people."

"Still young enough, Bev," Gerald objected, "to cause the men some real damage."

Beverly glowed. Rachel pouted. Krista fretted. The aunts were beginning to get competitive and it was bound to grow worse.

Bottomless bowls of Samba salad followed, along with some of Gerald's favorite wines. Eventually the table was crowded with marinated meats, fish, Cuban-style potatoes and baskets of Brazilian breads.

Gerald did most of the talking for some time, expounding on his spacious mansion in a tonier suburb, the loss of his wife Gloria a few years back, the dreams he perpetuated with his family-oriented shops.

Michael took advantage of gaps—mostly during Gerald's chewing—to speak of his Chicago turf, his relation to the Larkins, his interest in the company as a growing entity. Krista was proud of his attempts to stake his own claim.

To that end, Gerald asked about Michael's doughnut entry. Michael explained the Kris Pineapple Kringle, its upside-down cake basis.

Krista meant no harm when she suddenly mentioned that years back, her aunts had been fond of making a pineapple upside-down cake of their own.

Beverly paused vacantly. Rachel admitted to not remembering.

"Oh, c'mon you two. There were pineapple rings, bordered by maraschino cherries."

"We have so many recipes," Beverly claimed. "It is

sometimes hard to remember every one. Especially with the passage of time.''

"I can just imagine a prized recipe box in your kitchen," Gerald said. "My late wife had such a box. Called it her treasure chest.''

"Oh yes," Beverly assured. "Ours is carved in wood. Right, Rachel?''

"Teak," Rachel confirmed with a sultry toss of her head.

"I imagine your cake is delicious," Gerald praised. "You must make it for me. Heaven knows, I have the oven space.''

If looks could kill, the aunts would have broiled, baked and grilled Krista on the spot. They adjourned to the rest room for a brief hot powwow.

"What's this nonsense about we Mattsons being cooks?" Rachel demanded.

Krista shrugged. "It all started when you kept pestering me with those phone calls at the newspaper. Remember, I pretended we were discussing a recipe? Then Judy added to the illusion at my place.''

"I don't remember that pineapple recipe," Rachel said. "Do you, Beverly?''

"I don't even care to remember.''

Krista clenched her hands. "But Gerald wants the cake!''

Rachel preened into the wall mirror over the sinks, then took lipstick from her handbag. "Surely you don't expect us to bake it.''

"We can't risk you disappointing Gerald right now. You must do it for Michael.''

"Michael is expecting too much.''

"Michael doesn't *know* he's expecting too much because he believes Gerald only has eyes only for him. When, in fact," she admitted begrudgingly, "it is you two Gerald seems to care about.''

Beverly gawked at her niece. "Let me get this straight. Michael believes Gerald is being nice to us for his sake, when the situation is the other way around?''

"Yes!"

Rachel applied her lipstick. "Maybe he isn't as smart as we thought."

"He is too smart! He's just too anxious to see all the facts. Now that you've stubbornly stayed on, it's only fair you cooperate. We must come up with a recipe for you to make for Gerald."

"We probably hated making that cake and botched it up good every time," Beverly declared flatly.

"As a child I remember it as very tasty."

"That makes you out to be as gullible as your new boyfriend."

Rachel struck a thoughtful pose. "Krista, I imagine you enjoyed the fun of preparation more than the result. It's a bit like sex, dear—oftentimes the foreplay is more memorable than the actual act—"

"Everything is like sex to you," Beverly cut in.

"Forget about sex," Krista beseeched. "We have to come up with a recipe before tomorrow if we hope to continue impressing Gerald."

"Maybe we'd have a chance with our original one," Beverly conceded.

Krista dug into her purse for her cell phone. "I'll call Judy. She can run over to the house. Where might she find it?"

"All the recipes are stashed away in the pantry."

"All this trouble for a bad toupee." Rachel looked unsure.

"All this trouble for Michael," Krista corrected. "Who I happen to—"

"To what?" they chorused.

"Like very much."

Smugly, the aunts marched out of the bathroom. Krista raised a brow and punched Judy's number into her cell phone. Within minutes she had Judy on the run, headed for the aunts' house and the key they kept hidden on the front porch.

The limo ride back to the hotel was quiet and companionable. It was late as they strolled into the lobby of the Imperial Majestic.

Gerald dipped into his pocket to check his pocket watch, and confirmed it was well after midnight. "Anyone care for anything else?" he asked.

Michael spoke up. "We were going to have a look at the contest site."

Krista gave his sleeve a quick tug, whispered near his ear. "Look, there is your little gang, inside that lounge to the left."

His gaze swept past the marble and gold terrain to a gated lounge flanked by palms, where Allan and Norah Larkin lingered with Randy and Beth Norquist. "Damn. We were invited to join them tonight. So excited about our dinner, I never did give them an answer."

"I bet the Larkins did some math when they couldn't locate you or Gerald, and have been stationed at a table just inside that lounge for some time. Seems no other explanation for their timing."

"Well, not a one of them would have turned down the chance for a one-on-one with Gerald."

"Of course they wouldn't, Michael."

Norah performed some overdone pantomime, expressing shock at their arrival, reporting it to the others. With a clatter of heels and chorus of greeting, the foursome made tracks to Gerald's party of five. Both Norah and Beth attempted to sidle up to Gerald, but he was light on his feet and got away. Probably not as cleanly as he'd intended, as his cheek was now branded by Norah's tangerine lipstick.

From a comfortable spot between the Mattson women, Gerald introduced the pair to the newcomers, explained the aunts' longing for a night on the town. The Larkins and the Norquists were polite, but steam was practically coming out of their ears.

"How nice to meet your relatives," Norah told Krista. "You never even mentioned them at lunch today. Why, they could have come to my house. I would've shown them around afterward.''

''I had no idea they were coming to town,'' Krista replied.

Norah was hardly convinced. ''How quickly things happen. They've already gotten to know our Gerald.''

As tensions thickened, Gerald proved anxious to depart. ''If you'll excuse me, I intend to escort Beverly and Rachel to their room. Good night.''

Any thoughts of visiting the makeshift kitchen faded away as the trio strolled off. Krista felt bad to see that even the normally chipper Beth was pinning them with a hard look. She gave Michael points as he tried to distract Beth with a compliment to her pink cotton sweater and white pants.

Allan clapped Michael on the back. ''You hear the girls were talking shop this afternoon?''

''Yes, I did,'' Michael replied evenly. ''I didn't know that went on, never having had a girl of my own involved before.''

''Krista's involved now. A full-fledged member of our tribe. Why, her logo sketch was a riot!'' Norah placed a hand to her stomach as if it ached to laugh. ''Though we mustn't make too much fun of Gerald's baldness.''

''I wasn't making fun of him,'' Krista began, only to catch Michael's warning look.

''Everyone knows you meant no harm, hon. Though I'd love to see that sketch.'' Michael gazed around the group expectantly.

Beth shrugged. ''That's up to Krista.''

''But I don't have it.''

''Must have gotten tossed away,'' Norah declared with a cluck of regret. ''Sorry, Mikey.''

''You wives always talk so openly about company business?''

A discontented Randy was first to speak. ''It's the first Allan and I knew of it.''

Allan nodded, none too happy. "Appears you have the only woman with any discretion, Mikey."

"I didn't know anything to spill," Krista protested.

"But that is all changed," Michael said, pulling her to his side. There was no mistaking the foursome's interest. "I was going to surprise her tomorrow in the kitchen, but she got it out of me. I named my entry after Krista. It's called Kris Pineapple Kringle."

"Isn't he the greatest?" Krista enthused, cuddling up close to Michael.

"ALL THIS SUBTERFUGE, it's hard to keep up." Michael had flopped onto the suite's sofa some fifteen minutes later, tearing at the tie still choking his neck. "Do you find it hard to keep up?"

If he only knew. Krista sat down beside him, kicking off her shoes. "You're doing fine."

"That was a tense moment downstairs. Gerald sure was crafty, using your aunts as his getaway."

"Sorry you didn't get down to the kitchen."

"It's okay. There'll be plenty of time spent down there. The first practice run is at eight tomorrow morning. Then there will be the second practice run the next morning, then the real thing the next."

"So, you feeling ready?"

"I've prepared for six months, experimenting with measurements, ingredients."

He sat up straighter, looking inspired. "How would you like to see my recipe right now? You can review it while I fill out my entry form, see if you can make any suggestions."

Such a request was akin to asking a seamstress to pull a tooth, a pharmacist to rough up a house. She yawned at the prospect. "You want to tackle all that tonight?"

"Might as well. I'm too keyed up to sleep." He searched her face in confusion. "Something the matter? Thought you were dying to be involved."

It was true she had shown interest—in every angle of the competition save for the contents and measures of the recipe itself. She was a promoter, a player. But as it stood right now, the only measurement that currently sparked her interest was his broad muscled chest. She guessed it at approximately forty inches.

There was no way she could give him any solid advice on his recipe. Still, her interest seemed most important to him. So what was one more bluff in this maze of smoke and mirrors? As long as she didn't harm the recipe, what did it matter? Obviously Michael truly believed it to be perfect already. She forced her hands together in anticipation. "Bring it on."

Krista moved over to the writing desk with him, pulling up an extra chair as he set his briefcase on top and fumbled with his key ring to unlock it.

"So this briefcase is identical to the one the Larkins gave Randy Norquist."

"Yes."

"The same key opens both of them. Norah admitted as much today. Even offered Beth another key."

"Randy loses everything." Unperturbed, he sat down and began riffling through a file folder of papers inside the case. He withdrew some blank contest forms and considered them.

"You do realize that either couple probably could open your briefcase at any time?"

"I wouldn't like the idea of anyone going through my stuff," he admitted. "But there would be nothing to gain."

"So your recipe never was in here? Even at home?"

"No." He looked amused. "Told you I am especially sensitive to contest security."

"I suppose everything will go off without a hitch."

"With your flair for drama, you'd love to catch someone in a compromising position!"

At this point in time, with his tie askew, sleeves half rolled over sinewy arm and hair mussed, Michael himself was the one she'd most like to catch in a compromising position.

As irritating as the aunts' observations could be, they had a keen sense of her barometer. She was flushed and excited and having the time of her life—all because of one stressed-out executive. Making love to him in one of their garish bedrooms was becoming a clear and distinct goal. But the timing would have to be right. Would they ever both be in sync to appreciate such a magical moment?

As he opened his wallet and bypassed the condom tucked inside to dig out a slip of paper, Krista was fairly sure he wasn't considering it now. But had he brought the condom along just in case they were to hit it off? He didn't strike her as the type to carry one around without a definite plan. One thing you could say about Michael was that he always had a plan.

The idea that he might have been that attracted to her from the start pleased her to no end. Despite all his frustrations, he was aware of his desires and would in time act upon them.

But it wasn't to be tonight, she realized as he handed her a folded slip of paper. With reluctance she took hold of his precious recipe.

"Take that over to a cozier place for a survey, while I fill out this form," he directed huskily. "Somehow, I can't concentrate with you...so close."

Krista did so, quite pleased with the compliment. Curling up in a chair she reached out to switch on a pole lamp. The ingredients on the paper, including flour, shortening, baking powder and eggs, might have made plaster of Paris for all she knew. As for the preparation—sifting dry ingredients, draining crushed pineapple, greasing pans—it was all gibberish to her.

Eventually, mercifully, she fell fast asleep.

Chapter Twelve

Krista could hear her cell phone ringing as she was stepped out of the shower the following morning. Then the only sound was Michael's rich baritone. Had he the nerve to answer her private line? Full of dismay, without a thought to the way she herself had invaded every corner of his life, she awkwardly wrapped a towel around her drippy body and dashed out.

"Oh, Judy, you're funny!"

He was feeling that familiar with her Judy? Krista stopped cold in their living area to find him sauntering around in khaki pants and red DD polo shirt, his feet still bare, looking incredibly sexy—and pleased. Suddenly she was overwhelmed with a foreign sense of possessiveness. Not that Judy in particular was any threat; it was a more general feeling.

"She's doing fine," he went on to say. "Has everyone snowed and charmed." He suddenly caught a glimpse of Krista in his peripheral vision. Whirling her way, his eyes lingered on her long damp body, wrapped tightly in a white towel. "Very charmed, in fact."

Krista sidled up close and he began to speak faster. "I'm sure it did arrive. A bellman just brought some kind of envelope to the door. She's here now. Hang on." He placed the phone in her hand. "It's for you."

Flashing him an infuriated look, she held the small instrument to her ear. "Hi, Jude."

"Hmm, what a man to wake up to."

"Yes."

"So you must have gotten the recipe I faxed to the hotel office."

She jumped a little as Michael touched her bare shoulder and handed her a hotel envelope. The intimate gesture made her quiver beneath her towel. Daring to meet his gaze, she found there desire, humor and pleasure. It went far to erase any doubt that she was, after all, the center of his attention. Still, it would all take some getting used to. She was unaccustomed to anyone touching her cell phone, not to mention her damp shoulder, at this hour of the morning.

"I'll just take a look inside the envelope, make sure it's the right fax," she told Judy.

"Dashed right over to the aunts' house last night," Judy reported in her usual bulletlike delivery. "Got chased by the tiniest dog I've ever seen."

Krista chuckled, working to loosen the envelope flap with her free hand. "Oh, I've had to handle that brute once or twice myself. He had the nerve to nip me once. In a very tender spot."

"Luckily, I got inside before *that* happened."

"Don't knock it until you've tried it."

"Hey, is Ms. Big actually messing with that incredible man?"

"Well, you know."

"I do know. Thought you'd outgrown the game after college."

"I've discovered I'm still a player." Krista flinched as Michael took back the envelope.

"I can either open this or hold up your towel," he murmured.

"Hmm," Judy broke in, "sounds like you do have this taming game down very well, indeed."

Michael opened the paper with some curiosity—not to

mention amusement, Krista couldn't help noting. "So you had no trouble finding the recipe?" she asked Judy, trying to regain her composure.

"Went directly for the cupboard you specified. You steered me wrong on the teak chest, though. The only box inside was a cardboard one dating back to the seventies, that once contained earth shoes."

Krista's eyes rolled. So much for the carved wooden antiquity. It was no mystery as to why the aunts' column was far too often larger than life.

"Among receipts for oil changes and take-out food, and recipes for cocktails and hamburger pie, I found one recipe for pineapple upside-down cake, clipped off a Readiquick box."

Michael was holding the fax open for her inspection. She glanced at the list of ingredients, picking up maraschino cherries, pineapple rings and sugar before averting her eyes. "I'm afraid I was too young at the time to recall details. But this must be it. Thanks." Krista pushed the disconnect button.

Michael thrust the paper at her. "I have to get ready."

"Why are you smirking?"

"After all the fuss, I guess I expected the recipe to be a bit more advanced."

"So this is an easy one?"

"Simple as they come." He disappeared into his bedroom.

She followed, studying the recipe. "What is this—this Readiquick?"

Michael grabbed a pair of socks from the dresser drawer and sat on the bed to put them on. "You know."

"I don't."

"It's an all-purpose baking mix. Makes preparing anything from pancakes to biscuits a whole lot easier."

"How will the ingredients for the contest be handled?"

"Each contestant was required to submit a list of desired

supplies. Those supplies will be reserved in a designated spot, I imagine.''

Her soft forehead furrowed. ''So, you think Readiquick will be downstairs?''

His smile was fond but patronizing. ''Certainly not. All the contest entries must be made from scratch.'' He rose from the bed and breezed by her through the doorway. ''You better get ready. Most of the others have probably been down there a long while, the ones using yeast, anyway.''

She tightened her towel and skipped after him. ''Exactly what is in this mix?''

He moved to the desk to cram papers into his briefcase. ''Oh, flour, baking soda, some oil, I imagine.''

''Things the aunts can get hold of, right?''

''Yes. Any decent cook can make the required substitutions.''

''Would you be willing to make the required substitutions?''

''Can't they do it?''

''Please, just do it. The cake seems to mean a lot to Gerald. I suppose with his wife gone, he misses her old recipes a lot.''

''You sure have the knack for considering everyone's feelings all at the same time.'' On a gentler note he snatched the paper away from her, set it on the desk and began to scribble. ''If your aunts substitute these ingredients for Readiquick, they should be fine.''

''You're putting down exact proportions?''

He paused to inspect *her* proportions with a rueful look. ''I can't think with you in that state. Get ready while I do some calculations.''

Krista scooted to her bedroom to dress. In her initial rush she had apparently missed it. On her bed lay a women's red Decadent Delights polo shirt, as well as a convention badge bearing her name.

From here on in, Krista had the power to enter any convention activity she wished, starting with today's all-important practice session. There was no mistaking the level of compliment behind the symbol. No longer a mere ornamental wife on his arm, Michael was taking her on the inside, a full partner, along for the dream. Everything would be perfect if he could come to see that she was the kind of wife he had needed all along.

A small crowd was milling around the basement entrance to Gerald Stewart's test kitchen. Two security guards were flanking the double doors, one checking convention badges against a list of contestants, the other handing out clipboards boasting several papers, a workstation assignment on top. The procedure was fairly swift, though thorough. Clipboard in hand, Michael eased Krista through the door.

The stations were set up against the three walls, partitioned into medium-size cubicles. The fourth wall was reserved for a large, heavily manned booth with an Ingredients sign overhead. The air was humming with noise and tension, and a cloying smell of frying oil.

"Which station are we looking for?"

"Station seven. Over there to the right."

Krista stood by while Michael inspected their station, opening the oven, testing the freestanding sink for running water. There was plenty of counter space; a rack held a variety of pots and pans, as well as the deep fryer, which he promptly set aside. Smacking his clipboard to the counter with nervous energy, he went over the papers. Krista noted that one paper was a copy of his entry form, another a set of kitchen rules.

"So, where is this special recipe?"

He tapped his temple. "Up here. Only kept that paper in my wallet to show you, honey."

The endearment was no sooner out of his mouth than Gerald and the aunts were crushing their way into the station.

"How are the 'honeys' doing?" Rachel chirped.

"Very well," Krista said, allowing a doting Gerald to kiss her cheek.

"That shirt looks splendid on you," he said. "You are a natural."

Michael intervened with a "Good morning, sir!"

Gerald nodded at him, then referred back to Krista. "I tried to get *my* honeys working on my special cake some thirty minutes ago, before the mad rush, but they say they don't have their recipe yet."

"All taken care of." Krista delved into her pants pocket and handed Beverly the fax, folded in a neat square.

Gerald beamed. "There, you see. Now it's time to get busy." He excused himself and wandered off.

Beverly was scanning the recipe with pursed lips. "Why is Readiquick circled?"

"Because they don't have it at the booth." She gestured impatiently to the paper. "See where Michael noted some substitutions, up here in the corner."

Rachel's eyes were as wide as a child's. "But we've used Readiquick in just about everything we've ever bothered to make."

"It is the miracle food," Beverly stated decidedly. "Everyone knows that! No fuss, no muss, no measuring, save for a cup."

Krista turned to see if Michael was smugly amused by the supposed chefs making such an admission, but he was busy adjusting the oven racks. He had every right, she knew, to feel the aunts were only in the way, like two busy bees buzzing in his ear. "I hate to be rude," she said in a firm tone seldom tested on the aunts, "but will you two kindly scram."

Beverly's heavy bosom rose. "Very well, Krista. If you're ready."

Michael was tuning in enough to catch this request. "Hang on, she is supposed to be helping me."

"Michael is right," she agreed. "I belong here. But I

suppose I can pop in and check on you," she relented under the aunts' terrified glares. "Where are you located?"

"We have a deluxe station," Beverly bragged, "right beside the booth marked Ingredients."

Krista noted Michael's stiff shoulders loosen some, once they were alone. "Before we begin, I have something to show you." With great care he lifted his briefcase onto the counter, opened it and removed two four baking pans. Each pan was stamped with a deep-set ring. "I had these made special by a toolmaker I know back in Chicago. The bottom of each ring is machined level, to give the top of my doughnuts a flat top to better hold crushed pineapple." Her ignorance must have been evident behind her smile because he went on to explain that most doughnuts would be blended with yeast, allowed to rise and then deep-fried. "Ours will be baked, you see. Similar to the coffee cake method your aunts are using."

Krista had a genuine appreciation for his strategy. "Thinking outside the box, that's the way to get an edge in a big contest like this."

"Exactly right." He grinned so broadly, she wondered if his face might bust in half.

"So give me an assignment," she said eagerly.

"You can go get my ingredients." He handed her a five-by-seven inch laminated card bearing the number seven. "Turn in this card and they'll deliver the stuff to us."

Just then Rachel popped her head back into their booth. "I hate to interrupt again," she said sweetly. "But we have a question about your changes, Michael."

He bit his lip. "Yes?"

Rachel flounced up to him with the recipe in a manicured hand. "It's the measurements, you see—"

"I'm sure the substitutions aren't in perfect balance, but by following them you should end up with a reasonable dessert."

"But exactly what are a tisp and a tibble?"

"Huh?" Michael followed her red-tipped index finger to the sheet of paper.

"This code. We're not familiar with this code."

He mustered the grace to be indulgent. "*Tsp* is short for teaspoon. *Tbls* is short for tablespoon. It's common to abbreviate the two."

Rachel tipped her blond head from side to side.

"You use measuring spoons." Michael sighed bleakly. "You can't cook worth a damn, can you?"

"Not very well," she admitted. "That's why we gave it up years ago. When we did make something, it was with Readiquick."

"Then, why did you tell Gerald you're good?"

"Because it made him so happy to hear it," Rachel said matter-of-factly. "We often tell men things to make them happy."

Michael clasped his hands together desperately. "Please, oh please, go back to your station."

"Our deluxe station. Given to us in faith. By your precious Gerald."

"I, too, have faith that you can make this dessert if you try."

"Do you, Michael?" Rachel smiled girlishly. "Coming from you that is high praise. I'll go back and tell Beverly."

Krista clicked her tongue over the exchange, doubting Michael realized that as with Gerald, Rachel had just turned on the charm with the express purpose of making him happy.

"I'm off, then," she said, waving the card bearing the seven.

"Feel free to check on the aunts, on your way back," Michael invited somewhat reluctantly.

"Thanks. I'll make it quick."

She dropped off the card at the ingredients counter and took several short steps to the aunts' nearby station. As purported, it was a deluxe model, perhaps double in size to the others.

But Gerald Stewart's presence somehow shrank it to doll's house proportions. He had somehow made his way back. The Mattson sisters flashed Krista some desperate looks as he appeared to be settling in on a stool.

"I thought you were cruising the room, sir," Krista said.

"I was, but ended up back here." He chuckled. "Decided to watch these pros in action."

Krista gasped dramatically. "Gerald, don't you realize you are a lethal weapon to us Mattson women? My aunts can't possibly concentrate with you here. You are way too big a distraction!"

"Is that so?" Gerald beamed as the aunts confessed it was true. He smoothed his toupee with an excited jerk of his hand. "In that case, I'll just run along before someone overheats."

"Strut those wiles, Krista!" Rachel cried once he was gone.

Beverly nodded. "You certainly have blossomed fast in the man-handling department."

Krista found herself glowing under the praise. "I've surprised myself more than once the past few days. Had no idea taming men would be so fun. Have you ordered your supplies yet?"

Rachel shook her head. "Though we did find the tisp and tibble, thanks to Michael." She lifted the ring of tin spoons and caused them to clink. "He's so smart."

Krista took their clipboard in hand. The only sheet of paper attached to theirs was a food order form. "I'll get you started by filling out this form. Read those ingredients to me, Beverly." That accomplished, she sent Rachel to the order booth. Then she attempted to reason with the more practical of the pair. "Aunt Bev, you can do this if you keep your cool."

"Always keep my cool!" she thundered.

"Well, yes—"

"Oh, go back to your own booth." She shooed her off

gruffly. "We can manage fine, now that Gerald's gone. It's no lie that he makes me feel all silly and incompetent."

Krista arrived back at station seven with their small shopping cart of ingredients. Michael's welcoming smile was bright enough to melt an ice cap.

"Let's get to work, partner."

The couple went to work shoulder to shoulder, assembling the miniature upside-down cakes, baking them, popping them out of their molds. Krista entered a whole new world as she drained cans of crushed pineapple, chopped cherries and sifted dry ingredients. Michael did the necessary beating of dough with a wire whisk and a strong arm.

As she paused to speak, Michael playfully dipped his finger in the batter and plugged it into her open mouth. "Don't worry," he murmured, "the eggs are pasteurized. It's completely safe."

There was nothing safe about it. A frisson of delight ran the length of her spine as her tongue tasted the batter, his skin.

Seemingly startled by the contact, Michael withdrew his finger from her mouth with a pleased grunt. "Like it?"

She smiled slyly. "I like it."

It was almost three hours later when Beverly and Rachel reappeared at their station. Both looked bedraggled, dusted with flour and sugar, smudged with fruity juices. Beverly had an added speckle of pineapple in her gray curls.

Krista laughed. "Sorry I didn't get back. We've been up to our necks in it."

Michael gallantly tried to stifle his chuckle behind a cough. "What happened to you two?"

Beverly's double chins quivered. "We're finished, that's what."

Krista rejoiced. "Where's the result? The oven? A cooling rack?"

Beverly voice was falsely high. "At this very minute?"

"Yes."

Her eyes narrowed to dangerous slits. "It's in the garbage."

"You can't be serious!" Krista cried.

"Oh, no?" Beverly strolled over to Michael's open briefcase and tossed the soiled fax inside. "I'm returning this recipe for torture and humiliation—this witch's brew. Since it holds such happy memories for you, Krista, perhaps you will make it for your grandchildren one day. But save this copy, as the original will be set aflame the minute we reach home."

Krista regarded them in exasperation. "It's a rotten shame, after all your trouble."

"Maybe it was wrong to show off for him in the first place," Michael ventured to say, "just because he expressed an admiration for good cooks."

"Oh, get off your high horse," Rachel snapped, flicking some brown sugar off her nose. "You'd think this was a lipstick convention, with all the kissing-up going on."

To Krista's relief, Michael laughed. "Touché." He offered the aunts doughnuts. In fact, they all paused to eat one. The ladies' high approval rating mellowed Michael out considerably.

"So what is your next move with the big guy?" he eventually asked the aunts, who had mellowed some themselves.

"I suppose you could consider telling him the truth about your ineptness in the kitchen," Krista said. "He's still bound to like you just as much—maybe even respect the truth."

Beverly hooted. "Any man sporting a hideous rug like Gerald's doesn't put a high value on truth in advertising. Like most men, he prefers gushy little lies that enhance his masculinity. Why a man would think any hair is an improvement on baldness is beyond me. Just goes to show you men are perhaps even more vain than..."

During this speech Krista was going through a series of contortions to halt the tirade on male vanity and gullibility. They were in the process of burying Michael with the ultimate snow job. It didn't seem wise to send him on a mission of self-exploration in the middle of the game. He might begin to question the whole deal.

Michael seemed to be taking Beverly's tirade with humor, though he did heartily approve when Krista offered her a second doughnut to keep her jaw busy. He went even further by offering the aunts the whole batch, swiftly setting the treats inside a red plastic DD storage container specifically made for storing doughnuts. "I wasn't planning to go back to our room just now, as there is a lecture on managerial skills starting in twenty minutes." He glanced over at Krista. "I'd hoped you would join me for that."

She tugged at her official red polo, feeling a part of things like never before. "I did have a look at some of your company literature, and would like to hear Jonathan Smithers live and in person." Truth be told, she had found the DD brochure frustrating and had many ideas to bounce around with someone in higher authority.

"We'll be off, then," Rachel said, taking hold of the red box.

"So, what will you tell Gerald of your misadventure?" Michael asked.

Beverly's reply was airy. "You hit a snag with the tibbles and called on us for assistance. Therefore we had to abandon our project completely."

Agog, Michael sank onto a stool. "Help me, Krista, I can't feel any of my limbs."

Krista and Michael were finishing the cleanup of their station soon thereafter, when Norah appeared, dressed in a red DD polo shirt and plain dark slacks, carrying a bulky napkin. "Hello, Mikey, Krissy."

"Ah, Norah." Michael leaned closer so Norah could peck his cheek. Krista couldn't help thinking that she had the best kiss-up lips in the bunch.

"How did your practice run go?" Krista asked politely.

"Well enough. How did you two fare?"

"Very well," Krista took pleasure in saying.

"I've brought you a sample of our cherry chip."

Krista and Michael split the doughnut she had wrapped in a napkin, sampled it and were lavish with praise. Michael went on to explain why they couldn't offer her a sample in return, which didn't please her much.

She wasn't offended enough to leave, however, and wandered around the small station. The area was clean and relatively bare, save for Michael's open briefcase. She stopped by the case and glanced down at the contents.

"Krista tells me you're keeping an eye on my case," Michael noted with humor. "Surely you have no complaints about the way I'm taking care of it."

She broke from a thoughtful frown to say in delight, "Of course not! Just can't stop mothering you."

Michael sighed after she left. "Do you think I tease her too much?"

"I think you'd explode if you didn't have a sense of humor."

They shared a chuckle. Michael went over to his briefcase. The first thing he saw was the grease-smudged fax. "You want this recipe from your hapless chefs or shall I toss it?"

"I want it," Krista assured. "It'll be interesting to prepare it at home according to directions, without relative interference."

He closed the briefcase, then, putting one hand on her shoulder he used the other to brush some flour from her forehead. "I noticed something today."

She felt her heart flutter. "What was that?"

"That you aren't all that comfortable in the kitchen yourself."

"Oh?" She averted her gaze.

"You gotta admit your dicing, slicing and beating skills can use some work." He captured her chin to make eye contact.

"Well, I may not be quite the kitchen aid you thought."

"That you led me to believe, you mean."

"It all started with the lasagna back at my place," she confessed anxiously. I would have gladly confessed that it was frozen, but Judy insisted I try and impress you by taking credit for preparing it."

"I suppose the salad and bread that went along with it were—"

"Prepackaged. It's partly your own fault, Michael. I quickly discovered that I like your admiration. Think how disappointed you would have been to learn that I can't whip up simple dishes with ease."

"I suppose so."

"Sometimes charades in a relationship are for a better good."

He gave her a quick impulsive kiss. "The very idea that you can so easily wiggle out of things with me, Krista, makes you a very dangerous woman indeed."

"I think I can come to like being dangerous. Like it very much." She kissed him then, slowly and deliberately.

Chapter Thirteen

The meeting room hosting the managerial workshop was one of the larger ones. This didn't surprise Michael in the least. Demand was bound to be high as Decadent Delight franchise owners very frequently managed their own shops.

He was surprised that when left to lead them to seats, Krista chose two front and center. It was his choice, as well, when attending an important lecture or seminar. Funny, he would have imagined the temptress behind "Simona Says" at the rear of any gathering at the newspaper, ready to duck out if proceedings got bogged down with mundane issues. But more and more, Krista was an ill fit for the Simona veils of impish mystery.

Even now she was shifting in her chair, straightening her spine, watching Gerald's ace assistant Jonathan Smithers take the podium with dignity in a sober black suit and dapper bow tie. He was an exception to the rule of wearing red polo shirts. Even Gerald was wearing a polo today.

"Good afternoon, everyone," Jonathan began with trademark aplomb. "I trust those of you who entered the contest had ample time to get here. I find it rude to enter a lecture in progress. We will be discussing managerial skills for the next hour. I will lecture for three-quarters of the time, then will allow questions for the last leg…"

Despite Jonathan's dry delivery and hard-line tactics, Michael felt the lecture was thought provoking. Jonathan spoke on how to curb absenteeism, how to keep employees honest and loyal. Michael took copious notes on issues he hoped to debate with Randy and the other fellows later on. To every employee who knew him, Smithers was a thorn in the company's side, a narrow-minded leader who tended to crack the whip. But he was also a man Gerald held in highest regard. So no one challenged his authority. Ever.

Never in Michael's imagination did he expect Krista to fire up the question segment of the hour. With a blowtorch.

When recognized, Krista stood, with notes of her own jotted on a company notepad. "Mr. Smithers, I can appreciate the idea of running a tight ship. But I find your guidelines a bit too extreme."

"Is that so?"

She glanced at her notes. "First off…"

First off? The room had fallen into a numb hush. Michael felt his throat tighten. He reached up to loosen his tie and realized he wasn't even wearing one.

"I'd like to address your theory on curbing absenteeism."

"You don't agree that requiring a doctor's written excuse will slow it down?"

"I hardly see it as an effective deterrent with part-time employees," she said, "many of whom are liable to be students. Take the truly sick first. A lot of young people rarely go to the doctor for treatment of the most common cold or flu because their young bodies can recover quickly or because they can't afford office calls for minor ailments. Forced to produce written proof, they will come to work, instead. Anything contagious can be hazardous when working with food."

Smithers, startled by the challenge, blustered, "Something has to be done to discourage the fakers."

"Sure, your plan will stop some cheaters from taking the extra odd day off. But the bottom line is that it will force many honest young people to come in while sick, and, in turn, cause a health risk to everyone else who enters the shop.''

Jonathan scanned the crowd as if searching for a question from another source, but Krista dug in again, tapping her pen to the notepad. ''And about employee incentives. Rather than dismissing the whole idea of incentives to keep the budget level, wouldn't it be worthwhile to try an experiment with different—''

''We haven't dismissed all incentives. Gerald Stewart's doughnut contest is a fine example.''

''Yes, but it is exclusively for the benefit of owners. I am referring to lower-level incentives, which you, sir, claim to be in charge of yourself.''

''The topic of commission is a long and hot one,'' Jonathan snapped. ''I see no alternative but to discourage it. Putting the clerks who run the registers at an advantage doesn't sit well with the rest of the staff.''

''Agreed. It is wrong to reward a few. I was going to suggest a group incentive. Such as a cash bonus to split among everyone if a monthly sales quota is met. If a shop cannot afford that, perhaps a doughnut party for an employee who comes up with a sales gimmick for the shop window. A designated parking spot for the employee who arrives on time for a whole month. Or, to put a positive twist on your sick leave threat, why not award an official certificate to anyone who is responsible about sick leave? That will go nicely in one's personnel file, and encourage good workers and slackers alike to make mature decisions.''

Michael sat up straighter in his chair, amazed and impressed with Krista's mind. Others were watching her, as well, with nothing less than awe and respect. She was revved, humming smoothly like a tuned engine. She was enjoying herself, mainly because she had nothing to lose, being outside the company. But somehow, this sort of debate seemed natural to her.

''Oh! I forgot to mention stealing,'' she went on gaily,

bringing a chuckle from the crowd. "I believe all these incentives will help deter employee stealing. Happy employees, especially young people still feeling around for their values, are more apt to feel guilty in betraying a manager who is who showing them kindness and respect." She took a deep breath. "Hang in there, Mr. Smithers, I'm almost finished. Just wanted to touch on DD's policy of charging employees for their polo shirts. You stated figures on how lucrative it is to give out only the first shirt free—"

"We lose many employees in the first two weeks as in any business dealing with young people," Jonathan argued coolly. "It is a waste to hand out shirts willy-nilly."

"Again, I feel the loyal employee is punished by the slackers, the quitters. I worked many odd jobs as a kid, and my father, a single parent, hated it when I was allowed only one shirt."

By now Jonathan's face was as red as a company shirt. "If you were satisfied with a job, wasn't it worth it to buy a couple more shirts?"

"My low wages didn't make the purchase a reasonable expense, especially because, in a scandalous thirst for profit, the companies in question inflated the price of the shirts! It is my understanding, Mr. Smithers, that it is DD's policy to inflate these prices."

To Jonathan's evident dismay, a ripple of approval crossed the room. "Perhaps we could look into selling them at cost."

"Good. How about issuing a second shirt after a month on the job. Better still, use free shirts as a performance incentive, in one of the categories I mentioned earlier—"

"It is my understanding, Ms. Mattson, that you aren't yet a member of the Decadent Delights family, that you are here by the grace of your fiancé."

"That doesn't make her opinion less valid." It was Michael who jumped up to her defense, standing so close their arms grazed. "Though I had no idea that Krista intended to speak, I am intrigued, as my colleagues seem to be, by the questions she's raised. And for the record, I especially agree with her complaint about the way the uniform shirts are handled. My first DD employers, the Larkins, never overcharged for uniform shirts. They issued two to every new employee right off the bat. The good deed had so much impact on me, in fact, that I have gone one better and never charged any of my employees a dime for a uniform shirt.''

There was a rumble of surprise from the audience, but it didn't stop his admission. "It has cost me, but I eat the expense. When young people start working for me, I remember that I myself couldn't afford even one shirt. Rather than take the chance of burdening them, I pay the freight. One thing I do ask is that if and when they quit, they return the shirts so someone else can put them to use. The program has worked out well.''

The mood of the crowd was remarkably changed. The guarded atmosphere always surrounding a Smithers lecture was suddenly electric with action, the invisible barrier drawn between himself and his associates shattered. Hands flew into the air now, people spoke up. It was pandemonium.

"Hope I didn't go too far.'' Krista asked the question of Michael some fifteen minutes later at an open café near the conference rooms.

"Compared to whom?''

She shrugged, pouring sugar into her coffee. "To your average Decadent Delighter, I guess.''

"Well, I blanched as your hand shot up, but quickly began to cheer on your common-sense approach. There sure is a practical side to you, Krista. One I like very much.''

"I probably shouldn't have jumped in, but I got carried away. Saw some solutions and couldn't resist sharing them. I'm surprised others weren't ahead of me.''

"Perhaps being on the outside, you found it easier to speak your mind. For as long as I can remember, Smithers has been Gerald's right arm.''

"His strong arm, you mean. I didn't mean to get so involved, but he's annoyed me since the moment we met. Then to hear his 'my way or the highway' approach to human relations, why I just couldn't help wanting to incite a riot!"

"Well, don't be too critical of us who have let Smithers run free. It's common knowledge that an executive was fired for daring to mess with the tyrant."

"That's what's holding my people back from speaking up?" a deep voice rumbled.

Michael's head jerked up and he saw Gerald Stewart standing beside them. "Hello, sir. Care to join us?"

"I certainly would." He pulled up a white steel chair from an adjoining table.

"Coffee, sir?" Krista asked meekly.

"I'd love some." Hailing a waitress, he ordered a cup.

"You hear about the lecture?" she asked.

"Hear about it? I was there!"

"Hope you weren't offended," Michael said. "But it is high time someone yanked Jonathan's chain a little."

"Agreed. Hadn't realized he'd grown so distant from the mainstream, so unapproachable. But in Jon's defense, the exec who was fired a few years ago did more than criticize him. He was a bona fide slacker who really did take unnecessary sick leave." He leaned back as his coffee arrived. "Still, after listening to Jon drone on for nearly an hour, I must say I was uncomfortable with the image he projected in my name. The company is supposed to be fun. I don't think he means to, but he is choking off creativity. Partly my own fault, as I spent too much time feeling sorry for myself after Gloria's death. But things will swing back again, I assure you."

"As long as everyone is still friendly," Michael said.

"Of course. Jon and I will come to terms. His harder line is helpful at times. I merely stopped by to commend you both on being resourceful."

Their conversation was interrupted suddenly when a

small group of men hailed Michael. "Excuse me. If I don't see what they want, it'll never end."

As Michael retreated, Gerald glanced hastily at his watch. "I am pressed for time. But my business is really with you, I guess."

Krista felt herself blanch as he produced the napkin with her sketched logo on it. "I hope you weren't offended. It was an experiment, to see if your logo could be improved—"

"Hush." His leathery face lit up with humor. "I realize you meant no harm. Though, I was a bit annoyed at first. That is, until your precious aunt told me that she finds bald men most virile. She even insisted I take off my rug to prove it. I had no idea the bald head was considered an erogenous zone. Anyway, it was a freeing experience. I'm not ready to go public or anything like that. But it is a possibility."

Leave it to Rachel. "Do you mind if I ask who gave you this napkin?"

"Found it in my jacket pocket last night, upon our return from dinner. Thought you might have put it there yourself, especially after hearing you in that meeting just now."

"No, I sketched it at Norah's luncheon, then lost track of it."

"If someone was trying to upset me, they have failed," he said magnanimously.

They were well past the issue when Michael returned to his chair. "Sorry about that. They wanted some details about my polo shirt system. It really does work, sir."

Gerald's eyes flashed with interest. "I believe it. You are a very persuasive young man. The things you said about your poor beginnings really struck a chord. So much so, in fact, that I'd like you to write up the whole concept—including your personal experience—for the newsletter. I'll give you the front page, with a photo."

"Wow. Thank you so much, sir."

"Your promo expert here can help you."

Michael grinned. "If she likes."

Krista leaned over the table, her voice low. "Gerald had a bit more news. The napkin has surfaced."

"*The* napkin?"

Gerald nodded. "Don't you fret about it. Your lovely fiancée and I have made our peace on the matter."

"May I see it, sir?"

"Better yet, you may have it."

"THAT WAS A MIGHTY INTERESTING CHAT with Gerald," Michael remarked a short while later in their suite. "He have anything else to say that I should know about?"

Krista came out of her bedroom to find him lounging on the sofa, feet propped up on the coffee table, looking extremely pleased with himself. "Not really."

"You must have been talking about something. I saw your heads together."

"We were discussing the connection between virility and baldness."

"You weren't."

"We were. Presumably Rachel rescued us when the napkin surfaced, convincing him he was ever so sexy without the rug."

"Nice save. He complain about their aborted cake?"

"No, he didn't mention the cake."

"What a gentleman, eh, letting that go after all the fuss made to get them cooking. He's really been giving me the royal treatment."

She pursed her lips, then said, "You're getting the treatment, all right."

"This sketch is rather clever." Michael turned the recovered napkin over in his hands.

"Oh, sure. It's fine now that it's cleared through Gerald!"

"Hey, I was prepared to defend you on a bum rap, if it came to that. But it wasn't necessary." Still, he frowned. "What's troubling you, then?"

"I just hate the way this contest has gone so needlessly off track between friends. All that girl talk at lunch about our entries. Then the snatching of your sketch. If there had to be trouble, I wish it didn't involve one of the couples who means so much to me. But I clearly recall Norah and Beth trying to cuddle up to Gerald in the lobby last night, close enough to jam something into his jacket pocket."

"They were bound to feel threatened over the fact that we were out with Gerald. Someone acted on that fear."

"That 'someone' took the napkin in advance just in case a weapon was needed. As for any threat, the Larkins see Gerald all the time—even took the Norquists to his mansion last spring when they were visiting. I didn't object then. In the end those connections shouldn't matter all that much. The best-run shop should be respected. The best doughnut should win this race."

"Thinking in those terms, you shouldn't have needed a fiancée, either," she couldn't resist pointing out.

"I'm inclined to agree, now that I'm in the thick of things. In a way I sloughed off my own principles on honesty and hard work to save my pride, to do my share of sucking up."

"In your defense, your charade isn't constructed to harm anyone else," she consoled.

He pounded the sofa arm. "How easily competition brings out the worst in people."

She moved up behind him on the sofa and wove her arms around his neck. "Not all people. It's made us a team."

"Yes. I gotta admit you've been nothing but a joy to have along. I don't know how I would have managed without you. The hardest part," he admitted reluctantly, "has been allowing you to see my people treating me this way."

"It doesn't make me think any less of you, if that's what you mean." With massaging fingers she kneaded his stiff shoulders.

"That's what I mean." He moaned softly as she dug deeply into his muscle. "You've really gotten to me, honey. Somehow managed to niggle your way deep inside my psyche, where no one's ever gone before. I find myself watching you with fascination, wondering how and when I fell so helplessly into your hands.''

''You poor bewildered guy.'' She leaned over to kiss his temple.

''Don't you dare laugh at me!''

''I'm happy, that's all.'' She kept a grip on his shoulders as he squirmed. ''Don't you think I have all the same feelings? This was an engagement of convenience. A debt owed by Simona. Even though I was instantly attracted to you, I didn't expect feelings to deepen, expand.''

He turned his head to gaze upon her with boyish delight. ''You were instantly attracted to me?''

''Aren't you more interested in how I feel about your psyche?''

''No.''

She sighed indulgently. ''I've never been much of a sweet talker—no matter what the column reflects. But I do believe we have a very charged chemistry,'' she added shyly, ''judging by the sparks...''

He twisted free of her then to spin around on the sofa. ''It's time to start a real fire between us, see where it leads. We'll break away from our routine, our troubles. From now until dawn we are going to forget all about the convention, about everyone even remotely connected to it.''

''You wouldn't dare.''

''I do dare.''

She was astonished by the dangerous gleam in his eye. ''You must have commitments.''

''The hell with the commitments! All I've done this past decade is work hard, and look where it's landed me. My only friends are business acquaintances that I can't completely trust.''

''I have an image of people hunting us down like wild game.''

He grinned. ''Not a chance. I've been here before and

know some of the smaller places downtown, where the locals hang out.''

Krista was brimming with anticipation. ''Let's do it, Michael. Let's do exactly what you used to do.''

''It'll mean cheap burgers, domestic beer, blackjack and lots of smoke.''

She gazed upon him with dancing eyes. ''They say where there's smoke, there's fire.''

He snapped up from the sofa. ''Oh, baby, I'm counting on it.''

Chapter Fourteen

Dressed in jeans, T-shirts and light jackets, Michael and Krista joined a group of tourists in a crowded elevator and stuck with them through the lobby and out the entrance. Taxis were standing by, and they wasted no time hopping into one. Michael directed the driver to the Glitter Gulch and off they went.

The cab dropped them off at the intersection of Main Street and Ogden. Michael explained that the heart of the downtown casino area was on Fremont Street between 4th and Main, a short four-block stretch. "What would you like to see first?"

"The hamburger joint," she replied promptly. "I am starving!"

Michael was gratified to find that Madge's, the place he remembered on 6th Street that advertised the best half-pounder in town, was still in business. Nothing about it had drastically changed. It still boasted the same retro decor with bright-orange booths, a soda fountain and fifties background music. The mainstay slot machines were even on the antique side, but in full running order, judging by their flashing lights.

It was close to five-thirty and the place was filling up fast, mostly with locals dressed in uniforms of all kinds, from casino personnel to hotel staff. There were two empty stools at the end of the U-shaped counter, and they moved fast to claim them.

There were advantages to their chosen position. It was easy to read the menu on the back wall, and counter service was prompt. A friendly teenage girl in a gingham blouse and lavender poodle skirt approached them with check pad in hand. Michael ordered a cheeseburger, fries and lemon phosphate, Krista a plain burger with onion rings and cherry cola.

Once the girl was out of earshot, Krista pondered how Madge's might handle what had to be a hefty uniform budget.

"Excellent question," Michael commended. "Makes my polo shirt system seem cheap and simple."

"I'm glad that Gerald was on hand to hear your story. Personal anecdotes are always especially powerful."

Michael was gratified by her praise and was quick to return the compliment. "You initially got the ball rolling by bringing up the issue in the first place."

"Well, we're both damn good."

"Yeah, partner." Their drinks arrived and Michael lifted his glass of lemony liquid to tip it into her cola glass.

"I can appreciate that must have been rough, sharing a childhood memory that wasn't especially pleasant. I don't know if I could have."

Michael stalled for a moment, feeling a rush of old emotions that he generally managed to block out. "I don't bare my soul very often. But you have a way of getting me energized so I forget my usual caution. And sitting there as you leapt into action just inspired me beyond reason." Catching her sheepish look, he added, "The instinct to speak up was just right under the circumstances. There is finally enough distance from the hard times to make the memories tolerable."

"I'd like to hear about your life," she said.

"Norah already gave you some idea of how things were. I never knew my father. Mother claimed to be confused about his identity, but I don't know if she really meant it. She was a drinker and lived in a haze most of the time. When I was a bit older I came to realize the power of free enterprise. I started working for the Larkins and suddenly I had not only an income, but a purpose, new friends. I threw myself into the job, buried myself in it, really. It was like my porthole to another planet, far away from our two-bedroom apartment with drawn curtains, droning television and a scent of booze and self-pity. I realized that good things happened when you worked hard. Guess I soon became addicted to work.''

To his surprise, Krista was nodding. ''For most of my life I was raised in a one-parent household in California,'' she told him. ''Just Dad and me. My mother died giving birth to me. Thirty-six years old and she had a heart attack in the delivery room. Anyway, Dad was—is a wonderful parent. He did everything humanly possible to mother me—sewing on buttons, mending scraped knees, getting to know the parents of my friends, encouraging me to confide in him, getting involved in the PTA at my school. What he couldn't handle, his sisters Beverly and Rachel took care of. They would take turns during the school year to come and stay with us. Then, during my breaks I would join them in Minnesota. For years it was my reality, all I knew. But later I did come to better appreciate all that Dad did beyond the call of duty, especially the way he was generous enough to share me with female relatives. There were so many unique lessons he couldn't show me by example, insight into the artistic and passionate feminine mystique. He was man enough to know his limitations.''

''I'm anxious to meet this man.''

''He's always interested in my friends.''

Their meals arrived and they began to nibble.

''Michael, women don't like to be stared at while they're eating!''

''I know.'' He looked remarkably unrepentant. ''Just

can't help thinking you look so much better without heavy makeup.''

"I didn't even bring it along, so it isn't an issue.''

"The more I get to know you, the more baffled I am as to how you ever got involved with the 'Simona Says' column in the first place.'' Was he imagining it, or did fear flash in her tempting sapphire eyes?

"Rather reluctantly,'' she said guardedly. "It was the aunts' idea. A way to earn some income while I was still in college.''

"You do seem to have a knack for promotion, what with your napkin sketch and all the points you covered at the workshop. Have you ever considered using it for good?''

"I'm using it for good right now,'' she said defensively. "Playing the best darn fiancée imaginable! Under the circumstances.''

"I just want to sort things out, scope the middle ground we walk on.''

"You are leading up to something. What is it?''

"I want to discuss the letter, the one that got me running to your place.''

She had the grace to redden. "That letter was written in a fit of panic. Looking back, I see it as nothing but a pack of nonsense to divert your attention, stop you from suing.''

"I won't have anyone criticizing the best letter a guy could ever receive,'' he retorted gently. "It was charming, insightful, suggestive, and made the most generous offer imaginable.''

"I would just like to forget that letter.''

"Nope. Impossible.''

"Okay, let's get it over with. I know what it is. That 'I'm too sexy,' line was ridiculous—''

"No, that was fine! I mean it was true. You were too sexy. Way too sexy. I couldn't think straight at all. It's part of the reason I was so flustered, unable to reason with you. No, it's what you said about being finished with the Simona schmooze. Did you mean really that?''

"Oh boy, did I ever!" She pulled back a little, as if weighing her words.

"If there is anything I can do to help you redirect your life—"

"I don't want to discuss it right now," she erupted. "Ask me anything else you want, about my feelings, my habits, my political beliefs. But let's not touch on the column, not in the middle of…everything."

It was difficult to understand why she didn't want to discuss the matter now. Still, there was no sense in spoiling everything over it. So he shrugged and bit into his hamburger.

As they shared a hot fudge sundae for dessert, Michael brought up the safer subject of gambling. "Were you sincere about trying the blackjack tables?"

"Blackjack's just twenty-one, right? The object of the game being to get a hand adding up to twenty-one, or as close as possible without going over that amount."

"Yes. And to beat the dealer's hand, of course." He regarded her with amusement. "You play twenty-one?"

"Very well." Diving her spoon into a mountain of fudge sauce, she withdrew a huge scoop and drew it to her mouth. "Mmm, this is yummy."

"Ah, I can envision you now, at some after-hours joint back in the cities, playing a high-stakes game in that little red dress of yours."

She gawked at him. "You sure have a rich fantasy life, don't you."

"Is my image that far off?"

"Try in my college dorm, dressed in gym clothes, playing for some very low stakes."

"What were the stakes?"

"Chits of a sort, small squares of paper. Each chit had a privilege written on it, like dibs on the television remote, private time in the bathroom, food tickets to the cafeteria."

"How'd you do?"

"I never missed an episode of *E.R.,* took long hot showers, and had as many Twinkies as I could handle."

"Wow."

"I have a photographic memory, you see, so if I concentrate, I can remember every card played."

"No kidding."

"Then it is a matter of figuring out what is left in the deck."

"Guess it is sort of a card counting system."

"Really? It has a special name?"

"Yes." Propping an elbow on the counter, he rested his chin in his hand and stared hard at her. She was the most exquisite creature on earth. Krista was lovely, brainy and confident. And she could count cards.

He smiled dreamily. If this wasn't love, it oughta be.

"It's nothing, really," she claimed with a wave.

"Nothing? Your memory is a gambler's dream." He glanced down, vaguely aware that she was finishing the sundae herself. "So you've never played twenty-one for money, in a casino setting?"

"Nope." With a clatter her spoon fell to her plate. "Strange as it may seem, I spend a lot of my time working, just like you. So, do you have one of these systems to help you win?"

"I count cards, too. Or try to with my limited brain power. My system is a well-known one. It's a matter of assigning certain values to each specific card." He watched her forehead crunch. "I think you're better off not knowing anything about it, and going with your own instincts. That is, if you would like to give the tables a try."

She leaned close to whisper, "I have fifty bucks on me." Then she clicked her tongue and winked at him.

He smiled. If this wasn't a glimpse of heaven, it oughta be.

There were several casinos to choose from. Michael settled on the Golden Horseshoe on 4th Street. It was an older building with low ceilings, narrow aisles and drink bargains. The gamblers fell into two outstanding categories: the older tourists and the blue-collar locals.

Even if the stray conventioneer did happen to wander downtown, the odds of him choosing this place for adventure were poor, as no guidebook had been especially kind in its assessment.

For the first time since their arrival they were free to relax in a casino. They stood just inside the large rambling space, bathed in a dull yellow glow. There was no mistaking Krista's excitement. Somehow, the celebrated columnist was more than pleased with this cheap, no-frills adventure. Though his memory wasn't photographic, he could remember well enough that he hadn't a single date in the past five years who would have been satisfied with tonight's itinerary, who would have brought her own gambling cache.

"The first trick to being a skilled player is to blend in with the other players," he cautioned.

"I don't think I can age thirty years," she teased. "But our casual clothing gives us a low profile."

"What I mean is, you look too excited," he clarified.

She gazed into the commotion. "Maybe because I *am* excited."

"Excited people have a greater chance of being watched. That will make your winning appear more of a spectacle and increase the odds that we may get booted out."

"They can kick us out for winning?"

"They sure can." To his chagrin, she appeared even more excited.

"Sorry," she mumbled under his frown. "I just feel so naughty."

"Hold that feeling for later."

She glowed all the more.

Willing himself to remain calm, he went on in a steady tone. "Other things to keep in mind. Don't move your lips while you count. Don't vary the size of your wager. Don't move your head to follow the cards as they're being dealt. Lastly, don't chat too much with me or anyone else.''

''Can I smile?''

''Only a little bit. Make it an in-between smile, serenelike.''

''Gotcha.''

Michael sighed indulgently. She looked about as collected as a kid on Christmas Eve.

He led the way through a room crammed with machines and tables. Stopping at a cashier's cage, he produced some bills to buy two cups of nickels.

''What are you doing, Michael?''

''We'll kill some time at the slots first. It'll give you a chance to dim a few hundred watts and perhaps enhance your tourist-without-a-photographic-memory image.''

They played the machines for nearly an hour, during which time they discussed a variety of topics, including some things that would happen at the table. ''Most players use chips. What you do is put the cash you want to convert to chips above the better's box. The dealer will give you your chips and push the cash through a slot cut into the table. If he offers you the deck to cut, don't get fancy. Take off a top portion and lay it beside the remaining half. Let's watch a few hands at the tables, then make our move.''

Moving casually, they observed a few of the half-circle tables covered in green felt. Michael remarked on the shoe holding the cards, the betting area and the Minimum Bet signs posted at each table. ''Notice how betters scrape the table with their cards if they want a hit.''

''Even we did that,'' Krista said with a laugh.

''Do you notice how players, when satisfied with their hands, slip them under their chips? It's bad form to ever touch your bet.''

After careful consideration Michael suggested they hit a blackjack game in the rear that boasted three players and a friendly young male dealer.

She detained him with a hand on the arm, tipping her

face to his. "Quick! Any changes necessary? How do I look now?"

"Too sexy, too sexy," he teased gruffly, leading her through the throng.

The dealer's name tag read Bert. He exchanged their money for chips, then asked for bets. Michael put down five dollars and Krista followed his lead. Bert then placed the deck in front of Krista to allow her to cut it. Michael felt a flick of annoyance as he sensed that Bert was admiring her. But was he really? Michael thought all men in the city were admiring her.

Closing his eyes, Michael willed himself to concentrate on the game. Could he manage it? Krista was at her most attractive in her plain pedestrian clothing, her complexion free of paste and powders.

Away from the convention's pressures, all he could think of was making love to her.

Bert dealt them two cards facedown in rapid succession, dealing himself one card down, the second up. Players studied their cards, and Bert's one visible card. Bert then went around the table to see if anyone wanted a hit. Krista and another man slipped their cards under their chips to signal that they were each set to stand on the hand they had.

Michael and the two women took cards.

Krista won the hand with two kings, for a total of twenty points.

Michael had the feeling Bert was finished flirting with his woman.

It was after midnight when they emerged from the casino. "So what now?" Krista asked. "Anything you want, my treat."

"That does seem a square deal, as you have all my money—and everyone else's—in your purse."

She grinned. "You aren't the sore loser type, are you?"

"I don't know for sure. I hardly ever lose."

"I'll split the thousand with you. After all, you gave me plenty of pointers—"

"No, no, that's all right."

She delved into her purse discreetly, pulling out a ready fifty. "I insist you take your stake back."

"No—"

"Yes," she said adamantly, pressing it into his palm. "I know very well you emptied your wallet in there, and I want to go dancing."

"You do?"

"We did all that practicing and have hardly used a step."

Michael took her to a lounge he knew down the street. It was a cramped smoky place that smelled of beer and bodies. The waitresses were full-busted with arms strong enough to carry trays of drinks above their heads. Little was left to the imagination as they were dressed in plunging T-shirts and short shorts. Michael would have anticipated that a sultry lady columnist who dated nearly every night had seen her share of such places back in the Twin Cities, but Krista appeared a trifle awed by the surroundings.

"What do you order to drink in a place like this, Michael?"

"I order beer out of the bottle," he replied quickly. Discovering a small table near the stage, he captured her hand and plowed through patrons and servers.

Calling the front section of the lounge a stage was using the term loosely. It was a narrow platform raised about six inches, and boasted a piano and a microphone on a stand. A dance floor fronted the platform. A bored young man with a ponytail sat at the piano and a woman of about twenty-two dressed in a glittery gold-colored dress belted out an energetic song.

A waitress approached to take their orders. Krista pulled her chair closer to Michael's and leaned in to him to speak above the din, telling him she'd have whatever he was having. He ordered two bottles of beer. The waitress departed and Krista continued to lean in close.

"Wanna dance?" he asked her.

"Eventually. Let's just sit here for a little bit. I need to chill out."

"I bet you do." He smiled. "Hey, that is probably my first successful bet of the night."

"Oh, you." She swatted his arm. "Surely a successful guy like you doesn't really mind losing to a lady once in a while."

"After sitting here, thinking about it, I'm amazed at how okay it is."

"That's because we're a team. When one of us wins, so does the other."

They sat through the remainder of the set and the duo's break, leaning against each other, drinking beer.

"You know," she marveled, thumping another empty bottle on the table, "I like this beer. Are all brands this good?"

"You've never had a beer?"

"No." Her eyes grew huge and she put a finger to her lips. "Don't tell anybody. I'm supposed to be the reckless kind."

"I can't believe no man has ever ordered you a beer."

"Guess I must look like a wine girl, because people always send over a wine."

"You must hang around some fairly nice places."

"Ah, but never had better company than I do tonight."

The duo returned to the stage then.

"Ready to dance now?"

She was.

To their delight the first song of the set proved to be a nice ballad. The singer had a soft husky voice that did better justice to a slow song than to the faster songs of the last set.

Michael had Krista locked snug in the crook of his arm as he guided her slowly about the floor among several other couples. Resting his face against her raven hair, he could still discern her fragrance despite the veil of smoke they'd been swimming in for hours. He'd come to recognize her scent, to take it for granted. Oh, how he'd love to take it for granted for a long while to come.

She tipped her head to catch his eye. "What are you thinking about?"

"Only that I can't imagine this convention without you."

"Well, it's been an exciting ride, sizing up the players, second-guessing their motives. I'm hooked on the intrigue."

"To no surprise, as you've caused a part of it yourself!"

"I only mean the best for you."

"I know that, honey." He squeezed her closer and twirled her around. "It amazes me how close we've become in such a short time, and on so many levels. This has never happened to me before."

"Probably because you're too careful in general," she suggested.

"That's probably true." He gazed down at her reverently. "Sometimes I feel you know me as well as I know myself."

She hesitated. "That may be because we have a lot in common—deep inside."

"Never would have guessed we'd be able to communicate so well, considering our different careers, personalities...."

"It's that chemistry thing I was talking about earlier. You know."

"I know." Dipping his head, he sought her lips with his. They continued to move automatically as they kissed. This was the first time Michael had used his tongue to explore the sensitive areas of her mouth. She closed her eyes and moaned softly. Loosening her body in his embrace she allowed him to make all the moves. Encouraged, he lowered his hand from her spine to her bottom, squeezing it gently.

"You are an angel. Or are you a witch?" he breathed in her ear.

She opened her eyes, which were now blue slits of fire. "Depends what time it is."

"I think it's time to go home."

The taxi ride back to the Strip and the Imperial Majestic and the trip through the lobby up the elevator were nothing but a blur, an inconvenience, a means to an end.

They were peeling at one another's clothes the moment they were safely behind the door of their suite.

"Your place or mine?" Michael asked.

"Mine." She placed a hand on his chest as he advanced. "Aren't you forgetting something?"

He held up his discarded pants. "I have a condom in my wallet."

"I know. I saw it. But you still have to go after the chocolate, the two pieces of Godiva the maid leaves under our pillows every night."

He was set off-kilter. "I've never found any chocolate under my pillow."

"That's because I've been taking them."

He gave her scantily clad bottom a tap. "That's stealing."

"All's fair with Godiva. Now scoot."

When Michael entered her bedroom a few minutes later, Krista was pulling down the covers. Cast in the dim glow of the bedside lamp, she was a model of an exquisitely built angel—long, lean and perfectly shaped. Also completely naked, save for the ball of chocolate between her lips.

With shaky fingers he tore at the foil condom packet to give himself a head start. Then, quickly advancing, he tossed the packet and the chocolates on the nightstand, grasped her by the waist, lifted her off her feet so they were at eye level and nipped the candy from her mouth.

"Hey, give that back!" Wrapping her arms around his shoulders and her thighs around his middle, Krista tore her mouth into his, sliding her tongue between his lips as if on an invasive mission for chocolate.

But her invasion was far more compelling than a hunt for candy.

Michael was suddenly consumed by waves of fire, the

heat source the very place Krista's moist opening branded into his belly. He burned in sweet agony, in desperate need as she rubbed against him wantonly. Never in his life had he been so anxious to consume a woman. To own her devotion.

As Krista clung to him, rocked in his arms and kissed him thoroughly, he became rock solid. She loosened her banded legs to allow for the change and suddenly her moist folds of skin were taking his turgid flesh inside. With a shudder he ran his hands up and down her satiny back, pressing her tight, as if to fuse her heat to him. It was all happening too fast. He wanted her too badly.

Dizzily, he toppled their bodies onto the huge circular bed.

Krista's arms and legs fell away from him as he landed on top of her. Her hair was a tousled mess around her face, she was breathing hard, she was watching him intensely.

Rising on his haunches he began to kiss her length, skimming her silken throat, tasting her nipples. Backing up on the endless mattress, he dipped his tongue into her navel, kissed her soft nest of curls. Her husky purr of contentment encouraged him to go lower, stroking her inner thighs, planting small kisses along the tender skin. As she squirmed in pleasure he slipped his hands beneath her, clamped firmly to her small bottom and tasted the petal folds of her opening, probing deep inside her with his finger until she gave a small guttural cry that was keening and foreign and perhaps the most erotic sound he'd ever heard.

Reaching out to the nightstand he got hold of the open foil package and the condom inside. Then, with swift movements he sheathed himself and drove into her. She released another small cry of pleasure and then another as he drove inside her again and again.

He savored the act as long as he could before his own climax. To his amazement, she climaxed for the second time.

Breathless, they clung to each other for a long time.

She finally said, "I'm ready for a boost."

"What kind?"

Her eyes twinkled. "A chocolate boost, of course. Hand it over."

He took her extended palm, rubbed it on his abdomen. "I believe some negotiation is in order. Say, a boost for a boost…"

Her eyes twinkled some more.

Chapter Fifteen

Krista awoke the following morning to find a man in her bed. The sexiest, most exciting man on earth, as far as she was concerned. With a gentle hand she stroked the fine hairs on his chest, tracing her fingers over his firm muscled belly. He groaned in his sleep with a hint of a smile. She would have liked nothing better than to slip over his length, awaken him with renewed lovemaking. And would have done just that had she not glanced over at the clock on the nightstand. It snapped her out of her reverie.

"Michael! Wake up!"

Michael rolled onto his side. His eyes opened and he reached out a hand to her creamy shoulder. His grin was lazy, his voice groggy. "I'm ready, honey. Maybe this time you can put on a little of that makeup and be Simona. And I'll pretend to be some important dignitary visiting your newspaper...."

As he went on with his scheme, Krista couldn't help thinking that he sounded as whimsical as her amorous aunt Rachel. With all her shenanigans, it appeared Krista had managed to create some kind of insatiable playmate. To her own surprise, the game he suggested struck her as rather tempting. At any other time.

"I bought you those slinky shoes you liked in the shop the other day," he intimated slyly. "They're in my closet. Why don't you go put them on and surprise me...."

"You wish!" She shook him. Hard. "C'mon, you have to be dreaming."

"If I am in your bed, I've been living the dream all night long."

"That is so sweet." She paused, touching the hair that had fallen over his forehead. "But it's morning now."

"Already?" He blinked in the darkness. "It's impossible to tell what time it is in this town."

"Don't let the heavy drapes fool you. We're already late as it is."

"Late for what?"

"Kitchen duty. We were due downstairs about half an hour ago."

"Damn!" Suddenly Michael was reacting, sitting up, rolling away from her. With a flourish his long legs kicked aside the covers. "Get ready. Hurry!"

The second practice run was in full swing by the time they arrived in the basement of the hotel, dressed in jeans and their red polo shirts.

"I bet the people using yeast have been here for hours," Michael grumbled half to himself.

"Don't worry. We have our strategy, our recipe."

Krista was by no means feeling any more confident in the kitchen, but she did know her duties and felt a closer kinship with her master chef. It was a lot easier to anticipate Michael today. His short temper didn't help matters, but all in all, the finished product was, in their estimation, worthy of high marks in presentation and taste.

"Hey, strangers." Norah Larkin appeared in their booth just as she had yesterday, but a bit earlier this time. "Here are the prized upside-down doughnuts!" She edged her way along the counter to the miniature upside-down cakes crowned with crushed pineapple and chopped cherries cooling on racks. "May I sample one? Or do Krista's aunts intend to rush off with this batch, too."

Michael flashed her an impersonal smile. "Help yourself."

Norah took a healthy bite of cake, her expression growing thoughtful. "They have such a unique flavor. What is that, Mikey?"

"Trade secret. At least, for now."

Norah frowned. "I should be able to figure it out, if it is a blend of common ingredients."

Michael put a hand on her shoulder, graciously steering her out. "I have every faith in you."

She halted in her tracks with a strained laugh. "I've come here to invite you back to our suite. Allan and I are hosting a small brunch. We're providing coffee, and everyone is bringing their doughnuts from today's run. Surely even you, Mr. Secrecy, can't object to sharing now."

She was staring Michael down, as if daring him to refuse the challenge. Krista couldn't help but think Norah was strung a little tighter than usual, if that was possible.

"Sounds nice," he said. "What time?"

"Immediately. Allan's already organizing things."

"We're still cleaning up here, but we'll be there soon."

Krista smiled once Norah left. "She's in top form today."

"Judging by her behavior, I'd say she just paid us the highest compliment."

"You mean she's all the more concerned about us as a competitor now that she's tasted your doughnut?"

Using his thumb Michael gently wiped some flour from her chin. "Exactly."

In keeping with the day, Krista and Michael were the last to arrive at the Larkin suite. They came straight from the testing area. Krista carried the red plastic storage box of doughnuts, Michael his briefcase. Randy Norquist opened the door to admit them. Behind him lay a sea of people in red polo shirts. Networking certainly was a Larkin strong point.

"Hey, gang!" Randy cheered, whisking the red plastic storage box out of Krista's hands. "An official batch of the Kris Pineapple Kringles have arrived!"

Applause swelled in the room. Krista noticed that it caused Michael to grimace.

"This was another bogus idea," he said under his breath. "The socializing should be kept separate from the contest. But here we all are, showing off our entries before the judging."

"It shouldn't cause any harm," she speculated. "Everyone is locked into their recipes now."

"I still don't like it, Krista. Some lines shouldn't be crossed in competition."

She agreed, in theory. But there was no turning back on this get-together. Everyone was in the community spirit. A larger crowd than ever before, in fact. She recognized the core group, Beth and Randy, Lucy and Kyle, Laurie and Ray, Amanda and James. "Guess all we can do is join 'em at this point, even the playing field by sampling the competition."

The long table that had held drinks and appetizers the first night during the VIP reception now displayed two coffee urns and a colorful array of doughnuts, sliced in cubes on platters. There were ten platters in all, each bearing the name of the contestant and the doughnut entry. Krista took a sample of each one.

"My, we have an appetite."

Krista grinned at Beth, who had joined her. "I have a furnacelike metabolism. Burn up everything I eat."

"I'm only kidding, out of envy." She patted her small rounded tummy. "Like everybody here hasn't tried every flavor." Spotting Michael's late addition, Beth promptly popped a cube of the cake into her mouth. "Mmm, this is fabulous. Just as Norah said."

Krista asked after the Norquist's entry of Cinnamon Spice. Beth pointed it out on Krista's plate. Krista took a bit of the dark, deep-fried doughnut with appreciation. "Wow. This tastes like the gingerbread cookies I buy at the bakery. Simply heavenly."

"Hope the judges find it heavenly enough to push it into

the finals. Then it will all be up to Gerald.'' Beth looked worried. "Big hurdles to jump.''

Krista looked around. "I expected Gerald to be here.''

"I suppose he's off someplace with your aunts. That's another thing Norah said, by the way.''

"I see.''

"You know what she is like, lady of the manor, guarding her territory.''

"She certainly does see Gerald as her territory, doesn't she.''

"Yup. She and Allan both do.'' Beth's expression grew inscrutable. "She's pretty frosted about the way you all have taken over Gerald.''

Krista fought to keep her sense of humor. "It's all Gerald's doing. My aunts came here with the intention of taking over Michael and me!''

"There's something about your group that he finds appealing.''

"Life is unpredictable.'' Krista watched her carefully as she went on. "Speaking of unpredictable, did you know my napkin with the sketch—you remember the one— landed in Gerald's hands?''

Beth appeared surprised. "Really? How very strange.'' She noticed Norah weaving through the throng with a carafe of coffee and called her over. "Krista has just been telling me that Gerald got hold of her napkin sketch.''

"It somehow took the scenic route all the way here from your house,'' Krista said guilelessly.

Norah's face contorted in melodrama. "You poor, poor dear.''

"Oh, I don't want either of you to fret about it,'' Krista said lightly. "It could end up with a very happy ending. Gerald is actually considering abandoning his bad toupee altogether.''

Norah froze, her nose in midtwitch. "Why. Well. How nice for you.''

As their hostess breezed off, Krista turned back to Beth, who was rummaging through her fanny pack.

"I brought some pictures of Katy with me this time—if you'd still like to see them." When Krista nodded enthusiastically, Beth produced a small photo album.

Beth held the booklet out in front of Krista while she nibbled on her doughnuts, explaining in proud detail the story behind every photo. Katy in the bathtub, Katy on the big slide at the park, Katy giving her daddy a jelly-smudged kiss.

"She is beautiful," Krista murmured sincerely. "Has your lovely red hair."

"Wonder what your first child will look like."

Krista's expressive brows jumped. "Excuse me?"

"Yours and Michael's. Your hair is so dark, his so golden. It's fun to wonder, isn't it?"

Perhaps. Krista allowed her mind to drift, imagining what kind of baby she and Michael might produce. A short week ago she probably would have sworn their offspring might very well pop into the world wearing a mini business suit. But now, knowing more about herself and Michael, she had the feeling the baby might be full of impish jelly-smearing surprises.

"The physical characteristics are only part of the mystery, of course. There are all the quirky personality traits to look forward to. Though I already fear Katy has Randy's crazy sense of humor. I can only imagine how she'll taunt him by the time she's, say, eleven."

They laughed over the prospect. Krista sobered first. "I hope the doctor can straighten out Katy's breathing problems."

"Oh, he will," Beth assured. "I'm sure Randy and I have been talking about it too much. But everything about that child consumes us. There is nothing we wouldn't do to make sure she has the best of care."

"Sounds like you're wonderful parents."

"Thanks. People we know don't think to say that very

often. Like us, most of our friends back in Chicago are parents, and parents don't tend to compliment one another. There's too much rivalry to raise the most superior child. That is one reason why Michael's friendship is especially refreshing these days. As a bachelor he has been the same old reliable guy, out of the baby loop, enamored only with our child. I honestly don't think there is anything he wouldn't sacrifice for Katy's sake.

"Not that we won't welcome you and your children into our life," Beth added as an afterthought. "I have high hopes that we will all get along very well."

Krista wasn't sure exactly what specific messages, if any, Beth was trying to relay. What struck her hardest was Michael's avid interest in the Norquist child. The discoveries she had made concerning Michael in the past eighteen hours were like precious hidden treasure she'd unearthed. Beneath his formal, businesslike facade he was not only a hot-blooded lover, but very promising daddy material.

Michael stared at Krista from across the room and couldn't help wondering what she was thinking about. Her expression was distant, dreamy.

Could she possibly be thinking of him?

"You hear me, Mikey?"

His head snapped back to Allan Larkin. "What?"

"I was saying there are rumors that Gerald is intent on expanding his operations to unexplored states."

Michael kept few secrets from Allan. Therefore, his first impulse was indeed to blurt out that Krista had heard that rumor from the big man himself, right here in this room. But in light of this convention's unusually intense professional warfare, someone's dirty trick with Krista's sketch, he stopped himself. Until this contest was over, there would be no revelations, no confidences.

"I thought maybe, with the stronger bond you've made with Gerald, you might have heard something." Allan was looking at him hard, as if trying to read his mind.

Michael worked to keep a passive demeanor. "Gerald hasn't said a word to me, Al."

"But you're getting on so well with him. Spending so much time with him."

"Not that much—"

"Gee, I feel like I've been robbed. You and I have barely talked."

"Sorry, Al."

"I do miss the old days back in Chicago sometimes. Guess I took you and Randy for granted back then."

"Guess you just like being a surrogate father too much."

"Without a doubt." He waved a beefy hand. "Say, if you do hear any buzz about an expansion, let me know. Or maybe I should just go to the source," he said grimly. "Those interloping aunts of Krista's!"

"They do seem to have Gerald's ear. It's so nice of him to take an interest in my little ladies' club."

Allan looked as if he were about to say something, but refrained. Michael used the brief silence as an excuse to escape, expressing interest in the brunch table.

"SOUNDS LIKE YOU HANDLED Allan perfectly." Krista was curled up on their suite's sofa later that afternoon, giggling like a young girl as they recounted events of the brunch.

Michael regarded her affectionately. "I have mixed emotions about shutting him out the way I did. There is the rivalry, but there is also our history."

"I'm sure he does miss mentoring you. But he is the one who moved here from Chicago."

"True."

"In a way, the Larkins have been spoiled by your attention. Until now you've never had a significant other at your side. They've had you all to themselves. Any good mentor should be willing to let go a little bit, even if it means some competition."

"I hate to think the Larkins view me as a threat." Before she could jump in, he added, "But I know I can't completely trust anyone, not with the stunts being pulled all around us.''

Intent on another kind of stunt, Michael reached out and coaxed her onto his lap. Slipping a hand beneath her thick, rich curtain of hair, he began to stroke the tender back of her neck. She in turn snuggled cozily into his lap, wove her arms around his neck and locked her lips with his. With soft needy moans they tasted one another and began to slide to the cushions.

He was just reaching up into her polo shirt with eager fingers, when the telephone rang. Cursing mildly, he struggled to rise on his elbows and reached out to snag the receiver.

''Hello… Yes, I recognize your voice.'' His voice strained in mild exasperation as he gave Krista a knowing look. ''We have been busy. Here to win a contest…. Oh, really? That would be nice. What time did you say? Yes, she is here. Hold the line while I call her. Krista!''

Still half draped over him, Krista took the receiver and deftly cupped the mouthpiece with her palm. ''Which snoop is it?''

''Gerald.'' He watched her blue eyes widen. ''He's invited us to his place tonight.''

''Why does he need to speak to me?''

''Dunno. Use some finesse and find out if the aunts are invited along, too.''

She held the receiver to her ear. ''Hello, Gerald… I see. No, that shouldn't be a problem. Until tonight, then.''

Michael hung up the phone. ''Did you find—''

''The aunts are already at his place.''

His gold-colored brows formed a disgruntled line. ''The old fox sure has a funny approach to things, always taking us on as a four-pack.''

She stroked his forehead. ''You're a fox yourself, acting as though the call were a nuisance. I assumed it was Rachel or Beverly.''

He shook his head dazedly. ''I'm beginning to see the

three of them in a single blur. What did he want to tell you in particular?''

''He's still waiting to sample that pineapple upside-down cake recipe the aunts were supposed to make; but didn't make, because they were helping us with our entry.''

''So they did actually give him that outrageous excuse. You gotta admire their nerve.''

''He knows I have the recipe and wants to make sure I bring it along.''

''No problem. It's still in my briefcase.''

She rested against his chest, kissing his rigid jaw. ''You won't mind guiding them through the recipe, will you?''

''No. Wouldn't want Gerald to think I'd hook into a family of culinary bunglers.'' Closing his eyes, he drew a pensive breath.

''All in all, I'd expect you to be leaping for joy right now.''

He shifted her pelvis over his strained zipper. ''Plainly, I am in no condition to leap anyplace at the moment.''

''Are you trying to tell me in your own frisky way that I come before even Gerald?''

He grinned wickedly. ''At this moment, you come before all others. Now, where were we?''

''Your hand was in my shirt.''

''Oh, yeah…''

IT WASN'T UNTIL MICHAEL was dressing for the evening that the recipe turned up missing. Krista's wail brought him rushing from his bedroom to the suite's desk, where she was rummaging through papers.

He stared at the contents of the briefcase with a grunt. ''Relax. This isn't even my stuff.''

''What?'' She half turned, glaring up at him in surprise.

''This case is Randy's.''

She picked up his key ring from the desk and held it in his face. ''As I told you, I managed to open it with the community key.''

"I'm sure this is an innocent screwup. The cases simply got mixed up at the Larkin's brunch."

"Even so, we have to switch them back, get that recipe. Fast!"

Michael sifted through the contents. "Randy won't like this, either. His contest forms are in here, even his ID badge. Funny he hasn't missed it yet." He reached for the phone and dialed the Norquists' room. After a brief conversation he hung up. "Randy is coming over."

"He seem surprised?"

"A bit off his game, yes. Stuttered an apology, too long an apology."

She tapped her chin. "Wonder what that means."

He grew impatient as his close friend came under her scrutiny. "Krista, the Norquists have no reason to want access to my briefcase at this point. Even if my recipe was in there, it wouldn't put them ahead. And you yourself said, their Cinnamon Spice doughnut is spectacular."

"Maybe the switch was just a fluke."

He thrust an extended finger at her bedroom. "Get in there. Put some clothes on."

"I like you better when you're taking yours off." Pivoting on her bare heel she marched off.

Moments after a knock sounded on the suite door, Krista emerged from her room, wearing a short-sleeved powder-blue sweater and white capris. She moved to the open doorway where Michael stood talking to Randy, who presumably now had his own briefcase in hand. He was dressed rather sloppily in gray sweats, with sandals on his feet.

"Hey, Krista," he said awkwardly. "What a crazy mix-up."

"It is strange."

Michael smiled easily. "We've realized both our cases were in the Larkin bedroom during the brunch."

Randy smiled anxiously. "Yeah. I sent Beth after mine. We left first, remember? She just grabbed the first one she saw."

"You did seem in a rush to leave," Krista noted.

Michael grimaced. She was going out on a limb to intimate that the couple was anxious to view the contents of Michael's briefcase. Seemed a silly accusation. Just the same, when the normally assured Randy flushed, Michael couldn't help wondering why.

"Look, I don't know what you guys are thinking," Randy blurted out. "But—well, this trip is like a little second honeymoon to us. Sure, we're deep into the contest, just like you. But after you've been married a few years, have a kid, some things have to be scheduled. Including sleep, movies, even trips to the grocery store!"

Suddenly Michael threw back his head, laughing uproariously. "So I got you out of the sack. No wonder your shoes don't match!"

Randy jabbed a finger at him. "Ham it up, big shot. Your time will come. Kids change everything."

Michael made an effort to sober. "I expect they will. I intend to be the most attentive suffocating father on earth when the time comes. But seeing you, the ultimate operator of the old neighborhood, standing there looking so disheveled, I can't help enjoying the moment."

Michael closed the door on his retreating pal with a grin. "I would've expected the amorous Simona to crack that mystery first. Relationships are your specialty."

It was Krista's turn to flush. "Oh, give me that case. Finish getting dressed."

No sooner had he disappeared into his bedroom again than she was summoning him back with another cry of dismay. "It's gone!" She sank onto the sofa amidst strewn papers. "The recipe is gone."

Chapter Sixteen

Gerald had sent his limousine for the couple but the luxury was wasted on them. Someone bothering to take the recipe from Michael's briefcase was a strange twist in the game. The question was, who was the culprit?

They were out beyond the glitter of the Strip now as their driver sped along I–15 toward Gerald Stewart's home in southwest Las Vegas.

They traveled far beyond the Larkins' middle-class suburb into a posh neighborhood of open space and gated mansions. The limo halted at a residence providing a stately anchor for a boulevard corner, pressed a code into a keypad and drove through yawning gates.

Michael squeezed Krista's hand as they made the trek up a long ribbon of drive. "This is the pinnacle of success," he said in hushed reverence.

The grounds, illuminated by generous lighting, were a spectacular array of palms, scrubs and rock formations. The house itself was a sprawling three-level masonry structure full of windows. There was an attached garage on the left, as well as a second freestanding building with a row of garage doors. The driveway jutted two ways, circling up near the front door on the right. The moment they emerged from the back seat of the limo, the front door opened and the aunts came outside.

"They're here!"

"Welcome!"

The sisters descended on the couple.

Beverly captured Krista in her strong arms, her breath hot and fierce near her ear. "You got that blasted recipe?"

"No," Krista whispered. "Lost it."

"Don't worry," Michael said, peeling the small clingy Rachel off his chest. "I'll help you every step of the way."

"And in return," Krista bargained, "you will help Michael shine before Gerald."

Rachel rocked back on her spike heels. "Gee, for someone who misplaced a treasured old family recipe, you're pretty snippy."

Krista replied irritatedly, "You are the ones who insisted I take it back. Said you intended to burn the original!"

Michael stepped into the fray. "Surely you two can slip out of this silly obligation. Why not use your persuasive talents?"

Beverly's bosom puffed along with her ego. "Normally, I too would call this task unnecessary silliness. Any man with a doughnut empire should be able to satisfy his own sweet tooth. But as it is, we've made sort of a compromise. We bake the cake, he shakes the rug. As we all know," she said with feeling, "that rug has to go."

No sooner were the words out of Beverly's mouth than the dapper mogul was out on the doorstep dressed in a western shirt and jeans. His bald dome shone under the stoop lights.

"Good evening, Gerald," Krista greeted him uncertainly.

Gerald nodded at the newcomers, quickly breaking the ice. "Must say, there is a unique pleasure in feeling the cool night air on my scalp. But let's not stand out here when there's a special dinner waiting for us inside."

Several house staff bustled in the spacious interior of the house. The decor was modern, with large leather furniture and mission pieces.

Krista pointed out some iron sculptures and the pink marble fireplace as especially unique.

"Built the whole thing up from scratch when Gloria and I moved out here back in the eighties."

"Where did you get your start, Gerald?"

"Dallas, Texas, where both Gloria and I were born. Started with one shop. Within three years expanded to five. The rest is history."

Dinner was soon served. The long dining room table was laden with choices. Huge slabs of roast beef drenched in barbecue sauce, corn on the cob, biscuits and a variety of salads.

Rachel cast Michael a sly look and announced that he was looking particularly dishy tonight.

Krista bristled. This wasn't the kind of attention she meant for the aunts to bestow on him! But it was, in fact, the only kind of attention Rachel bestowed on a man. She was sincerely trying.

Happily, it brought Gerald out in the open. "As busy as I've been, Michael, I haven't been able to shake your uniform shirt program from my mind. What amazes me most is that I never before gave the issue a bit of thought. Coming from a middle-class background, there was always cash from my father for any expenses. Charging for uniforms just seemed routine procedure from my point of view."

Michael went on to supply some anecdotes to further boost his position.

The conversation took a sharp unyielding turn to business. For the next two hours the aunts blended into the woodwork, while Michael, Krista and Gerald discussed everything from display cases to insulated sacks to the ramifications of adding a delivery service. Krista even proposed the idea of a theme song. Though she didn't say so, she helped promote many a company with the help of a tune.

"I feel as though I'm swimming in a virtual think tank!" Gerald came to say.

"Beverly and I are drowning in it," Rachel grumbled.

"It's okay," Beverly said in a sweet voice virtually foreign to Krista's ears. "All this shoptalk is growing on me."

Rachel popped up from her chair with a toss of her blond head. "I think I'll go call my boyfriend, if no one minds."

Gerald waved her off with his fork. "Be my guest. There must be twenty phones in this place."

When Rachel returned some thirty minutes later, all aglow, the conversation was finally winding down. Gerald made it official by dabbing a napkin to his mouth. "A wonderful spread," he announced to his cook, Mrs. Beacon, who had come out of the kitchen to check on them. "All that is missing," he said significantly to the ladies, "is the pineapple upside-down cake for dessert."

Michael cleared his throat and rose from his chair. "Mrs. Beacon, if you will show us around your turf, we'll get started. Won't we?" he said firmly to the shrinking aunts.

Krista was left to her own devices when Gerald begged off to make an important phone call to Jonathan Smithers at the hotel. She wandered around the house, appreciating the recessed lighting, beamed ceilings and inlaid cabinetry.

It was in Gerald's study that she lingered. At her leisure she perused his shelves of books, his abstract prints. By the time Gerald discovered her, she was holding a framed photograph in her hands.

"Ah, Krista."

She whirled toward him with a start. "Gerald! I didn't hear you."

"This is exactly the place I intended to bring you."

Her eyes darted with a nervous appreciation. "It's quite a nice place for escape, I imagine."

"Yes." Shoving his hands in the back pockets of his jeans, he sauntered closer. "Gloria and I would sit in here to unwind. We'd read books to each other, listen to music."

They both looked down at the silver frame she held tight enough to make her thumbs red.

"What you are thinking, m'dear?"

Krista laughed shortly. "I am thinking that for the first

time, Aunt Bev has trumped her sister in the man department.''

Gerald gently took hold of the photograph of himself and a woman Krista presumed was his late wife Gloria. "It's true that Beverly bears a remarkable resemblance to Gloria."

"No wonder you made a beeline for us that day in the lobby. I did wonder about the draw at the time. Though Rachel was the most obvious assumption. She is an outrageous flirt with amazing magnetism."

"Rachel is attractive in a flashy way, of course. But under no circumstances would I ever prefer her to a modest and stable woman like Beverly. In any case, it soon became clear that Rachel's flirty act was merely a game. She never had any real interest in me, having a boyfriend at home."

Krista was amused. "Obviously, you have her number."

"Rachel is the type of woman who craves attention from all men. It's harmless. I, too, like the limelight. Now, a woman like Beverly better understands the value of commitment." His eyes crinkled. "After forty years of marriage, commitment is what I do best, what I miss most as a widower."

"I assume Beverly knows about this resemblance?"

"Told her today. Reason I've waited this long is that I wanted to test my own intentions, take some time, however brief, to get to know her as a unique personality. If we didn't click, I figured she'd never have to know any details. As things have turned out, Beverly is a fascinating woman in her own right, someone I've quickly grown very fond of."

"I can see now why you've tried to entertain my aunts separately, away from the convention—in order to preserve your secret!"

"I was buying time, I admit. There was always the chance that someone might clue one of you in on Beverly's resemblance to Gloria. It's the reason I hustled her away from the Larkins the other night. If it had happened, I would have dealt with it.''

The robust man wilted a little as he placed the photo back on the desk. ''Now that I am ready to court Beverly, there will be some people, among those who knew my late wife, who will jump to the petty conclusion that I am looking for a duplicate companion. That is the reason I invited you out here tonight, Krista. I want to explain to you my intentions. Assure you that I have nothing but the highest regard for Beverly and would cherish her.''

''To think I've viewed you as nothing more than a carefree threesome!'' She paused, then gasped her own twist on words. ''You know what I mean. Don't you? Three innocent people. If Rachel can be regarded as an innocent.''

He chuckled indulgently. ''Despite Rachel's big vamp act I suspect she is fairly devoted to her boyfriend back home. Though I had no idea he existed until today. With her pride, I'm sure she wouldn't like to hear me refer to her as the perfect third wheel, but her presence has given me the chance to move in on Beverly slowly, deliberately. It's been three buddies at play up until this afternoon. While Rachel enjoyed a relaxing soak in my spa, I stated my case to Beverly. Miraculously, she welcomes my advances. The next and final step for me, is to convince you, a most valued relative, of my sincerity.''

''How very sweet, Gerald. Though there's really no need to convince me of anything. Beverly is mighty picky about her relationships. Even though she has been known to dole out poor advice to others, she's very careful about her own moves.''

He chuckled. ''She is a woman with an opinion. Sure took an immediate stand on my toupee. Plucked it right off my head in the heat of…negotiation.''

Krista sized him up approvingly. ''Must say, my sketch didn't do you justice. You look very distinguished.''

''If I decide to redo my company logo, I hope I can count on your help.''

"Of course you can." She gave him a gentle hug. "Welcome to my world, by the way."

"That's nice. Very nice."

Breaking free she linked her arm in his. "Shall we go see about that cake?"

It was close to one a.m. when all except Gerald made the return trip to the Imperial Majestic in Gerald's limousine. He was forgoing a night in his penthouse suite at the hotel to attend to business from his home office.

Rachel's repining started even before the vehicle left the driveway. "All that cooking for nothing! I shouldn't even have had to help."

"You didn't help," Michael replied evenly, settling back on the seat.

"Why should I, under the circumstances!"

He sat up straighter. "What circumstances?"

"A wonderful job you did, Michael," Krista broke in to praise. "The cake was delicious. Gerald had three pieces."

"Men!" Rachel wailed, clapping a ringed hand to her cheek. "You can't understand them. You certainly can't trust them."

"So what if he's fallen for me," Beverly crowed. "May as well pull up your girdle and accept it."

"Gerald has shown interest in you, Beverly?" Michael was astonished. "That's the circumstance Rachel's talking about?"

"We've sort of clicked," Beverly admitted with pride. "Just told me today that he'd like to see more of me."

"Wow. I had no idea."

"Hard to say if it will go anywhere, but he is a nice man."

Rachel gave her sister a sharp nudge. "I don't wear a girdle."

"Do so."

"You're the one who needs one with your wide—"

"Rachel!" Krista intervened. "You have nothing to gripe about. You have a boyfriend, Bob Freeman!"

"Your boyfriend is Bob Freeman?" Michael asked. "The managing editor at the *Minneapolis Monitor?*"

Krista's heart raced. This revealing argument was bound to put unwelcome strain on the fabric of their lies—at a very unwelcome time. Here was Michael, on the brink of the big contest, and he was sorting through inconsequential details that would do him no good. His fragile ego was still in no way prepared to handle the news that Gerald's interest in him was generated by his connection to the aunts.

As for the aunts' connection to her boss at the newspaper, it was just another clue as to the real identity of Simona.

It was plain the charade was beginning to burst at the seams, as it was bound to eventually. But all she needed was tomorrow. The bake-off was in the morning, the judging in the afternoon and the award ceremony in the evening. After that, the truth would in no way interfere with Michael's professional aspirations. He might need a stopover in a rest home to reenergize, but he would be in good stead with the Decadent Delights empire.

How he would feel about her as a lover, a life partner, she didn't want to even think about.

"Bob Freeman," Michael repeated in disbelief.

Rachel turned snappy eyes to Michael. "I didn't cheat on him with Gerald, if that's what you're implying!"

"It didn't occur—"

"Harmless flirtation is all it was. A lady likes to be hit on even if she has a boyfriend. It's the thrill of the chase. The rousing male scent." She breathed deep, as if stocking up on male scent.

"Freeman sure never had an impartial view of my complaint to the newspaper, did he?"

"Quit thinking so hard," Beverly advised. "Foolish exercise when you're getting what you want."

"You should be the last to whine, master chef," Rachel crowed in support of her sister. "Beverly's actually prepared to sleep with this Gerald character if necessary."

"Not on account of me, she won't! Gerald and I have our own understanding."

"Of course you do," Krista said hastily, flashing a warning look to the pair of rowdy hens. "Enough said."

Rachel sniffed. "Just the same, you could show a little gratitude for all our kindnesses."

Michael flung himself back on the car seat in defeat.

KRISTA EXPECTED SOME FIREWORKS once they retreated to their suite. Securing the chain on the door, she turned to find Michael stoically staring out the window. She mustered the nerve to ask him how he was feeling. It was like lighting the fuse on a stick of dynamite.

"Those women are trying to drive me insane, you know!"

"They don't know you well enough yet to try that."

"It's true, I tell you." He paced around, arms flying. "Beverly and Rachel are here to conduct some weird experiment on an innocent male. Realizing I'd be cornered in a tight jam by our charade, they closed in for the kill."

"Oh, Michael."

"First order of torture, find me in the masses. Second order, cozy up to my boss. Third order, wiggle into contest kitchen to bake cake for boss, a cake they neither recall or care about." He raised a finger as she prepared to speak. "Fourth on the list, storm boss man's house, force me to finally finish their aborted cake mission under the worst imaginable conditions."

"The cake turned out beautifully, thanks to your talents."

"Wish you had been there for the talent show. That pouty, difficult pair screwed up every task I tried to give them—even argued about the pronunciation of *alum*."

"I don't remember that being in the recipe."

"Rachel was going through the spice rack and pulled out the jar because the contents were white. After all, any white powder belongs in a cake mix, right?

"I suggested she take a sniff, and she ended up dumping half the jar all over the place." He marched over to pull his shirt away from his chest and give her a whiff. "Does that smell like something for a cake?"

"No?"

"It's used to *pickle* things." He smiled dangerously, leaving her to wonder what he'd like to pickle, given the chance.

"You'd think they'd be battle fatigued by now," he raved on. "But no, there's the clash in the car. Suddenly Beverly's seducing Gerald. Rachel's in cahoots with Bob Freeman."

"Why should either relationship matter to you?" she soothed.

"I don't know that they do. It's just the element of surprise, the unlikely connections, the dabs of glue bonding your aunts to my backside." He shook his head in bewilderment. "I'm used to being in control of my world, of forging clear-cut relationships. But the higher I climb on your family tree, the more disoriented I feel. All the Mattson branches are entangled with one another. You and me. You and your aunts. My secrets and your aunts. Your aunts and your boss. Your aunts and *my* boss. So many women doing so many things. To me!"

"I am right in assuming you've never dealt with more than one woman at time, much less three from one family?"

He nodded. "Is it always this hectic?"

She bit her lip, gave him a hesitant nod.

"I don't like all this confusion, Krista. Don't like it at all."

"We'll sort everything out. After the contest," she added emphatically. "That's where your head should be now, on tomorrow's strategy."

"I can only hope to think straight enough to pull it off!" He raked a hand through his blond hair. "This is exactly why I stick to business all the time. Personal hassles only drag me down.''

Despite any blame she might feel, Krista was beginning to get irritated. She had fought her reserved nature to bond with this man she'd known for such a short while. Even if she hadn't completely revealed herself to him, she had opened up her heart wide. Now all she heard was him backing off.

''It must be possible to run a successful business and have a relationship at the same time,'' she reasoned. ''Gerald managed well for a thirty-year stretch and is at it again. I bet he isn't making the fatal mistake of analyzing every single angle he doesn't completely understand.''

''Maybe Gerald's wearing rose-tinted glasses because he's lonely. Too lonely for his own good. I say he's better off on his own.''

Tough words meant to drive her off. With a man less special, her pride would have driven her to her room by now with a slam of the door. But surprisingly, she held tight to a wiser perspective. The pressure of the evening had most likely put in place all the barriers Michael had originally built during his troubled upbringing. He was on the defensive and feeling isolated.

Krista knew full well that it was up to the person with the happy childhood to be the one to yield.

''Rose-tinted glasses are very popular with lovers, Michael,'' she said gently. ''It helps smooth out the flaws we all have to make love possible. And if anybody around here is too lonely for his own good, it is you.'' Impulsively, she cupped her hands to his face, stood on tiptoe and kissed him.

''But, Krista—''

''You think too much.'' She deepened her kiss.

He groaned in yearning as her tongue explored his. Soon her hands were tearing at his clothes and he was a goner.

Thanks to fevered lovemaking, Michael slept well until dawn. They'd ended up in his bed, so it was his alarm clock that buzzed on the nightstand. He shut it off and rolled back on the mattress to find that Krista was gone. Probably best, as her presence under the sheets was an irresistible temptation. He rose, quickly showered, shaved and dressed. Then he moved into the living space to order lots of coffee from room service.

Krista was way ahead of him, already dressed in her red polo shirt and dark slacks, transferring breakfast goodies from a room service trolley to the table.

"Morning, beautiful."

She whirled around with joy, her long black hair a shiny banner on her shoulders. "Hey, I was beginning to wonder if you'd ever rise and shine. Thought I was going to have to come in there and shake you."

"That probably would've put us both back in bed."

She smiled like a contented kitten. "Come, have something to eat."

He joined her at the table, allowing her to fix his coffee the way he liked, with a dash of cream.

"Maybe this isn't the time to start a real discussion again about our affairs, Krista—"

"No, it isn't," she said brightly. "Not on Michael Collins day. Today is the culmination of everything you have worked for. Nothing should intrude."

He covered her hand on the table. "Just want to say…"

"That you never should've blown up last night?"

"No!" He snatched his hand back. "I wasn't going to say that."

She shrugged and began to butter a slice of toast. "Told you this wasn't a good time for talk."

He tore the bread away from her mouth. "But I want to talk. Need to talk." He dropped the toast on her plate. "I've been thinking about some of the things you said last night, especially that I think too much. I'm sure I do. But I sense that you do, too. On one hand there is this wild Simona streak in you, but it only goes so far. When challenges fall in your path you get serious, react like a seasoned operator.

I feel you react like me.'' He shook his head. ''I find your signals very confusing.''

''You aren't far off the mark with your assessment of me. There are a lot of things we'll need to sort out. When we have the time.''

''But you must realize that we can't always interrupt discussions with sex,'' he objected. ''We'll never completely connect if we do.''

She traced a finger along his jawline, more delighted than ever. ''We'll make it all happen. And soon.''

''Just not today?''

''Just not today.''

THE KITCHEN'S ATMOSPHERE was humming with tension on this, the third and final round. As Krista stood in line at the ingredients booth with her number seven card, she noted that there was very little chitchat between fellow contestants. Everyone was going through the motions with care and efficiency.

After she set her card on the counter, she turned to discover Beth in another line. She couldn't help pausing to say hello.

''Hi, Krista.'' She tucked some stray red curls behind her ear. ''Tell Michael I'm sorry about the briefcase mix-up yesterday. I was so anxious to escape that party that I wasn't paying attention.''

''Could have happened to anyone,'' Krista assured.

''Also tell him I intend to tease the daylights out of him once he's desperate for some private time with you!''

Krista laughed. ''I will tell him. Promise!''

When she returned to their station, Michael was setting out his utensils and pans on the counter. ''Any problems?''

She touched his back. ''Nope.''

''Took you a while.''

''I was speaking to Beth. Wants you to know you're in for some heavy teasing once you're looking for a romantic escape from the realities of parenthood.''

He chuckled. "Unfortunately for Beth and Randy, I am too clever to get caught with my...briefcase open."

She gave his rear end a smack. "You are the wise one today, aren't ya."

The sound of voices startled them. They turned around in unison to find Jonathan Smithers at their station, flanked by two security guards.

Michael placed his hands on hips, facing them down. "What's all this about?"

Smithers's face gleamed with ill-concealed triumph. "Pack up your toys, Collins."

"Excuse me?"

"You are disqualified from this contest. Now take up your possessions and leave this area immediately."

Chapter Seventeen

"What's this all about?" Michael demanded. He and Krista had been cooling their heels for nearly an hour in a small room off the kitchen, used as a command post for the contest. Finally, Jonathan Smithers had chosen to make an appearance.

"You know what it is about." The dapper man simmered with self-righteous triumph.

"It's about our challenging you at the workshop, isn't it," Krista surmised.

"Ms. Mattson, you and your partner here have breached contest rules. That means an automatic dismissal from the kitchen site."

"That's bull," Michael raged.

"I don't like either of you, it's true. But I cannot punish everyone I don't like. Would be highly impractical. As things stand, I would have been forced to act, no matter who the entrant. That the entrant happens to be you two, well, it doesn't break my heart."

"You can't hope to get away with this, Smithers."

"I am only enforcing the rules. Your credibility has been questioned and I had no choice but to yank you from the lineup."

Michael clenched and unclenched his fists in his lap. "Start explaining, Jonathan, before I explode."

Smithers glanced back at the security guard near the door. "I wouldn't advise any theatrics—"

"Explain, dammit!"

"Very well." Reaching into his jacket pocket, Jonathan Smithers extracted a folded sheet of paper. "This is only a photocopy. The original is in the hotel safe."

Michael snatched the paper from him. On it was the recipe faxed through the hotel to Krista. He waved it as if it were litter. "This is nothing!"

"It is a breach of contest rules. The rules state that no premixed ingredients may be used in the preparation of said entry. The use of Readiquick is strictly out. And, may I say, a pedestrian choice of ingredient."

"I didn't use Readiquick, you fool! This is not my entry!"

"I understand that it is."

Michael stared at Krista, then back at Smithers. "Who made this accusation?"

"It was made in confidence."

"I bet it was. You know why Gerald is a class act? Because he would've checked the validity of such a claim before taking action."

"Unfortunately for you, Gerald leaves a lot of things to me, including this morning's bake-off."

"Surely we can reach him and settle this matter in time for me to proceed. I could still get my doughnuts made with *my* recipe. In fact, Smithers, you could watch our every move. That would prove everything was on the up-and-up."

"I'm too narrow-minded and negative to help employees," he said. "Remember?"

"Where is he?" Michael demanded.

"I believe he took some lady friend on a drive out to Mount Charleston."

"Some lady, huh?" Krista peeped.

"Oh my God." Michael turned to Krista with a look hot enough to incinerate.

They returned to their hotel room. On the faint hope that the lady in question wasn't Beverly, Krista went into her bedroom to call her aunts' suite. Rachel was there, by herself. It seemed that Beverly was indeed off with Gerald today. No, her aunt had no clue as to when they would return. But it would be before noon, as it was such a big day for Gerald's company.

She returned to the living area to find Michael pacing the living space.

''Michael—''

''I can't believe this has happened!''

''I'm afraid it is Beverly with whom Gerald—''

''No doubt about it! Would have to be one of the Mattson gang, and she's the logical choice.''

''I put Rachel on alert. The minute she hears from Beverly, she will relay the problem.''

''Goodie.''

Krista wrung her hands fretfully. ''Have you considered who might have betrayed you this way? Maybe if we confronted this person, he or she could speak to Smithers—''

''That would do no good. The fax is all too real. Even I must admit that on the surface the evidence looks bad. It appears that I may have cheated. With that miracle food, Readiquick. Face it, the damage is done.''

''Perhaps Rachel could explain to Smithers.''

''Krista, only Gerald can fix this mess. He knows about the coffee cake recipe, knows it is separate from my recipe.''

''Maybe he'll return in time.''

''He won't.''

''I am so sorry.''

''You should be! This is all your fault.''

She was astounded at his charge. ''What about the lousy traitor who turned you in? Who slipped my napkin to Gerald? Odds are it's the same person, a Norquist or a Larkin. This person is the one who has done the damage.''

''You don't have to rub in the fact that someone I care

for betrayed me. I get it. Loud and clear. That person gave in to the pressure of the contest. But as I see it, Krista, it's pressure that wouldn't have existed without you.''

"What?"

"All my troubles stem from my association with you. The napkin wouldn't have existed without you. The fax with that awful recipe wouldn't have existed without you.'' He slapped his forehead. "I don't know what came over me, allowing a two-bit advice slinger to seduce me into this kind of web.''

"Hey, you came to Simona, remember? Simona to the rescue. You were so grateful.''

"If you recall, I originally came for a retraction to win my fiancée back, not a benchwarmer to take her place.''

"But we've decided she was all wrong for you.''

"Well, maybe so. But if not for your column, she and I could have coasted through this convention without a fumble. All I wanted to do, Krista, was make the best damn doughnut possible for the contest. Just try to imagine this contest, without you and your aunts' interference.''

"You've got to believe I've had the best intentions. Helped in every conceivable way,'' she said in her defense.

He expelled a breath. "Okay, I admit you tried on some levels—''

"Some levels? I bonded with your friends, was charming to Gerald, made your dream my own!''

"It might have worked if you had kept one crucial promise—if you had sent your aunts home when I asked you to. But I suppose that would have been the boring way out, as it was my convention that was providing their headline entertainment!''

Krista was quaking with anger as she held up a shaky palm. "I can't believe how naive a normally intelligent man can be. But you are standing here, the living proof. I hoped it wouldn't come to this, I hoped you could go on believing in your charm, your magnetism, your need for a fiancée in the first place.''

"What are you talking about?"

"It's about time you know the truth about my aunts, Michael. I did intend to send them away when you asked. Hey, I didn't want them hanging around, either. They are pests who never know when to back off."

"Don't tell me your love for them stopped—"

"I assure you I love them. But it was not a question of my affection. It was Gerald Stewart."

"Excuse me?"

"I was giving them the heave-ho with some success when Gerald spotted us in the lobby."

"I remember. He invited us to dinner."

"He invited *my aunts* to dinner," she clarified hotly. "You and I were an afterthought. In fact, we've been an afterthought ever since. Like it or not, Beverly in particular was the bait he intended to reel in."

Michael shook his head forcefully. "No. Gerald's liked me for ages. *Me.*"

"No. Gerald didn't know you from Adam when we first arrived. I noticed it right off at the cocktail party in the Larkins' suite. I was speaking to him and quickly got the impression that most DD owners and managers were a blur. Part of Jonathan Smithers's job is to refresh Gerald's memory on just who the players are in the DD family. Smithers is of great value to him, despite his steely methods. He knows his stuff. He's the one who knew of you."

"Damn." Michael rubbed his face. "So all the favors, all the attention was due to those two meddlers."

"You have proven yourself since, Michael. By now Gerald knows exactly who you are—"

"Fat lot of good it does me." He gazed upon her in disappointment. "I hate that you kept all this from me for so long, Krista."

"There are other things I would like to tell you—"

"No. Please don't. I can't bear to hear another word about you or your wacky relatives. Plainly, any plans we had aren't going to work out. From my perch, your whole life looks like an endless maze of deception. I can't handle any more of it.''

"But it isn't as it seems!"

"Nothing is as it seems with you Mattsons. And I can't afford to care about that. I keep life uncomplicated, on an even emotional keel. Another single day with you might be enough to crack me into a million pieces." He marched to the door, only to turn back briefly.

"I suppose you've figured out the saddest part of all, haven't you? Gerald never took personal note of my engagement when it appeared in the company newsletter. He had no intention of following up on it after his brief announcement at the opening reception. As for my friends, they would have been far too caught up in the game to take notice if I'd made a lame excuse for coming alone.

"So much for the big family plan. I never needed a partner in the first place."

On that sorry note, he left.

KRISTA HEADED for her aunts' suite. Rachel answered after a series of hard knocks. She was dressed in a skimpy pink terry-cloth robe.

"What took you so long?"

Her huge eyes bounced and rolled as she pointed to her bare feet. "I was just relaxing. Having a snack, painting my toenails. There's a big shindig tonight, you know. We're sitting with Gerald at the top table."

Krista breezed inside. The room had Rachel's self-indulgent stamp on it, all right. The soap opera channel blaring on the television, a bottle each of red nail polish and polish remover on the coffee table...along with something else—a pineapple upside-down doughnut, also known as a Kris Pineapple Kringle.

Rachel had returned to the sofa and was about to take a bite out of the doughnut.

"Stop!" Krista cried. "Hold it right there."

Rachel's small pouty mouth sagged. "What's the matter with you?"

"Don't talk, don't even breathe. Just lower the doughnut to the plate. Easy now, don't damage it."

"But I'm hungry. And it's all your fault, making me wait here while my sister is out on a date."

Krista didn't look particularly sympathetic. "Have you any more of those doughnuts?"

"A few."

"Thank heavens for that!" With a joyous sigh she collapsed on the sofa beside her aunt.

"SO HERE YOU ARE!"

"We've been frantic to find you."

Michael shifted on his bar stool to find the Mattson sisters standing by. "Nobody's better at finding me than the two of you. So, what do you want now? A pint of blood?" He laid out his arm on the bar. "Go ahead, open a vein."

The ill-mannered greeting didn't stop Rachel and Beverly from sliding onto the empty stools at his right. Or from ordering their usual beverages.

"We want you to know everything is fixed," Rachel chirped with a toss of her blond head.

"It sure is." Shaking his head he sipped his whiskey.

"Listen up," Beverly ordered brusquely. "We had a long talk with Krista and we understand the ramifications of the whole mess."

His profile remained set in granite. "Go away." As the waiter brought their drinks, he gestured to the martini. "That should have two olives."

"See how sharp you are?" Rachel gushed. "No need to feel like a loser."

He turned with a thin smile. "Why, thank you."

"Let's get down to it," Beverly went on. "You should know that you aren't out of the contest."

"Of course I am." He tapped his watch. "It is five in the afternoon. The panel of judges chose the three finalists two hours ago. The finalists were sent on to Gerald, and he has probably already made a decision on the winner and the two runners-up.''

"The conclusions you jump to.''

"So negative, too.''

"Ladies, I've never considered myself homicidal, but for your own safety, I suggest—''

"Oh, we understand about powerful emotion,'' Rachel assured. "I was once homicidal over a Patrick von Clark. I felt like killing him when he dumped me for a tramp at a peace march, just because she was carrying a bigger sign.''

"It wasn't her sign that was bigger,'' Beverly crowed.

Michael blinked. "Peace sign? When was this?''

"Back in 1970.''

"I was homicidal then, too,'' Beverly confided. "I felt like killing Rachel for being such a weenie over a married man.''

"Divorced.''

"Separated. And not legally.''

Michael hailed the bartender. "My check please, add up all our drinks, extra olive and all.''

Beverly laid a hand on his arm. "You aren't going anywhere yet.''

"Dear me, no,'' Rachel trilled, "not after all the trouble you've put us to.''

Angry with himself for being curious, Michael gave them a hard look. "I'll give you five minutes.''

It proved to be a very interesting five minutes. According to the aunts, Krista had thought to submit his doughnuts from the first practice run to the contest. Gerald made an exception to the rules because he felt there was fault on the side of the company, he in inviting the aunts into the official kitchen area, Jonathan Smithers in his rash handling of the accusation.

Michael sighed. "Despite this last-minute save, I have no illusions about my chances. The doughnuts are two days old, a tough comparison to pastry fresh out of the oven. Even if by some miracle I do win, contestants will be protesting from here to eternity.''

"The doughnuts were kept reasonably fresh in that box,'' Rachel countered. "I ate three this morning and found them delicious.''

"As for the matter of favoritism,'' Beverly said, "any doughnut that makes it past the panel of judges to the finals is certainly worthy of top prize. You know how dynamic Gerald is. If he declares your Kris Pineapple Kringle a winner, it shall be a hit!''

Michael did have to give them points for tenacity. "It's a nice sentiment, but I'm fairly sure it's all over. As humiliating as it is for me to accept, without you two, I wouldn't even have gotten near Gerald.''

Rachel shrugged. "Well, if Beverly here hadn't looked like his late wife, he probably wouldn't have seen us for spit, either.''

Michael was startled. "I didn't know that. Anyway, I appreciate your efforts and want to officially thank you. As for Krista, I especially admire her ingenuity. I was too upset to think of any kind of solution and, as usual, she stepped up to bat for me.''

Beverly smiled. "That's the nice thing about partnerships, Michael. When one person stumbles, the other is there with a safety net.''

Rachel jerked a thumb at her sister. "Listen to her, a few days into a romance and she's the expert.''

"I meant our partnership, Rachel,'' Beverly snapped. "Look how well our collaboration has worked out.''

"Oh. Yes.''

Michael paid the tab and eased away from the bar. "When you see Krista, tell her—''

"Tell her yourself,'' Rachel scoffed. "We don't wish to get involved in your affairs.''

"Don't wish to get involved!'' He stood frozen, glaring at the pair of chins held high in the air. "I've come to watch my step in the shower every morning, expecting to find one of you handing me the soap!''

The very idea brought a round of chortles.

"What we mean to say," Beverly clarified, "is that we no longer feel we have the right to be involved. Our responsibilities have been met, our debt paid."

"Not that we like the way you've shown your gratitude to Krista, who knocked herself out to help you—"

"We don't like it a bit, especially as you two are the perfect match."

"Debts? Responsibilities? A perfect match?" He sat back up on his bar stool. "Start making sense. If you can."

Michael sat. Accepted the drink they bought him. Listened.

"You two are the character Simona. For real?"

"For real. Krista was duping you to keep us out of trouble. In real life she is the queen of Bigtime Promotions, Ms. Big to her employees. Messing around with you is about as wild as she has ever gotten."

It was shocking. It was comforting. It was the best news ever. "So that means that all the while I was trying to transform Krista into a lady, she was trying to behave like a—"

"Careful what you say about Simona," Rachel snapped.

He rubbed his forehead. "You know what amazes me most about your family, is the extraordinary lengths you go to, to help one another. Because quite frankly, a lot of the time you don't even seem to like each other!"

"That's what a healthy family is all about," Beverly assured him, dabbing the corners of his mouth with a cocktail napkin. "Just wiping off some peanut crumbs."

"Guess I forgot to eat a decent meal today."

"Well, go collect Krista and have yourself a nice dinner. Talk things over."

"Yes, I will do that."

Michael dashed to the nearest elevator, jammed inside

with a bunch straight out of the swimming pool, and took the longest ride of his life.

"Krista!" he shouted as he burst into their suite. There was no reply, however. On the table there was a note.

As I now seem to only be in your way, I have opted to take care of my own business. If you're ever in Minnesota and feel like talking, let me know.

K.

She was really gone. Michael had never felt so alone.

"SOMEONE TO SEE YOU, Ms. Mattson."

"Thank you, Courtney."

Michael watched the gum-chewing girl retreat on a swish of hip. "I think I recognize your inspiration."

"Hello, Michael." She sat behind her desk, dressed in a smart tweed suit and white chiffon blouse.

He, too, was dressed for success in dark wool. He slid a rectangular box onto her desk. "I'm here to see Krista Mattson's alter ego."

"You know very well Simona isn't really—"

He pressed a finger to his lips. "We both know all about the elusive Simona. But I'm sworn to secrecy about her identity, so we can't even discuss it. No, I'm talking about the formidable Ms. Big, owner of Bigtime Promotions."

"Oh, I see." She leaned back in her chair, folding her arms across her chest. "The aunts might demand confidentiality in their affairs but they certainly don't offer it to others."

"They do have your best interests at heart. Most of the time. Not bad old gals, really. A refreshing change for a man with no family."

Her mouth softened. "Sorry had to miss the big dinner. But my regular sky writer was ill and I had to find a replacement, fast."

"A sky writer emergency is a decent excuse," Michael said with a grin. "Anyway, it was pretty much over by then. No one paid any attention to me for the rest of the evening. I crashed in my room about eleven. Slept fifteen hours. By the time I woke up, most of the conventioneers were gone."

"I'm sorry you didn't win the contest, Michael."

"I am, too."

"Thought for sure when I presented Gerald some of your first practice-run batch, you'd have a decent chance to make the finals."

"In a way, I'm glad I didn't make it. The way things shook out, I don't think anyone ever would have believed I hadn't cheated somehow—not with Gerald having the final say. We'd grown so close to him, he knew all about my entry. What means the most to me is that you tried to help, even after our quarrel."

"I did want you to win, even if I was furious with you."

"You don't look mad anymore."

"Well…" She trailed off with a smile.

"Exactly how long were you mad?"

"I've been back one week and four days, been better for about a week."

"You could've called."

"Oh, Michael. I really didn't think so. Not after the way I tricked you so completely. Besides, you could've called me, too. You had all the facts by then, knew I was behaving like a nut for my family."

"Your family still scares me a bit. I had to take some time to sort things through. And I've been very busy at work."

"So you know the winner of the contest?"

"Not personally. Some New Yorker with a caramel doughnut. Not bad tasting, if you like caramel."

"I like caramel."

He smiled ruefully. "You and Gerald."

"I hear the Larkins were runners-up."

"Yeah."

"You don't look too happy about it."

He played with her bronze paperweight. "It was difficult, as Norah was the one who messed with the napkin sketch and the fax. She ultimately confessed."

"I see. So she does poke around in the briefcases she gives as gifts."

"Yes. You called that one well in advance."

"Must have been hard to accept that it was Norah, after all she's meant to you."

He nodded. "She's assured me that she was wearing her 'business hat' versus her 'surrogate mother hat' during the convention, all in keeping the contest fair and honest."

"That's a crock."

"Sadly, she's committed to her beliefs. May never come to understand why I've lost faith in her."

"Have you come to realize she might not be the model wife, after all?"

He smiled ruefully. "Yes, Krista. Her focus on Allan seemed flattering from a distance, but it certainly is that same narrow-mindedness that drove her to rivalry madness."

"What prompted her confession?"

"In a way, it was due to your aunts." He smiled at her surprise. "Discovering in the final hours that Beverly strongly resembles the late Gloria Stewart was the key. Remember when our party of five met the Larkins and Norquists in the lobby? As you know, only Norah and Beth got close enough to pass Gerald the napkin. By far, Norah had the most reason to freak out. Only she would have known of the resemblance, having met Gloria. Neither I nor the Norquists ever had that pleasure."

"At the time, it did seem strong retaliation for one evening out with the boss," she agreed. "I suppose Norah was on the edge, though, and seeing Beverly was enough to tip her over. Guess you would've figured it all out sooner if I'd told you of the resemblance."

"You knew?"

"Not long. Gerald told me at his house the night before, while he was seeking my blessing. But I was already holding so many secrets, and you were so disgusted with the aunts, that I didn't consider telling you anything."

"Wouldn't have mattered in the long run. The damage was done."

"I'm afraid I must agree."

"So, how did the Norquists take the loss?"

"Not as bad as you might think. Allan, in his remorse over creating a self-serving monster of a wife, has given me their fifty grand in prize money. I, in turn, handed it over to my godchild Katy Norquist. Her parents fussed a bit, but Katy promptly stuffed the check in her toy purse and gave me a slurpy kiss. An even trade in anyone's mind, so they had to accept it."

"Seems you still have devoted friends in the Norquists."

"A man can't have too many good friends," he said tenderly. "Or slurpy kisses from girls of any size." Fighting for control, he cleared his throat and began on a more professional note. "Now, about this business with Ms. Big."

A flash of disappointment crossed her eyes but she was careful to remain a good sport. "All right. I'm ready." She sat up straighter.

"On behalf of the Decadent Delights Corporation, I am empowered to offer you a job as an assistant director of the new tristate territory. Minnesota, Wisconsin and Iowa are about to be introduced to the best doughnut known to mankind."

"So that was Gerald's expansion plan for the midwest?" she enthused. "Pretty big plans."

"I'd say so."

"Being that you are Gerald's representative, is it possible that you've been given a top slot in this venture?"

"I am trying not to be a self-centered jerk by blowing my own horn, but yes, I have been given top slot."

"Congratulations!" Clasping her hands together she popped up from her chair and threw his arms around him. He nearly fell off the edge of the desk as he caught her.

"So how did Gerald come to choose us for his tristate echelon?"

"We both made an impact on him at the convention," he said matter-of-factly. "Apparently once he saw me 'for more than spit,' to quote Rachel, he realized my value. As for you, I imagine you're in through nepotism, being the niece of his lady friend."

"Very funny."

He chuckled. "Seriously, you know you made an impressive showing the whole time. And he never did see you as anything but a promotions specialist, as you honestly claimed to be. You're certainly in on your own merit. I stayed on at his place a few days after the convention per his request, and he couldn't stop talking about you."

"You and Smithers in the same town, under the same roof? What happened?"

"We've managed to reach a truce. He'd always held Norah in high esteem and was mortified to learn that she'd jumped the gun about my cheating. It's made him a humbler man."

"Speaking of the Larkins, how did the revered Allan get passed over for this expansion?"

"A little matter of his arthritis, being so intolerable to midwestern climate. If it was a lie to get himself to Vegas, it's come back to nip him hard!"

She smiled wistfully, pressing her cheek against his. "I can hardly believe you're here. A large part of me thought I'd never see you again. After the runaround we Mattsons gave you, I'd have understood."

He pulled her flush against him. "Don't think I could have stayed away for long, even if you were exactly who you pretended to be. You quickly proved addictive and very necessary. As it happens, though, your aunts gave me the sales pitch of the century back in Vegas, after confessing to be Simona themselves. Explained that in reality you were nothing more than a plain, boring workaholic.''

"Plain! Boring!''

"Krista, the very idea that I could find love with a lev-elheaded professional like myself is a dream come true. And we both know you're neither plain nor boring.''

"No?'' she said breathlessly.

"You're a firecracker by day. And oh, by night, you transform into a sexy and sassy goddess that makes Simona look like an amateur.''

"I do?''

"You know you do, Ms. Big.'' He smiled as she blushed. "With that in mind, I have a gift.'' Positioning her back in her chair, he grabbed the box off the desk and dropped to one knee beside her. Inside the box, nestled in tissue paper, lay the pale-green glittery shoes she'd pre-tended to prefer back in Vegas.

"I thought you were still dreaming when you claimed to have those shoes!''

"I had 'em all the time.''

"But you hated them!''

"No, I hated the idea of anyone else seeing you in them.'' Very gently he slipped off her right pump. Dipping into the box he took the right sandal and slipped it on her foot.

"What does this mean, Michael?''

"Will you marry me, Krista? Wear these shoes in my bedroom, bear me beautiful, well-behaved children, help me run an empire?''

She looked out into space as if weighing the options. "All those challenges do sound very exciting, especially the marriage proposal. As for the job offer, I do have my work here, too.''

"Oh. I suppose you could turn Gerald down.''

"Hey, don't be so hasty. I can juggle both jobs if I hire on an assistant for Judy.''

Their eyes met in an understanding twinkle, making the

solid love connection unique to a pair of hopeless workaholics.

Deftly, he slipped off her left shoe and prepared to replace it, too, with a sandal.

Krista moaned softly as his hands stroked her leg. "I'm
sure arrangements can be made to satisfy…both companies."

"I love you with all my heart. To me, you are the most
fascinating woman in…the whole tristate area."

At that moment, Courtney burst into the office followed
by Judy. They stopped short at the sight of Michael on
bended knee.

"Oops!" Judy halted apologetically. "Courtney thought
you'd cried out my name. I didn't know you were here,
Michael."

"Would you look at those crazy shoes!" Courtney exclaimed, scooting closer to the desk. "Are those the shoes
you called me from Las Vegas about?"

Krista smiled firmly. "Get out."

"Yes, Ms. Big." Judy gave them a wink and a thumbs-
up before hustling Courtney back out the door.

Securing her new shoes, Michael eased her chair forward
and kissed her lips. "Can I call you Ms. Big, too?"

She smiled against his lips. "Why, Michael…what have
you in mind?"

"Creating a fantasy that would make Simona blush,
that's what."

"Then, please, carry on…"

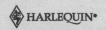

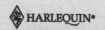

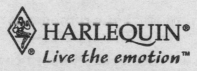

Coming in March 2003 from

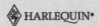 HARLEQUIN®

AMERICAN *Romance*®

SURPRISE INHERITANCE
by
Charlotte Douglas

The latest book in the scintillating six-book series

MILLIONAIRE, MONTANA

Welcome to Millionaire, Montana,
where twelve lucky townspeople
have won a multimillion-dollar jackpot.
And where one millionaire
in particular has just...
received a surprise inheritance.

MILLIONAIRE, MONTANA continues with
Four-Karat Fiancée by Sharon Swan,
on sale April 2003.

Available at your favorite retail outlet.

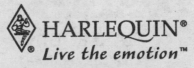

HARLEQUIN®
Live the emotion™

Visit us at www.eHarlequin.com

HARSI